Silvia Kwon is the author of *The Return* (2014). Silvia has a BA in Art History from the University of Western Australia and a MA in Creative Writing from the University of East Anglia (UK), where she was a Malcolm Bradbury Scholar.

Vincent & Sien

SILVIA KWON

MACMILLAN
Pan Macmillan Australia

Pan Macmillan acknowledges the Traditional Custodians of country throughout Australia and their connections to lands, waters and communities. We pay our respect to Elders past and present and extend that respect to all Aboriginal and Torres Strait Islander peoples today. We honour more than sixty thousand years of storytelling, art and culture.

First published 2023 in Macmillan by Pan Macmillan Australia Pty Ltd
1 Market Street, Sydney, New South Wales, Australia, 2000

A catalogue record for this book is available from the National Library of Australia

Typeset in 12.5/17.5 pt Adobe Garamond Pro by Post Pre-press Group

Printed by IVE

The paper in this book is FSC® certified. FSC® promotes environmentally responsible, socially beneficial and economically viable management of the world's forests.

To Pamela Peelen

'For one human being to love another;
that is perhaps the most difficult of all our tasks'

– Rainer Maria Rilke

In early 1882, Vincent van Gogh moved to The Hague to further his artistic career. Towards the end of winter, he met a prostitute, Sien Hoornik, in the street, and they soon became lovers.

Part One

One

The Hague, January 1882

It is winter, the evening bitterly cold. The north-westerly is so sharp it feels like pins. All day it has been battering this precarious coastline as if determined to return the sandy contours once more to the sea.

In Geest, where the city's poor live, a small barrel tumble-rolls down an alley, an abandoned broom knocks urgently against a door while awnings flap and furl, and shutters bang against the brick like a chorus of hammers.

The crowds, swaddled and hunched against the wind, are heading home, their working day finished. They rush past a mother and child wending their way towards the centre of the city. For this mother, Sien, her working hours have only just begun. As she pulls the black shawl tighter around her shoulders, she takes care to leave a glimpse of her modest décolletage. Her belly, however, she keeps well hidden beneath the garment's thick woollen folds. She is tired, her energy sapped by the fledgling life inside her. But her rent is due the next day, and she cannot afford rest. She must find at least two clients – preferably three – if she is to have enough for her jenever as well.

Feeling a tug on her skirt, she looks down. Maria's cheeks are red-raw like beets, and her nose, which is never dry in winter, glistens.

'I'm hungry, Mama.'

'Hush, maybe soon,' Sien murmurs, refusing to indulge the girl with pity. Pity, like rest, is something she cannot afford.

Above, a smattering of stars is piercing the bruised sky. Soon twilight will give way to night and, worried the wind will not only thin the crowd but keep the men indoors, Sien presses on, her steps brisker than before. Maria scuttles along behind in her wooden shoes, struggling to keep up.

It is not long before they are traipsing the narrow streets of Kalvermarkt. Despite the weather, the taverns are doing a roaring trade. Sien should have known: wind or no wind, the men flock to them like thirsty pigs to a trough. Laughter, throaty and beer-swollen, erupts from their doorways while their fogged windows glow with warm yellow light. Sien quickly averts her gaze. She'd like nothing better than to join the men and drown her sorrows in their sodden company. Born with cocks, they are free to carouse, leaving women to huddle at home with their shivering children as they stoke the dying embers of the fire and pray the men will remember to return with a coin or two in their pockets.

She is sure there is no better proof of God being a man.

But whether from the heavens or Geest, she no longer cares,

as there are no men for the likes of her. Has she not always found herself abandoned? Pushing out their babies alone? And afterwards, too? Thankfully, the two others beside Maria – sickly, pitiful things – were smart enough to depart the world early.

At last, spotting a familiar figure stepping out of one raucous venue, she hurries towards him. She has no trouble recognising Johan's peculiar gait – his legs are always bowed as if he is astride a horse – even in the busiest of streets. It is said that an unfortunate curse afflicts him, leaving that eleventh finger between his thighs as hard as a rod, day and night – though some would argue his condition is far from a misfortune. But it is one that he must seek 'treatment' for outside his marital bed because his wife, having tended to him for twenty years, refuses to have anything more to do with it. And who could blame the poor woman? Luckily for Johan, he does not have to suffer, for the city teems with girls and women more than willing to relieve him of not only his hardship but his coins.

Because it has been some weeks since their last rendezvous, Sien sidles up to him and flashes a knowing smile. But when Johan pushes his cap over his eyes and attempts to swerve past her, Sien, bristling, quickly blocks his path. Well, the nerve of him! Surely, if anyone should do the snubbing, it should be her. A butcher, that tallow stench of slaughtered meat clings to him as indelible as skin. And what of his collars, which are always sprayed with gouts of rusty-red blood? How these games tire her, forcing her to play the seductress when she'd prefer to be no more than a whore. But aware that it is often her sweet-talking that stirs the men's loins, and fearing he may be the evening's only customer, she holds her temper and purrs, 'Come, Johan, I'm wet already.'

But instead of giving her a dissolute smile, tonight he steps back as though to avoid a fast-moving carriage, tucking his chin so deeply into his neck that his doughy jowls concertina like a ruff collar.

In the end it is Maria who changes his mind. Now exhausted and on the verge of tears, the girl wails again, 'I'm hungry, Mama.'

Johan, a man with five of his own, sighs, resigned.

Sien seizes his arm and leads him to the stable behind the tavern. Inside, two horses resting in their stalls flick their tails and snort at the intruders as the air chokes with the pong of manure and the sour-damp of loamy hay. Normally, she would not even pinch her nose, but today, overcome with nausea, she can't help but gasp as she hoists herself onto the bales of hay stacked against the wall. Maria, knowing what to do, hides behind the door.

Ha – just as Sien expected, Johan's one-eyed eel has sprung up beneath his shirt tail as hard as the tip of a broomstick, casting his earlier rebuff in a doubtful light – more an act, and a churlish one at best. How glad she is for the dimming light. For at such hair's-breadth distance, as their features turn beast-ugly, it is the men's faces more than their prodding that repulse her.

Over time, her mind – that clever thing – has learnt to grow wings. So, at these moments, as her head knocks against the mortar and her shoulders slam against the brick, it duly takes flight, detaching from her just as would skin after a burn, and she is somehow at once both outside and inside herself. If not for this neat trick, as indispensable – if not more – as that split flesh between her legs, she is convinced she would have been sent to the cells long ago for digging her nails deep into a man's back or sinking her teeth into an ear.

A part of her, having now become aloft, hovers below the rafters, and she finds the bird's-eye view both touching and amusing. As Johan's raspy breath begins to lengthen, the rocking ebbs and, knowing that it will end soon, Sien's lips curl in a smile. As a rule she would have pulled away from him before he could spray inside her, but on this night, she lets him be. After all, what difference will it make? And besides, the method has proven to be anything but foolproof. So, she allows him to take his time, but as he withdraws from her, his hand brushes against her stomach, and he stammers, 'What in the . . .'

'It's alright – it's not yours,' she reassures him quickly, though of course she has no way of knowing this. But pointing fingers is never good for business, and if pregnancies are a trade nuisance for her, these rendezvous are far from guilt-free affairs for the likes of Johan, who is now hauling up his trousers so hurriedly he nearly trips over his own feet. After flinging coins at the ground, he flees as if the stable has been set alight.

At Johan's clumsy departure, Sien chortles and shakes her head. No doubt it will be some time before she sees him again. The word will soon spread, but so too will her girth, and she will have no choice but to take on sewing, a dependable earner but never enough to pay for anything more than the lamp's oil she requires, working late into the night.

Plucking a handful of hay, she wipes the slimy trail from the inside of her thighs before picking up the coins. Johan, in his haste, has left her an extra quarter. Perhaps she will have enough to buy her jenever after all. Reaching into her basket she pulls out her battered tin flask, a gift from an English sailor, and swallows a good mouthful. The fiery drink never fails to console her, and she can no more do without it than she can do without a pair of thick stockings in winter.

She calls out Maria's name and, hearing only the swish of the horses' tails in reply, she checks behind the door and finds the girl curled up asleep. Too tired to pick her up, she gives a small kick to her shin. 'Come, wake up. We can have supper now.'

It is late, but Sien is still in need of another guilder. Near the Prinsegracht, her feet begin to drag on the pavement as a feverish chill overtakes her. Staggering towards the stoop of a house, she drops onto the marble. Her shawl slides off her shoulders; Maria crawls onto it and promptly falls asleep. Sien, hugging her shivering body, slumps forward, convinced she will meet her end this very night.

Suddenly, a man's shadow looms over her. Too weak to look at him properly, she can only glimpse his polished boots, the tail of his coat and the brass ferrule of his cane, but they are more than enough to fill her with a small dread.

'Move along – this is a private residence,' he snaps, tapping his stick impatiently.

'I would, if I could,' she hisses, only just able to raise her head.

Stung by her reply, he shuffles awkwardly before skip-stepping around her and opening the door. The tinkle of a piano and a woman's hyena-like laugh escape into the night air as he disappears inside. Though Sien knows better than to expect this man's help or sympathy, her heart knocks with such anger that her chest lifts almost as high as her belly. But it seems to have taken the last of her strength, her body sinking further into the stone. In this darkest of hours, she is hardly afraid, nor disappointed. Her quietly slipping away from this world would mean an escape from the men, the babies, her hungry family and this failing body of hers. Besides, no mystery surrounds the fate of her soul; the possibility of her salvation is more remote than the furthest star. She only pities the servants of this house who, after being awakened by Maria's cries and screams, will have to scrape her body off the cold stone in the morning.

Then she hears someone say, 'Are you alright? Shall I fetch a doctor?' The voice also belongs to a man but it almost trembles with concern.

She shakes her head. A doctor? Who can afford a doctor? Even at the threshold of death, no one she knows would dare to ask for one. She assumes the man, whose speech is educated, that of a gentleman, is one of those religious do-gooders who like to wander the city in search of souls to save.

Ill or not, she knows she cannot stay here. Carefully, she rights herself, but immediately stiffens at the face that greets her. Yes, the first man was typical of his sort, but this one is irksome in a different way – his expression drips with pity, and because she detests this useless sentiment more than her predicament, she demands, 'What business is it of yours?'

The man blushes and stutters, 'I – I – I . . . just . . .' Then, catching sight of Maria asleep on her shawl, he winces.

Sien takes him in with a frown. A gaunt face, bearded, topped by an oversized bowler hat. And though his too-naked gaze seems to belong to a man without guile, she detects, in his sharp cheekbones and knitted brows, a man of flinty character: he is no fool; rather, someone to be reckoned with. She would like to see the back of this man too but, still short of a guilder, and sizing him up as the type who may be willing to pay for a room, she is about to proposition him when the door behind them flings open and floods the porch with golden light.

'Take your woman and clear from here, or I'll call the police.' It is him again with the fancy cane.

To her shock, the stranger leaps onto the porch, hands balled to fists by his side and shoulders thrust forward like a boxer. 'Are you blind? Can you not see this woman is ill?' he shouts, his temper flashing around him like a lightning field.

The man in the house gapes, astonished at the outburst, and Sien gazes at the good Samaritan in wonder. When has anyone stood up for her? As she blinks against the sting of salt in her eyes, she thinks: ridiculous, this near tears. How silly of her to be undone so easily by kindness – however unexpected, however rare.

The householder, unrepentant and unmoved, nevertheless lowers his voice. 'I'll give you a few minutes, but no more,' he says before banging the door shut.

They are returned to the pallid light of the streetlamps. The man stares at her; his eyes are so wide that it is their whites she mostly sees. And though he is bound to have a guilder, his gaze unsettles her; it is too fervid, too much in want of something she cannot guess at, something other than her body. And now, convinced she ought to be rid of him too, she says, 'I think I'll be alright, now.'

But as she attempts to rise to her feet, the pavement spins before her eyes, and to avoid losing her balance, her hand closes swiftly around his wrist.

'You are with child?' he asks, steadying her.

She nods.

He scans the street. 'The wind seems to be getting stronger,' he observes. As if he controls the weather, a sudden gust dislodges his hat and his arm shoots up to catch it. 'I have a warm apartment not far from the station. You're welcome to rest there.'

At his absurd invitation, she draws back. Does he not realise she is working? But rest, he had said. Rest. Suddenly her body yearns to drop onto something warm. Then, remembering her rent, her near-empty flask, she blurts out, 'Men pay me to go with them.'

'Yes, I understand,' he replies, a slow smile forming.

She supposes the rouge on her face and the low-cut blouse could point to no other possibility.

'Come, we'll find a cab,' he says, picking up the sleeping child and hoisting her gently over his shoulder.

Then, deftly, he loops Sien's shawl around her neck. As he does, the lining of his coat, torn, slips out tongue-like from the inside of his cuff; clearly he has no one at home to mend his clothes. Because he is already striding off towards the square, she can do little but follow him. A cab, he had said. They were to take a cab.

Near the rank, he signals urgently to a two-horsed one. As it draws alongside them, the driver, taking stock of their threadbare garb, does not hesitate to raise his whip once more. But before he can pull away, the Samaritan's temper flares for the second time. 'What're you doing? I have a sick mother and child here, and you dare to drive away?' he shouts.

Startled, Sien turns to him, mouth open. How wrong she was about him belonging to that pious company. If anything, his soul seems as troubled as hers. Still, his words wrap her heart like a warm blanket against the cold while the driver, with little choice but to heed this irascible customer, grudgingly drops his gloved hand.

They climb inside the small carriage, and as they trot through the familiar streets, Sien's heart beats as lively as the clip-clop of the horses' hooves on the stone. Too rapt to speak, her attention riveted to the small window and her feverish chill forgotten, all she can do is stroke the waxy leather seat, smooth beneath her palms. The city glides by, appearing as if in a dream, and convinced they are almost floating above the ground, she finds herself, impossibly, sympathising with the rich. Now she knows. Now she knows why those accustomed to sitting this high look down upon the likes of her as if they were no more than ants. Who wouldn't, when one is able to size up the world from such height?

'I gather you've not been in a cab before?' her saviour asks, grinning.

Sien shakes her head. Preoccupied with the view – she doesn't want to miss a thing – she ignores the amused delight with which he regards her. Maria stirs awake but, less impressed than her mother, she simply stares out the window with a tired frown.

As they leave the city centre, the streets begin to darken and quieten. They soon come to a stop at the end of a deserted street. Sien, disappointed the journey has been so brief, hangs back while the man pays the driver and lectures him: 'See, I have the means to pay you. I'd think again before refusing a fare on the basis of one's appearance.'

'Look, you are here, are you not?' the driver retorts, pocketing his coins.

Sien and Maria disembark, and the driver urges his horses on with a flick of his wrist.

Now back on the ground, and disorientated by the near silence, the unfamiliar street and the absence of carriages, of life, Sien glances about her with more trepidation than curiosity. The neighbourhood is new to her, on the other side of the train tracks, and in the gibbous moon's crisp silver light, the double-storey building in front of them looms castle-like, not quite real. It is taller than all the houses in Geest, she is sure. As she is sure that the man who has brought her here must have more than a guilder.

'My apartment is just up there,' he says, pointing to the first floor.

A part of her would like to turn back, but her legs, tired, ignore her doubts and follow him, as if they know better.

The apartment is not altogether bare but furnished with only the necessary: a table and three chairs, an iron bed, a large trunk in the corner, an easel and a taboret. It is even more bereft of domestic warmth than her little house in Geest. But there is a good stove, still warm, while the walls are alive with pictures of people doing all sorts of things. Old women sewing; a man with clogs; a delivery boy; a porter, his legs almost disappearing under the sacks of coke he is carrying. She turns to him, confused. Who is this man obsessed with the poor?

'I'm an artist,' he explains, following her gaze.

He is suddenly all energy, excitement, his limbs erupting in jerky, spasmodic movements, suggesting he has never had a visitor to his home before. That he should shower her with such attention, treating her as if she were an important guest, makes her stare, wide-eyed. When has anyone ever fetched a chair for her? But she sits, grateful to be relieved of her body's weight, while Maria, without waiting to be invited, climbs onto the bed and nestles her head into the pillow.

Pleased, he rubs his palms so vigorously she thinks he means to ignite them. Beaming at her, he announces, 'I'll get the stove going.'

As he squats before it, her eyes are again drawn to the walls. Though she can barely read, she can make out the name printed neatly on the bottom corner of each drawing. 'Vincent,' she says.

Smiling, he looks up inquiringly.

'Clasina,' she answers. 'But everyone calls me Sien.'

'Well, Sien, make yourself at home,' he says, closing the stove.

'Who are they?' she asks, pointing her chin at the figures on the wall.

'They're models who pose for me. As I said, I'm an artist. I'd be more than happy to pay you to pose.' His words tumble from his lips in one breath.

'Pose?' she repeats, shaking her head slowly.

'So that I can draw you,' he replies, unfolding his body and standing.

'*Me?*'

'Your face is just like Delaroche's *Mater Dolorosa*,' he murmurs, eyes narrowed so they seem to be boring through hers. It is then she notices the tic just near his cheek; it reminds her of a trapped insect trying to free itself.

Though his piercing gaze unsettles her, the mention of money quickly allays her suspicions.

'You would pay for this?'

'Yes, a guilder for each drawing.'

An extraordinary amount to do very little, as far as she can see. And even more bewildering that he should want to draw *her*. Has he not seen the grey that weaves through her hair, though she is only two and thirty? And her pockmarks – though faded and faint now, they are still visible.

She considers the figures in the drawings more closely. So ordinary, they hardly seem worthy of the paper used. After all, who would want the likes of her on their wall?

'Why do you draw them?'

'*Why?*' he repeats, as if stumped by her question. She can only assume he has not been asked this before. He rubs his chin, eyes searching his work. 'Well, how shall I tell you? It's . . . it's a matter of the heart,' he replies, face lighting up.

'Heart?'

'Yes, you could say they fill my heart.'

His answer makes little sense to her, and she stares at him blankly.

'Look, it's like this,' he says, beginning to pace. 'It's about expressing what I see – and I see a great deal. But it's more than just seeing; I have to express what they *do* to me.' Then, seemingly surprised by his own explanation, he halts to glance at the walls.

'*Do* to you?'

He turns and meets her eyes. As if all his thoughts have gathered in his brows, they are pitched together, causing the flesh above them to corrugate. Then, as his face relaxes, he explains, 'Yes: what I feel when I see a person with a certain face, a gesture, or sometimes a tree, alone and bare. I feel a – a quickening in my heart.'

His penetrating gaze leaves her no choice but to ask herself, *What does he feel looking at me?* She cannot recall one person, not even from her family, ever telling her she made them feel something. Over the years, a few drunken men have slurred sweet words, but they would no more remember these the next day than the amount of beer they drank.

Sweeping his arm to take in their surrounds, he says, 'As you can see, my home is not a palace, but it is a room in which we can find some rest. Though the posing is far from easy, I must warn you. It's hard work for both of us. But I'll pay you, and you will be warm and dry.'

His words leave her speechless. First, he appears suddenly

by her side as if spun from nothing but the cold, thin air, and now – moved merely by the sight of her, apparently – he is promising her money so that he may draw her. She is overcome with confusion and incredulity more than the relief she always imagined on having her long-held wish to quit the streets granted. His offer sounds like a charlatan's make-believe. Too good to be true, her mother would scoff if she were here. The Hoornik family could be accused of relying too heavily on this saying, but it has only ever proved accurate. Better to refrain from entertaining fanciful notions than to bear the crushing disappointment of their inevitable hollowness. Yet, Sien wonders if his proposal could be genuine. After all, these people on the wall – had they not done this very thing he speaks of?

Two

She wakes with a start. The bed is not familiar, nor the room, but finding Maria asleep next to her, snug in a blanket, Sien settles back into the mattress. The stove has long burnt out, and her breath escapes her mouth as a trail of wispy vapour. From the floor rises a steady but wheezy splutter of snoring. Propping herself on her elbows, she is astonished to discover Vincent sprawled on the hard boards next to the stove, knees folded, head on a pillow of magazines, his coat thrown over him. He has given up his bed – for her.

As she realises the events of the night before – the stranger appearing out of nowhere, the carriage ride – were far from a dream, a hushed feeling overtakes her. The last thing she can recall is the heavy heat of the stove, and the even heavier lids of her eyes. Her clothes, still buttoned, have not been touched. Stunned, she sits up, now wide awake.

Overnight, the air has turned stagnant and now reeks of a young man's thick, musky scent, the same as the one that lingered stubbornly in the attic room she shared with her brothers for many years. It triggers in Sien the morning sickness that still comes and goes. It is quickly forgotten, however, when the drawing on the table catches her attention. Quietly she leaves the bed and picks it up. Turning it to the window for better light she is startled to see it's of her, in slumber. She drops it as she steps back, her breath trapped in her throat. Is it really her? She reaches for it again, tentative, suspicious. Yes, but it's also not quite her; on paper, she is beautiful and serene. Even that unsightly bump on her nose is somehow less ugly. And what has happened to the pockmarks?

Hearing Vincent stir, she puts the drawing back on the table.

First, he rolls slowly onto his back, but then, as if struck by a realisation, his eyes flash open. Then, almost throwing his coat aside, he not so much stands as leaps to his feet. The man moves like a stick insect, she observes.

'I'll light the stove and we can have some breakfast,' he says, his smile dazzling.

As the apartment begins to warm, the mood becomes almost festive as Vincent strives eagerly to play the generous host. Maria, having just woken, stares at him in that way children often do at strangers – unwavering and for too long. When Vincent offers the girl a slice of dark bread, she snatches it quickly, her hand like a bird's beak. After gulping it down, she runs outside to join the children who can be heard playing in the street.

The deep aroma of coffee wafts through the apartment and

Sien's head swims giddily, her mouth watering with anticipation. She has rarely drunk it, chicory her staple refreshment, and as she holds her nose to the rim of her cup, something inside her shifts, like an icicle breaking off a windowsill.

The wind of the previous night has swept away the city's sombre atmosphere, and the long-absent sun has decided to make an appearance. As it peeks through shroud-thin clouds and lights up the dust motes, Vincent darts about the room like a busy maid, whipping the air so that it seems to crackle around him. One moment he is scooping cinders from the stove, next he is refuelling it; then, turning to consider the furniture, he rearranges the table and chairs before pulling the drapes apart just so – all the while stealing frantic glances at Sien, as if he is afraid she will prove to be a mistake of his eye, or a ghost. Sien, unaccustomed to such persistent attention, feels more self-conscious than flattered, and wonders if something is awry with her appearance. Smoothing down her hair, she re-pins it into a bun.

Sien's only encounter with art has been those paintings glimpsed in the windows of elegant shops but not once did she stop to admire them; it would never have occurred to her to do so. Many years ago, when she was a young girl, an elderly widow for whom she cleaned had a few paintings on her walls, but she can recall little more than their dark palette.

Yet in this studio on the Schenkweg, aware that the mysterious hand of God may have finally touched her, she silences her misgivings and is more than a willing student. Whatever posing is, however hard, she is certain it could never match the gruelling work of enticing drunken men with her tired, worn body night after night – although it is not lost on her that she has once again been hired for her body.

In preparation, Vincent rolls up his sleeves, revealing thin arms covered in bright copper hair. His hands, slender and animated, remind her of a pair of wings in flight, for they do not cease, wiping repeatedly on a towel and playing with his pipe, tamping its bowl, packing it with tobacco. She is tired just watching him.

Finally, he is ready for her.

He gestures her to the rush-seated chair then, fetching a foot-stove, he bends down to place it under her feet. 'Here: this will keep your feet warm.'

Sien assumes posing will be merely a matter of remaining statue-still. But she soon realises her mistake. She has sat in a straight-backed position, her legs together, and is startled at Vincent handling her like a flower arrangement. It's clear he has very particular ideas about her pose. Taking her hand, he gently plays with her wrist until it dangles just so on her knee before tucking her chin into her other palm and adjusting the angle of her head. 'Like so,' he says, dipping his head to demonstrate for her. At his touch, her skin quivers and her cheeks warm. Struggling to heed his instructions, she is dumbstruck when Vincent suddenly drops to his knees and fiddles like a dressmaker with the hem of her skirt.

Then he begins.

Her pose is far from comfortable, given the gouge-dig of her elbow on her thigh, but she denies even the sneeze that tingles her nose, the urge to wriggle her toe, the need to rub her itchy brow. But she manages to steal a sideways glance at the artist who sits nearly as motionless as her but for his arm, which jerks back and forth like the brace of a train's wheels. Immersed in his task, his mind seems to have gone to an unreachable realm while his body has become as efficient as a machine.

Occasionally the shouts of children – Maria's squeals among them – and the toot of a train float up to the apartment as fleeting reminders of a world beyond this room but they may as well be coming from the moon, for the cosy silence within these walls cocoons her.

As the sun climbs the sky, Sien comes to understand that Vincent was right; the business of sitting still has proved to be surprisingly arduous. The longer she sits, the more cumbersome she feels. Her fingers have become heavy, her neck stiff and her bottom sore. But, cramped as she is, she wills her body to hold. After all, has it not withstood the screwing of hundreds of men, if not more? If nothing else, surely it has by now acquired the stamina and patience of a draughthorse.

To her surprise, it is the artist who loses his composure first.

'Arrrgh,' he cries, standing abruptly and sending his chair clattering to the floor. Then, glaring at his hands, he shakes them as if he would like to be rid of them. 'Why won't they obey me? I may as well have sticks for fingers.'

'Can I stand now?'

'Yes, why not?' he replies, swatting the air with the back of his hand.

At last. While Vincent appraises his work, Sien, despite her belly, almost cat-springs from her seat and ambles to the window feeling the cords in her neck slacken and the knots in her shoulders unwind as she takes in the view. In the distance, the open land meets the sky. Closer, a few shrivelled cows graze on the islands of grass in a boggy meadow. And even closer still, pale-frosty sheets billow in the drying ground of a laundry, while next door two men are bent over a sawhorse in a carpenter's yard. A neighbourhood where the sky is not a canopy but the very thing that it is – endless and depthless – and where the clouds seem to hang low enough to invite one's touch. So different, yet how much nicer it is than her Geest, with its grime-coated alleys that provide more a lively warren for rats than human thoroughfares and rows of houses, so small, they could easily be mistaken as a village built for dwarves.

Her reverie is cut short by Vincent clearing his throat. 'Shall we?' he says. 'I'm nearly finished.'

Returning to her chair, she attempts to replicate the pose but it does not satisfy him. Striding to her, he turns her wrist before lowering her chin a fraction. Then, taking up his own position once more, his hand seems keener and hungrier than before.

This time, as his palm brushes across the paper over and over again, a gentle rasp, like rush swaying in the breeze, drifts from him.

So, what seems like another hour passes.

Hearing Vincent's chair scrape against the boards, Sien gladly breaks her pose. She eyes him warily, expecting another outburst, but this time he appears transfixed by what he has done, though his hands continue to flex by his side.

'Would you like to see it?' he asks without looking up, his gaze concentrated on his work so fiercely his expression is almost a scowl.

She joins him, curious.

Even before she has taken a look, he blurts out, 'The ear always gives me trouble, but I'll get better.'

He is right. Her ear is simply a pear-shaped thing with a black circle inside it.

But her ear doesn't hold her interest for long because this woman, again familiar and yet somehow not, tugs at her heart. In this image, unlike the one of her asleep, her open and downcast face speaks only of sorrow.

She turns away, her eyelids fluttering. How is this possible? How can a drawing make her feel such pain? Yes, it's one thing to feel sad, but to have it mirrored like this . . . well, he may as well have opened her heart and taken a peek.

But what does she know about art? Where she's from, paper, if there were any to begin with, would be used to patch the walls or light the stoves before anyone would think to draw on it. She returns to the window once more, her back to him.

'Well . . . don't you . . . don't you like it?' he mumbles. 'I'm still learning, so you mustn't think I can't do better . . .'

'Am I so pitiful then?' she demands, turning to face him.

But instead of answering her, he is scrutinising her face with such absorption she would not have been surprised if he'd reached for another sheet to draw her again right there and then.

In a voice that is almost a whisper, he tells her, 'It's beautiful, though.'

She frowns, wordless, incredulous. Is he mocking her? She would not hesitate to exchange her so-called beauty for something else. But for what? Happiness, she supposes. Not that she knows anything about that.

His expression sharpens. 'Don't you see? It's because you have struggled, because you have truly lived. That's where the beauty comes from. Those gay women on the Plaats, their noses turned up, twirling their parasols, have nothing on you.'

'Ha, I wouldn't know anything about that,' she scoffs. Even if she really were as beautiful as he says, she cannot see how her beauty could surpass those women's. All she can do is shake her head. But when she searches his face she realises that he means every word.

'Believe me,' he says, 'most people wouldn't know real beauty if God himself pointed it out.'

But then again, is it not true that all those figures on the wall are from her world? Workers who have become almost invisible to her, familiar as they are, just like the stones she trod every day. Though their clothes are tattered, and their hands thick and callused, they are hung like stations of the cross. Where are the men in top hats, or the women with porcelain skin and delicate features? She has come across many who, made guilty by their money, have wanted to save the poor but never one who worships them.

He rifles through his trunk and plucks a picture from its depths. 'This is the picture I mentioned last night,' he says. 'Delaroche's *Mater Dolorosa*.'

She peers at a woman looking heavenwards, expression imploring.

No, it cannot be. 'The Virgin Mary?'

He nods, pleased that she guessed correctly.

'You think I am like . . . the Virgin Mary?' she almost shrieks, shoving the picture back towards him. 'How dare you! You must be mad.'

She expects him to apologise for his audacity, confess he made a mistake, but he does no such thing. 'Not at all. In fact, your portrait is even better than this pure, alabaster version. Don't you see? Yours is marked with the weight of real life. With *real* suffering.' Then, shrugging, he sighs heavily, as if yet again he has been forced to repeat a truth so obvious anyone with eyes would have no trouble seeing it.

They are interrupted by a noisy footfall – wooden clogs landing on timber – on the stairs outside the door. Maria enters, her nose streaming, her pinafore smeared dark brown. But her eyes, looking up at Vincent, sparkle clear.

'I'm hungry,' she tells him, lifting her chin.

Sien scowls at the girl's demanding tone, but Vincent does not hide his delight, chuckling, a hand on her crown. He steps into the alcove kitchen and retrieves the dark half-loaf and this time also a block of cheese, whistling. The girl, impressed, tilts her head back and, pointing a finger at him, says, 'You're a bird.'

'I learnt it as a boy in the woods at Zundert,' he says.

He tells them about the excitement he felt imitating a starling while wandering through the woods surrounding his childhood home, imagining himself as that bird flittering in the trees, trying in vain to merge with nature. 'My brother Theo begged me to teach him but even though he is four years younger his tongue refused to loosen. It was too rigid, you see. But that's Theo for you.'

He offers Maria a slice of cheese and this time, in a surprising display of grace, the girl reaches for it slowly. When Sien notices the saliva pooled in the divots of Maria's lips, she lowers her eyes, reminded that though she herself may be intimate with hunger after years of hand to mouth living topped up with soup kitchens' fare, her daughter is still compelled to heed the gnawing in her stomach. But in time, she too will learn to ignore that persistent rumble in her belly – because she will have to.

Before letting her dash outside again, Sien bends down to wipe the girl's nose and attend to the stockings that have spilled around her ankles. Straightening, she finds Vincent looking at her differently, almost helplessly. Next, his mouth swoops onto hers, fastens, and she has no choice but to push him off her in order to reclaim her breath. He detaches reluctantly, wearing a smile that makes it clear he has no time for bluff or games. Amused, she returns a smaller, crooked one.

Nimbly, his fingers dart over buttons and braces until the garments drop to the floor. Then, grinning, he stands with his hands on his hips, his gaze by turns warm and wilful. Sien gulps at the body before her. She's seen many – hungry, thin, fat, tall – but this one is a ravaged terrain of drawn flesh. His pale skin is spotted and mottled. Did he whip himself like those foolish church people?

Yet this wiry man is a welcome change from her usual yeast-bloated clients with their milk-sop faces, and she can't help but be swayed by his confidence; almost guileless, it seems nothing short of a declaration of his feelings. In her experience, most men are only ever interested in the expedient purpose of her and, not seeing her as a person, they barely bother to impart a glance, never mind a word. But this man regards her in an entirely new way – with respect, even admiration.

He enters her cautiously but then he is all flailing limbs, so eager he is for her. She can't recall the last time she had a man who was so keen, prompting her to wonder: when was his last time with a woman? As his body settles into a rhythm, he looks down at her with such raw tenderness that he makes her shudder, as if he has touched her very heart. And because no man has ever made her feel this way, this time her mind refuses to budge, instead clinging to her flesh, and she realises this is a far cry from the perfunctory service she normally provides. That she is apprehended as a person rather than a receptacle for the male appendage. For the first time in her life, she feels seen, instead of seen right through. It dawns on her that she might not be a prostitute but a woman he desires – yes, for her body, but also something else. Something more exalted. As if he can see her very soul.

Soon his body flips back and he lets out a groan, as though he is racked with pain. Then, as would cloth taking on water, he becomes limp and heavy, and from the weight of him she can be sure that it has been some time.

'I've had women before . . . but this . . . with you,' he stammers, rolling onto his back. 'How can I describe it? I was sure my desire went beyond me. In fact, beyond the flesh to another realm. As though both my body and my spirit were there inside you.'

He is crying, or is about to. Though she can't deny the unusual intimacy she felt, who speaks like this after just one time? Speechless, she turns to him. His eyes are indeed wet. As for his candour, she has not once, in all the years, known a man to confess his feelings like this. But does he not also speak for hers? More than just his cock, did she not feel something else? She would not have believed that it could be different, but she can't deny it: with him, it was.

'Is there anything that can compare to the touch of another? To the touch of a woman? A few months ago, I went to a rendezvous house in Amsterdam. That woman, like you, had a young child. But we talked more than screwed,' he admits, sighing.

She nods. She too has been paid extra on occasion to stay and talk. Usually about a girl they were in love with, or about the troubles they were having with love. Though she managed to relieve the ache in their groins, there was little she could do to help with the one in their hearts.

She sits up and buttons her chemise.

'Where are you going?' he asks, raising himself on one elbow.

'To my family.'

'You're married?'

She shakes her head. 'Just my mother and sister at home.' Though she was nearly married once, she is about to say, but changes her mind. Perhaps after all these years she is not yet over Hendrik. Or perhaps she is still angry at him for promising to marry her then disappearing on a ship bound for America.

'Some married women walk the streets, you know,' he says sourly. 'When their men should keep them near the family hearth.'

'It makes no difference,' she says, shrugging. 'When there's hungry mouths to feed one can't afford to be so high-minded.' She is tempted to tell him about the young girls escorted into the night by their own mothers. Instead, aware that afternoon is approaching, she reaches for her clothes.

He bounds from the bed, again more grasshopper than man. 'Then marry me,' he says, eyes dilating wildly.

Too stunned to respond, she stares at him, blouse half-buttoned. Who is this man? She waits for him to retract his words or at least apologise for speaking so rashly, but when he does neither she bursts out laughing. His proposal of marriage after one heated romp seems more an absurd joke than a question. Even more disturbing is that he should think such a thing possible between him, a gentleman, and her, a streetwalking whore from Geest.

Her reaction does little to dampen his conviction, however; he merely twitches his mouth, his expression not only serious but almost reproachful. 'Well, why not marry me?' he asks offhandedly. 'We'd be good for each other.'

Shaking her head in exasperation, she stands and begins to gather her things.

But he does not give up. 'As long as you can live with a poor artist,' he continues.

Out of habit, she is about to clean up the sticky glob on the edge of the mattress with her handkerchief, when he does something that truly astounds her. Fetching a towel – 'Here, let me' – he dabs at it. She cannot recall a single man ever bothering to clean up after himself, and she is more flabbergasted by this gesture than his mention of marriage.

'We can be poor together,' he says, dressed now and standing straight. 'Struggle is always much easier with a companion by one's side.'

However true, the more he speaks the more he begins to grate on her nerves, echoing those folks who stand on street corners waving their pamphlets and trumpeting to the passing crowds that it is only God who can save them. What does *he* know about marriage? Very little, she suspects. In her experience, it's always those prepared to speak easily about such matters who know the least about them.

'It's still a guilder for the sex,' she informs him tartly.

Ignoring her, he sits and reaches calmly for his pipe and takes his time filling it.

'Perhaps it's sudden, but I know what I feel in here,' he says, pointing to his chest and taking a deep puff. 'And I'm even prepared to say that I know of your feelings for me. For I also felt them here.'

He leans back in his chair, smiling.

Though he may be right, she refuses to play his accomplice, for his talk seems as foolhardy as wishing she were born a princess.

'I take it you do this often? Ask strange women to marry you?' She folds her arms across her chest as she does when Maria tries her patience.

'No, but I have complete faith in my heart because I believe it to be more truthful than my head. I have lived enough to know. I am nearly thirty, after all. Besides, we can look after each other, so you don't have to walk the streets.' A pause. 'And keep each other from being lonely.'

'I'm not lonely. Hungry, maybe.'

'Whatever the case, you cannot deny that it's good for you to be here with me,' he says, tapping his pipe with a deliberate but unnecessary force. 'To wake up with one's love next to you is the most vital condition of being alive. With such love, one can do almost anything.'

'But I've heard it before, you see,' she says.

'The father of the baby you're carrying?'

She shakes her head, amused that he should think she would know who that is. 'No, a few years ago with my second-born. Someone I was naive to trust. A clergyman. I was younger, of course.'

He jumps as if his seat has suddenly caught fire.

'Ah, what a cowardly scoundrel. Abandoning a mother and child. And a man of cloth too.' He waves his pipe. 'Perhaps it's useful to know they have the same needs as any man. Look at my father, six children.'

'Your father is a priest?'

'A pastor.' He explains his flight – actually his eviction – from his parents' parsonage the previous Christmas. 'All because I refused to attend church. As if I had committed the gravest of crimes.' And how right he was to abandon his plans to follow in his father's footsteps. 'The church, well, it's riddled with all sorts of inconsistencies and false posturing. In any case, I've learnt that art is my true calling.'

She nods. But she cannot help but also arch her brow. That he, the son of a pastor, should have the pluck to absent himself from church on the holiest of days and have no regrets about doing so.

A headstrong man, she gleans. Though she stopped trying long ago to fathom the mysterious business of saving souls, his action would appear as disloyal, even impudent, and his father's decision to throw him out seems more reasonable than not. Gathering her shawl and basket, she doubts she could have dreamt this man up, even if she wanted to.

He pays her. Astonished by the amount, she does not close her palm but stares at the coins. There's a guilder for posing, another for screwing – the easiest one she has earnt in all her years of walking the streets – and an extra one she didn't count on.

'Don't be so surprised,' he says. 'I could not have done without you today. To be able to draw you, a person who lives and breathes – well, for me, nothing else quite compares. I think my brother Theo will be impressed with the work.'

'Your brother?'

'Yes, he is an art dealer. I send him my work.'

She nods.

Tentatively, he adds, 'Can you come again tomorrow?'

Sien, touched by his vulnerable, anxious gaze, feels a tussle in her heart as the chambers expand and shrink, leaving her too tight-chested to move. It's only on hearing Maria's shouting below that she is spurred into action. She rushes out the door without answering him.

Three

They are sitting on the kerb: Maria and another girl, taller and older. Between them teeters a tower of stones, while nearby a group of boys are playing with hoops and sticks. After daintily placing the last stone on its peak, Maria stands back and, like a satisfied worker, dusts her hands on her pinafore, which no longer has a patch that is clean.

In Geest, camouflaged by that neighbourhood's sooty colour and air as well as the company of other children just as bedraggled, her daughter's filthy clothes would barely have drawn a glance. But here on the Schenkweg, next to the girl whose ruffle-edged pinafore is hole-free, hair tied with a ribbon and feet sheathed in neatly buckled boots rather than clogs, there can be no mistaking Maria as anything but the street urchin she is. Clearly, the Schenkweg is for those who have their feet a few rungs higher on the social ladder.

'Maria, let's go home,' Sien says, taking the girl's hand.

Maria wrenches free and stares at the pile of stones with a puckered face before aiming a determined kick at the wobbly stack, as if it has somehow wronged her. Straight away, the other girl lets out a wail distressed enough that the boys stop their play to turn in their direction. But Maria, ignoring them all, dashes ahead of Sien towards the corner and swiftly disappears around it. Perhaps the girl will fare better in the world than her, Sien muses; she hopes so.

In the city, it is only early afternoon, but the sun is already casting long shadows. The light is thin, but its glare is enough to cause eyes to flinch and bestow a languid mood on the city, so that its people have lost their harried manner of the evening before. Even the labourers on the canals, unloading the barges onto waiting drays, take their time.

Today, Sien walks with her head lifted rather than down, feeling almost carefree. How different the world seems when she has a few coins jangling in her purse. Even the sliver of cold air nipping her toes – the stitching of her boot must be coming apart – does not fill her with worry as it would normally have done. Still, she hopes they will see her through this winter for a cobbler's fees are hardly trifle. Though now, with this posing, she may be able to afford a used pair. A guilder, did he not say? It takes her breath away; quickly she sucks in the air.

Entering Geest, she could be forgiven for thinking the sky has darkened. The cramped streets, the blackened houses sitting cheek by jowl, seem to press against her, and the smell of sewage is so thick she is almost sure that she can see it. Everything is exactly as it was yesterday, but why is she gagging? It is as if she has been away not just one day but some months. Already, she yearns for the Schenkweg.

Then, passing the distiller, she realises she has not taken a sip of jenever all day. But she is far from surprised that it should have been forgotten in the company of such a man. Her steps become tentative as she casts her mind back to the previous evening, for the streets she has trod for years have failed to yield anything or anyone as interesting as Vincent.

At a familiar sharp whistle, she turns her head. Jan, who works in the storeroom of the distillery, puts down the barrel he is hauling and beckons her with a crooked finger, smiling. He is built just like the stout goods he handles and always appears as if there is nothing else in the world he'd rather be doing. But because today she hesitates, Jan furrows his brows as he holds up a stone bottle and points at it.

She goes to him not only out of habit but because she is uneasy at the thought of giving him a cold shoulder. After all, has she not always relied on him to fill her flask when her money ran short?

Maria is given candy and told to wait outside the door as they retreat to a dank, darkened corner where, flanked by towers of barrels, she lets Jan touch her. When he shoves her against the staves to do more, she lands a swift palm across his cheek before pushing him away.

'No, no, you're doing it again, Jan.'

He stumbles back, his lips glistening, eyes lowered but a sly smile lifting one cheek.

'You can pay a guilder or give me bottles rather than just filling my flask,' she tells him, straightening herself.

He sighs. 'I would give it to you if I could,' he mutters, picking up his cap, which was knocked from his head during their brief tussle.

She does not enjoy his sulking. Without a word, she hands him her flask. The jenever trickles like pleasant music in her ears and, now overcome with thirst, she snatches it from his grasp and takes a gulp. Smiling wider now, his spirits seemingly restored, Jan tops up her flask, erasing any ill will from his clumsy overreach. She gives his ribs a playful nudge before collecting Maria outside.

With money for the rent and a full flask of jenever, she surveys her neighbourhood more sympathetically than earlier. As she passes the butcher shop, she allows herself a peek at the window. Eyeing the strings of plump pink sausages hanging above the counter like decorations, she gives in to her yearning and enters the shop. Then she continues on to the greengrocer, where she buys potatoes and green beans.

Near home, Maria disappears from her side, swept up by the tide of the neighbourhood's gang of children. Together, they pour through the nooks and crannies of Geest as if almost one body, searching for mischief while evading the rough tongue of the grown-ups, always on the lookout for an opportunity to ease their constant hunger – a baker's cart upended at the moment he is attending a customer, a crate of apples upset from the back of a wagon.

The Hoornik house on the Noordstraat is quiet. In the sitting room, Sien's mother Wilhelmina is sewing buttons next to the stove which is only just warm, wrapped in all the blankets of the house.

'Where have you been?' Wilhelmina asks, her ashen face quickly reddening.

'I went back to an artist's apartment.'

'Well, I thought something had happened.'

'Something did happen. He offered me a job.'

Her mother's eyes bulge. 'Does he run a rendezvous house, does he?' she asks, smiling at her clever question.

Sien returns a smile sweeter. 'No, you stupid woman, he has a studio. I sat for him.'

'Huh, you mean you sat *on* him, don't you?'

But Sien ignores her, for she has the last word, removing the contents of her basket onto the table. And now her mother's eyes nearly pop from their sockets.

'Oh, and here's the money for the rent,' she says, dropping the coins into Wilhelmina's palm, her tone breezy.

The older woman's eyes dart from the shopping to the coins and back again; she is barely able to hold back a gasp. A moment so rare, Sien cannot help but savour it. *See, did I not do good?* She is sure that in all of Wilhelmina's fifty years and more, this is the first time one of her children has arrived home with a basket so laden.

From the back of the cupboard, Sien pulls out the heavy pan, so seldom used that it has bloomed a patchwork of rust, and today as she peels the potatoes, she finds the near-blunt knife that usually has difficulty slicing gliding easily under the floury skin.

Wil, Sien's ten-year-old sister, lured by the unmistakable aroma of cooked meat, runs in from the street and, astonished that such a decisive answer to her hunger awaits her, peers keenly at the pan, her nose nearly touching its rim. Suddenly, Sien wonders if she made a mistake bringing meat into the house, where for days the smell will persist not only in the rooms but in their hair and clothes as a bitter memory. Then, in awe of this feast, the family sits down to eat in a silence more hushed than the one inside a church.

Four

There was never a chance she would not return to the Schenkweg the next day.

He opens the door, bright-eyed, a towel hanging over his shoulder.

'You are just in time,' he says, his gaze lingering. Under it, her skin tingles.

Inside, she stops short, surprised to see a woman, younger, more a girl, standing with a broom in her hand. Sien makes no effort to hide her irritation, giving the girl her most withering glare. The girl immediately drops her head and briskly resumes sweeping the floor, seeming to make the point that the broom in her hand is no mere prop. Is she another model? Sien wonders. How many does he have? Or is she only a charwoman? Because Vincent's drawing board is propped on the chair and she can see the girl, broom and all, on the paper, she assumes the girl is both.

She hesitates, in two minds about staying.

'I've nearly finished with Geertje. There is some coffee in the pot over there,' Vincent says, waving a hand towards the kitchen. Then, picking up his black stick and his drawing board, he sits.

The promise of coffee too enticing to resist, Sien removes her shawl and bonnet. After pouring herself a cup, she retrieves some sewing from her basket. Because many of the women in his pictures are busy with a needle, and thinking posing is bound to be more bearable if her hands were occupied, she brought the household's stockings in need of mending. Then, her attention caught by a scrap of fabric flapping bunting-like – it's the torn lining of Vincent's coat – she decides to repair that as well.

Vincent watches Geertje as if she is performing an extraordinary feat instead of cleaning his apartment. When he instructs her to hold still, the girl, caught in mid-sweep, frowns with a sidelong glance, half-ready to flee. As Sien takes stock of Geertje's dirty, threadbare apron, her flaky skin and the long, sunken face with a pea-sized mole below her mouth, she regrets her earlier hostility; it is quite likely the girl has even less than she does.

The drawing done, Vincent pays Geertje. At first, the girl eyes the coins eagerly, but then her face darkens. 'You promised me a guilder – this is only eighty cents. I might be a charwoman but I can still count you know.'

Vincent, flustered, makes a show of patting his pockets. Sien, unable to bear the awkward performance, takes out the shortfall from her own purse and offers it to the girl, who snatches the coins and scurries out the door with her broom.

Sien returns to her sewing, but Vincent, in the silly mood of an excited child, pounces on her. 'Watch out for the needle,' she warns, raising her hand above his head.

'It's nothing more than the sword of an angel,' he replies, nuzzling his face into her neck, his beard tickling her. 'Did I not say we would be good for each other?'

His affection is not unwelcome, but she wriggles free from his embrace, for she hardly enjoyed parting with those coins. 'I thought I was to be your model,' she mumbles, pushing the needle through the toe of Maria's stocking.

'But you see,' he says, reaching for his pipe, 'I need all sorts of models, old, young.' Then an idea seems to strike him. 'What about your mother and sister? Would they like to pose for me?'

His question lands inside her with the weight of an anchor. Her head down, she continues with her sewing, silent. For as much as she would like to see her family earning, she would also like nothing better than to have Vincent and this apartment entirely to herself. She had woken that morning filled with a rare pleasure, relishing the prospect.

'So, you earn all the bread for your family?' Vincent asks, stroking her shoulder. His touch caresses her skin as would a fresh morning breeze.

Looking up, she nods.

'Walking the streets to provide for them. Well, I admire your strength and courage. I can only imagine what a heavy load that must be,' he murmurs.

Her sewing drops onto her lap. No one else had ever acknowledged her ordeal, nor expressed admiration for her efforts. So she gives herself permission to admit something she could never previously afford to do: yes, the load is heavy. And yes, she has for a long time wanted to relinquish it. Suddenly she is stripped of her familiar bearings, as if he has cracked open her very core. And yet, strangely, it is as though her very soul has been glimpsed by another. Perhaps he has succeeded in boring through her after all. Afraid she might cry, she quickly purses her lips. 'My mother takes in sewing, but her eyes are dim now, so . . .' She picks up her needle once more.

'And I hear it pays poorly.'

'Not even enough to scrape by.'

'It would seem they would do better if they were to sit for me.'

For a moment, she is tempted to dissuade him, but she suspects her words would not only be futile but ring false. In any case, there is no avoiding her family turning up here against her wishes, barging in and demanding to know what she is up to, demanding to see this so-called artist and his studio, their interference no more than an assertion of their rights.

In truth, she knows she could never have kept Vincent her secret. After all, anything she earnt, anything anyone earnt, was always shared; no one dared to save anything for themselves because no one ever had an inkling of what the following day would bring. Even if they were blessed with two meals in a single day, they were just as likely to find themselves with nothing at all the next. They managed to survive because they pulled together, sharing not just coins but stolen buns and the clothes on their backs.

So, though his offer elicits a pang of disappointment, she suffers a deeper one at the thought of denying her kin the chance to earn a few coins. And she understands she cannot dismiss that mysterious calling of blood; it is too loud, too strong for her to ignore.

The next day, Sien delivers Vincent new models: her family. Not only curious about the gentleman artist but mindful they have been extended an invitation far from ordinary, they are wearing their Sunday best. Wilhelmina wears her most cherished bonnet, the one with a brim and ribbon for ties, and Wil, her pinafore fresh, has donned her prized velvet hairband, sweeping her locks back smooth and neat. But though Maria's face has been scrubbed, her dress, impossible to keep clean, appears as it does every day: dirt-smudged.

As if Vincent has been listening for their footsteps, the door swings open even before they reach the landing. He greets them, face burning, exuberant. His eyes roam hungrily over the Hoornik women while his hands are busy rolling his sleeves up one moment only to push them down again the next. 'Come in, come in . . . how wonderful . . . three generations,' he says.

It is Maria who scampers inside first and makes herself at home, snatching a piece of chalk on the table to draw on the back of her hand. Shy Wil remains behind Wilhelmina's skirt and peers out rabbit-faced.

After they are seated around the table, Vincent prepares the coffee. Sien catches her mother assessing the apartment, unimpressed. What sort of gentleman has furnishings that are even more drab and bare than those in their little house? Though the artwork on the walls are hard to miss, Wilhelmina pays the pictures little heed. Sien now regrets bringing her mother here.

Vincent brings the coffeepot to the table and begins to pour. On a plate is a raisin bun bought for the occasion, already sliced. He pushes the plate towards them earnestly and Wilhelmina's expression brightens. Basking in his attention, a silly smile remains fixed on the woman's face as she answers his questions.

'Eleven children, you say? Oh, that is remarkable,' Vincent mutters, studying Wilhelmina with such interest that she blushes like a girl. For the first time, Sien is able to picture her mother not only young but also pretty, before marriage, before all the children, before widowhood. What has happened to the woman whose ill temper is renowned throughout Geest? A woman who, witnessing her son receiving the blows of a baker's fist after he was caught stealing bread, did not hesitate to snatch an old woman's walking stick and thrash the man's head with it, making it bleed – long after he'd let go of the boy.

Vincent is too jumpy to linger over his coffee. He gulps down the last dregs and suggests Wil as his first model. But the girl, cowering in her chair, shakes her head so determinedly it appears as if it may not be attached to her neck, prompting Wilhelmina to quickly volunteer herself in her place.

Vincent, as he clears a space for Wilhelmina, almost sprints around the room. When he asks her to put her hat back on, she complies eagerly. He then offers her the still-warm foot-stove. At this kind gesture, Sien's mother again turns crimson. 'That is very thoughtful of you,' she coos in a too-sweet voice that makes Sien cringe. The girls retreat to a corner to play with a family of rag dolls Wil never forgets to pack in Wilhelmina's basket when they venture from home.

For Wilhelmina, Vincent issues no instructions. He simply lets her be. Sien's mother, nevertheless, seems to have made up her mind to give nothing away, assuming a blank expression so forced that she appears not only awkward but as stiff as a tin soldier. Maintaining it proves too strenuous, though, and after some minutes her mask begins to drop. What emerges in its place is a layer soft and vulnerable. Her face, framed by the frilled edge of her headwear, resembles a withered flower, her skin crumpled paper smoothed flat. Unexpectedly, Sien feels a rush of sympathy for the woman, and suddenly she can see her as Vincent sees her: a woman who has endured, despite all the struggle. She can almost hear him: *What is the value of pretty compared to life itself?*

Later, when Vincent's back is turned, she meets her mother's eyes. They flash with suspicion, even contempt, and she can almost hear her too: *Who dares to call this work? Sitting on one's backside?*

All the coffee has been drunk, and because the girls are tired after their sitting, Wilhelmina takes them home. Sien agrees to stay behind because Vincent still has energy to do more. He does not forget to pay Wilhelmina. The woman's smile lights up the room.

Alone, Vincent and Sien dispense with the work and quickly retreat to the bed.

Afterwards, discovering spots of blood on the sheets, Vincent is thrown into a state of near frenzy. 'Shall I fetch a doctor?'

'No, no,' she assures him. 'There is nothing wrong.'

'What if you are in danger? Or there's something wrong with the baby?'

Not in any pain, she is unconcerned; his agitation bothers her more than the red stain. 'It's probably nothing – just the baby growing.'

'So, it's happened before, with Maria?'

When she shakes her head, he is nearly livid. 'Well, how can you be sure everything is alright?'

That he should care so much baffles her; the child does not even belong to him. But she is not inclined to remind him of this fact, just as she is reluctant to disclose her wish for a stillborn – if he fears for the baby's wellbeing, then what would he think about her desire for its termination? Nor does she mention that this is her fourth pregnancy, for she is beginning to realise that for him the child inside her is not a cause for despair but a life he must save and, wanting to soothe him, she says quickly, 'Why don't I pose for you?'

He quietens then. Nodding, his eyes turn to his easel.

Five

It is the final weeks of this harsh season, and the frigid weather begins to thaw. Flushed with budding love, they have become as inseparable as any new lovers. Sien now spends most of her days at the studio, working diligently as Vincent's model, invigorated by her chance to escape her life.

Wilhelmina, assured by the regular guilders Sien earns, is able to give up sewing, that cursed thing, and does not complain, content to keep an eye on Maria.

Sien leaves early in the morning, joining the barge handlers, the streetsweepers, the porters as they begin their working day. She luxuriates in her leisurely stroll, the usual half-hour journey to the Schenkweg taking her nearly an hour. Rarely has she seen the city at such time. When she walked the streets, she never rose before midday, working through the deep of night before falling into bed, too exhausted to be able to tell whether it was night or morning.

Now away from Geest, and able to view the city in the vivid freshness of pink dawn rather than smudged by the purple of dusk and blurred by the orange vapour of gaslight, she realises it is rather elegant and beautiful. And because she no longer needs to search for paying clients in its streets, she finds it less hard, less mean. Did it also not provide her this man, Vincent? Just as a wispy, thin strand of hope rises within her, she picks up her pace, wishing to smother it before it has a chance to catch light. Her, Sien Hoornik from Geest, and a gentleman? It's too ridiculous, she reminds herself.

But as soon as she enters the apartment and finds Vincent up, smoking, drinking his coffee, she can't put her basket down and untie her bonnet with enough speed. It has become a sanctuary, a place where she can forget her family, her troubles. A place in which she can discover another side of herself: a woman relaxed enough to roam the studio in her undergarments; a woman who sits by the stove to smoke a cigar he offers; a woman who does not spend every waking minute thinking about the shortfall in rent, the empty pantry. A woman who has only one job: to pose for him.

She can even yield to those languorous urges to lie in bed, satiated by his attentions, while he works up his drawings. She enjoys watching him as he bends his sinewy arms and body towards the easel or drawing board, as though he means to embrace them. Fully absorbed, the effect of his concentration is nothing short of hypnotic, and even more impressive is how he can become instantly still by the simple act of holding a pencil or piece of chalk, coal, the lines seeming to emerge from his very fingertips. As he switches between the different materials, they end up behind his ear, sometimes in his mouth, so eager and impatient is he to avoid interruption of any kind. She can't help but admire and also envy his purpose, his pin-sharp focus and, most of all, his ability to escape the world. Because he seems to forget it exists. She suspects that even if rifles were fired at the windows or a blaze were to engulf the studio or the King himself turned up to stand next to him, they would barely register. Just as if she were to slip out quietly it would be some time before he would notice her absence.

Then, if he is happy and satisfied by the work, he joins her on the bed and they screw again, his intensity doubled now, suggesting the work he completed has given him new vigour.

'See? How can you deny what we have between us? It is just as Michelet said,' Vincent tells her, turning on his back.

'Michelet?'

'A French writer. He said life should not be lived alone but with another by one's side.'

'I've never lived alone, but I have yet to be happier for it,' she replies, recalling the crowded orphanage in which she and her brothers spent time, and the crowded attic room she shared with her siblings.

'No, Michelet is talking about a man and a woman. That if a woman is a man's joy, the salt of his life, then the man must be her protector, her strength.'

Afraid that Vincent will bring up the topic of marriage again, she stiffens. It is not that she is averse to or fearful of getting married; she wishes she already were so, living a quiet life with a hardworking man by her side and, more importantly, her children graced with their father's name. And even as she braces herself against the subject, a part of her also yearns to hear him talk about it. But her heart retreats from such fanciful musings. She knows the notion of marriage between them is little more than one of those fairytales she has always detested.

'Oh, yes, I always dreamt of being turned into salt rather than a poor whore,' she says, her tone mocking.

He chuckles. Then, burrowing his head into her neck, he begins to lick, murmuring how fond he is of salt, of its sharp taste; his tongue on her skin tickles her, and she writhes and wriggles, a chortle caught in her throat.

Some nights, too tired after posing, she stays overnight in Vincent's apartment, growing ever more reluctant to return to Geest. Captivated by his care and concern, the storm of misgivings inside her subsides, replaced by tender feelings for him. So much so that she asks herself: *is it love?* She assumes it must be. And though at times she is beset with doubts, she lets herself indulge in whimsy, imagining a future with him.

One early evening, just as she enters Geest, she hears a shrill, ear-piercing scream. Stopping at the entrance to an alleyway, she glimpses shiny blue fabric and a lock of reddish hair over a bare shoulder. Then two bodies locked in a fierce tussle. She recognises Rika straight away, despite the bruise of kohl around her eyes and her rouge-smeared cheeks. The girl is pinned against the wall by a soldier from the city's barracks. She is squirming, gasping, moaning, crying as her hair thrashes and whips her face.

Sien cannot bear it. Without thinking, she rushes into the fray. When her attempts to pull the soldier off the girl fail, she reaches into her basket, retrieves the small scissors from her sewing kit and jabs them into his side. It punctures his thick coat and he leaps back, staggering against the wall opposite, his cock still pistol-erect, his beer-soaked pupils dazed and glazed. Before he has a chance to recover, she grasps Rika's wrist and they scramble from the alley and make their way down the street Sien half-waddling, Rika half-stumbling as she clasps her torn skirt around her to keep her bare legs covered. They slip into the crook of another alley, both gulping for air. Rika turns and drops her head onto Sien's shoulder, her sobbing both violent and mournful. Sien remembers her own first time, around Rika's age – fifteen. It wasn't a soldier but an older man, grey-flecked and sombre but still vigorous enough to hurt her.

'It's alright,' Sien murmurs, stroking the girl's head. Though they both know that nothing is alright. They both know this is only just the beginning for Rika. Her hymen has been torn forever, and her future has already been written.

'I . . . I can't go home without any money,' Rika says, hiccupping now.

'How much did the soldier say?'

'Fifty cents.'

Sien takes out her purse and gives the coins to the girl along with her handkerchief. 'Here, wipe your face and go home now.'

Rika swallows hard then, hitching her skirt higher around her waist, she slinks off towards the courtyard at the back. Sien watches the girl disappear before straightening her own skirt, which had become twisted and bunched during their dash. Still a little out of breath, she leans her back against the wall. What is happening to her? She is beginning to care not only about her own fate but about others. Normally, she'd never part with fifty cents so easily. After all, it would have bought bread for a week, if not more. The old Sien would never have stopped for Rika, would have hurried off after a quick glance, her heart heavy but leaving the girl to her fate. After all, the incident was no more than a rite of passage for a young girl in Geest, just as it was for her and many other girls in their neighbourhood. But this new Sien is a woman who does not hesitate to give away fifty cents to a girl in distress.

Now she finds herself sorely regretting her actions. They were foolhardy. She fell victim to a momentary weakness, pitying Rika like that. While Sien is short of fifty cents, Rika will have to endure the groping of a different drunken soldier all over again tomorrow night. What good did she do – other than saving the soldier *his* fifty cents? Under Vincent's spell, softened by his attention, she wonders if she is starting to regard the world through his eyes. Since she has no doubt he too would have stopped and tried to intervene. The old Sien would have fought hard to keep hold of that fifty cents, knowing the difficulty of earning it.

Suddenly she feels very far away from Geest, as if she has left these streets altogether.

She enters her house, disturbed that it should be so quiet and dark. The lamp, or the candles at least, should have been lit.

What's happened? she wonders. Where is her mother, her sister, Maria?

The girls are not home, but she finds her mother sitting next to the window in near darkness, a towel in her hand, asleep.

As she searches for the matches to light the lamp, her mother wakes.

'Why is there no light?' Sien asks, finally locating the matchbox on the table.

'I was saving the oil.'

'But I told you this morning to buy some since I gave you half a guilder last night.'

The woman does not answer.

Sien lights the lamp but the flame flares for only a few moments before dying.

'Well?' Sien asks, looking about her. She can just make out the shaft of the half-candle in its holder on the mantelpiece. She lights it and brings it to the table.

Her mother sits up, her face glum.

'What happened to the oil you were meant to buy?'

'Karel came by,' Wilhelmina says without looking up.

Sien shakes her head. 'Don't tell me you gave him money?' Of course, Karel would have heard of Sien's new job, the guilders flowing through her pockets. But this is hardly the first time he has helped himself to her earnings, and nor will it be the last.

Wilhelmina's mouth is crimped tight.

'So he can go drinking? How could you –'

'Listen to yourself, Sien,' her mother breaks in, eyes blazing. 'How many times has your brother helped us?'

'Yes, but not lately and not for a long time.'

'Anyway, he said he's got some money owed to him and he expects to be able to settle with us in a few days or so.'

'And you believed him?'

Her mother shoots her a cold glance. 'While you're gallivanting around the Schenkweg posing for that artist, pretending to be a lady of the town, you seem to have forgotten who you are and where you're from. And even if you manage to forget while over there, don't you dare do it around here.'

'Why do you resent seeing me even a little happy? You . . . you ruined my life, and now there's this . . . this chance for me.'

Her mother sniggers. 'Ruined your life? It was the only way for us to eat. You know it as well as I do. We don't have the luxury to choose. And you don't have the luxury of laying the blame on anyone, least of all me. Do you hear?'

'Then you and Pa should have screwed less,' Sien flung at her bitterly. 'You should have kept your legs closed. All I've had since I can remember is a crying baby to help look after, when I was barely a child myself.'

Wilhelmina stands and swings her hand at Sien, who ducks just in time, her mother's fingertips only just grazing her cheek. As Sien storms out of the house, Maria runs towards her. The girl seems taller now than she had been that morning. Clutching Sien's leg, she shouts excitedly, 'Mama, Mama, I won. I had a fight with a boy and he ran home crying.' It is then Sien notices the crusty red chin, the scratch on her cheek.

'You did well. Go inside and tell Oma and then clean up. I'll be back soon and we can have supper.'

The girl rushes inside, her shoes clattering, her voice high like a whistle as she calls out, 'Oma! Oma!'

Evening has arrived, the shops are shuttering and the streets are quiet but for the noise of children in the distance. Their incessant chatter, their relentless, restless pursuit to sate their hunger, will keep them outdoors for some time yet. Why would she, or anyone else, choose to remain here if they had a chance to be somewhere else? She does not want Geest for Maria, nor for this unborn child inside her. She would like something better for them, someplace else and with a father's name. She has always felt this but now, possessing the courage to voice it, she knows that it is all Vincent's doing. Because of him she finds herself thinking about her life as more than a matter of survival; now she is beginning to care about her future.

Yes, she is willing to admit this place has already taken too much from her, making a mockery of the very notion of what it means to live. Here, there was never any room to assert herself, for her life never belonged to her; the struggle for survival had been foisted upon her and she does not doubt that in time it will be the same for Maria, and this baby growing inside her. She is already worried that if it is a boy, he will grow into another Karel. Despite what her mother said, she would prefer to forget this place, forget that she hails from here.

Six

One morning in early spring, she bleeds again. This time, Vincent is not swayed by her assurances, and he insists they visit the maternity hospital in Leiden, where she is due to have the baby; where she had the others, while young trainee doctors gawked at her as if she were a sow in a barn.

She is reluctant. In her experience, whenever doctors become involved it has always meant pain of one type or another. But he does not relent.

'Doctors can be miracle workers, you know,' he says, donning his hat.

She tries to persuade him that perhaps it would be better if she went alone. 'It's women's business, after all.'

But he shakes his head. 'Should I not learn how best to look after you?'

This idea is so unfamiliar to her that his question echoes in her mind repeatedly for a few moments before she has fully registered it. By the time her lips have opened to reply, he is already at the door.

'Besides, there is not just one life at stake, but two,' he says, turning the handle.

They are seated in the third-class waiting room at the station. But the activity of waiting is altogether impossible for Vincent – he has brought his sketchbook. His hand in constant motion, drawing their fellow passengers, only ceasing when their train arrives.

As they walk side by side across the platform, she can imagine everyone assuming them to be a married couple. Vincent hovers by her side, solicitous, a hand at her elbow to steady her, giving the impression he is aiding someone ill.

In the carriage, they sit opposite an elderly couple whose rheumy eyes glisten like those of fish and whose skin is burnished nearly to leather after working all their lives outdoors. And though their clothes are clean, they are somewhat threadbare from too many washes and too many pressings under a hot iron. A basket sits between them. Other than a quick nod they remain stone-faced, the corners of their mouths turned down. How long have they persevered together? Sien wonders. No less than decades. What must have passed between them during that time she can only guess at, but she finds herself contemplating the possibility that if she and Vincent were to marry, she may yet discover for herself the iron-wrought bond between a husband and wife so that words cease to be necessary. A lifetime with another by your side, but, she is also sure, a lifetime of toil and struggle. Then she chuckles quietly to herself because she wonders whether Vincent, even after many years, would be capable of such silence.

Next to her, entranced by the couple, Vincent eyes them too openly. When he takes out his sketchbook, the old woman stares him down with a gaze too frosty for Sien to ignore but which somehow fails to deter him, leaving her no choice but to nudge him with her elbow. He looks up and, meeting the woman's expression, slowly closes the book before returning it to the pocket of his coat.

Before disembarking, the old woman flicks her chin towards Sien's belly and mumbles, 'I wish you luck with your baby.'

They exit the station and head down the Stationsweg, a bustling street lined with coffee houses, shops and taverns. Sure that the wait at the hospital will be lengthy, they stop at the bakery to buy a large glazed bun. Then, as they are about to cross the canal near the hospital, Vincent freezes mid-step and, pivoting on his heels, begins to retrace his steps towards the station, leaving her stranded on the pavement. Confused, she turns and watches him before following hesitantly, wondering if he has changed his mind. Will she have to return alone to The Hague? She regrets agreeing to this needless trip. But then he spins around abruptly and paces quickly towards her. Taking hold of her wrist, he pulls her into a doorway.

She shakes him off, her patience deserting her. 'What are you doing?' she demands, glaring.

A finger at his lips, he shushes her. A vein is throbbing at his temple and his forehead is gleaming with sweat. Pushing the brim of his hat over his eyes, he peers out into the street, glancing cautiously left to right and back again, and she finally understands: he is hiding from someone. No doubt someone from his world. At last, satisfied the coast is clear, he steps onto the pavement once more.

'You see, I thought I saw one of my cousins,' he explains, his tic now roused. Is it an apology or an explanation? But it hardly matters, because this near brush with his family has sharpened a thought that has been nagging her: what is she doing in his company? And why is he getting involved with her? Though she can see how they could be mistaken as a married couple, given Vincent hardly dresses like a gentleman, and because the intimacy between them has allowed her to be accustomed to being his companion, she now sees its falsehood; they no more belong to each other than a man paired with a horse. Forced to see them through others' eyes, she is dismayed by her tempered heart. With a small tight shake of her head, she thinks, no, this will not do. She reminds herself she works for him, she is his model and no more, and she must resist – no, dismiss – the murmurings in her heart. It will only lead to her undoing.

When he reaches out to her, she ignores him.

The waiting room is teeming with women and children, and the queue is long enough for there to be no seats left. If it wasn't for this hospital, many poor women in this part of Holland would die giving birth, and there are more than enough women, more than enough bodies busy making other bodies, for this room to be never empty.

Small children, crusty-faced and rag-clothed, run amok. Some of the women are holding their bloated bellies, groaning, as a foul stench drifts through the building like the inside of a barn. She has seen it and smelt it all before. It's all the same, she thinks. The same drama, the same sweat, the same blood and tears whether people pushed out babies, horses birthed foals, cattle calves, ewes lambs and so on. All of them marching to the same end with none spared. Then all of it repeating again and again, like wheels spinning in mud, sort of pointless and stupid.

She leans against the wall, prepared to stand, as she has done in the past. But Vincent has other ideas. He disappears for some minutes before returning with a small wooden crate and urges her to sit. 'Here, you will be more comfortable with this. I can sit on the floor.' He helps her as if she were frail. But she discovers he is right. It provides a rush of relief to her back and legs. Taken aback by his attention, she wonders, Is this what artists do? Make a fuss? But more comfortable now, she cannot say she is not grateful for it.

Vincent is only the second man in the room. He glances about him as if he is enjoying a picturesque view. His anxiety at the close call with his cousin now forgotten, he reaches eagerly into his pocket for his sketchbook, telling her breathlessly about one of his favourite artists, Luke Fildes, an Englishman who made a fine woodcut of London's homeless as they queued for a bed on a winter's night.

'Don't you see?' Vincent whispers. 'This roomful of people nearly matches those subjects.'

She follows his gaze. She is unable to see any art; sees instead mostly stricken, unwell women who would like to see their suffering come to an end. His gawking soon attracts their scorn, one woman returning an expression so hostile that Sien – who can hardly blame her – reminds him in a low voice, 'They're not some goods in a shop window, you know.'

Disappointed, he lowers his gaze and returns his sketchbook to his pocket.

It is now near the middle of the day, so he unwraps the bun, causing a small riot among the children who have gathered around him. Playfully, he pulls faces at them, his eyes sparkling with delight at his usefulness. As he doles out small bites, he reminds her of a priest breaking bread at an impromptu service.

'So, Sien, another one?' asks Dr Thomas, peering at her with dark eyes that seem to have sunk deeper into his skull since she last saw him.

She reddens. She would prefer him high-mannered and haughty in that way so habitual to the men of his rank. But he is not, and she cannot help her embarrassment. She feels she has again let him down by her need to return to his clinic, and though she would find it easier if he were colder, she is also sure she would like him less if he were so.

Vincent, who has been shuffling behind her, now steps forward and pipes up, 'Am I to understand you have treated Sien before?'

'Yes,' replies Dr Thomas, raising his brows above his pince-nez.

Taking the seat next to her, Vincent leans forward with his elbows on his knees, fingertips touching. 'Then you're in an excellent position to advise us on the problem, because this has not happened to her before, despite the previous pregnancies.'

'And you are?'

Vincent does not answer straight away but, rubbing his palms too vigorously against his trousers, he fills the room with urgent, raspy music. 'Well, since you ask, I am intending to make her my wife,' he mutters, before swallowing hard. He then sits back calmly, looking pleased with himself, as if he has just been awarded an important prize.

Sien turns to him, indignant. Despite their moments of ardour and all the talk about Michelet, they have not spoken of it since his rash proposal. And now to hear him make this declaration in front of the doctor not only disturbs but riles her: it suggests she has agreed to it – as if this whore had the nerve to expect and accept a gentleman's marriage proposal for all the world to mock her: *How can she let herself be made such a fool of?* Then the fury subsides because his guilelessness frightens her. Where will it lead them? Especially her?

'I assume it is yours?' the doctor ventures.

Vincent shifts in his seat. 'Well, if you like,' he says, gesturing at her belly.

Dr Thomas, tipping his head to one side, considers Vincent with a bemused expression. 'I ask you, is it yours or is it not?'

'I don't see why this is of concern,' Vincent replies. 'It's a life we're trying to save here, is it not? An innocent life.

One who hasn't had a say about his coming into this world but one who is nevertheless fighting to do so.' His back stiffens, so his posture is like that of a proud bird. 'That's the issue, is it not? Not me or Sien – although I must admit she's just as important as the child.'

Despite Vincent's brief but passionate sermon, the doctor remains unmoved. 'So it's not yours,' he says under his breath as he picks up his pen. Yet after his scribble, he looks up and regards Vincent with twinkling eyes. Then, turning to her, he says, 'Well, Sien, I congratulate you on your man here. He may have been sent from the heavens for all we know.'

He bestows on her a warm smile. No doubt, very few women who have entered his hospital have been accompanied by a gentleman. That Vincent should be so concerned about an unborn child that is not his must strike the doctor as not only unusual but remarkable. And yet what does Dr Thomas know about him? Only that he speaks with fine, gentleman's words. And if Vincent really has been sent from the heavens, then why to her? What has she done to deserve him? After all, what church would have her? Should she now start to pray again, like she did as a young girl? Should she now start to care what happens to her? More familiar with contempt than this sugary talk, she feels a chill run down her back because she feels as if she no longer knows who she is.

She would like to flee this room, this hospital, but, like a chastened child, she can only look down at her hands.

*

'The baby is fine but it is in a breech position,' the doctor says after examining her. 'Instead of the head, the legs are pointing towards the birth canal.'

'Is the child in danger?' Vincent asks.

'No, not at this time. And it is quite likely the baby will turn before birth.'

'And if it doesn't?'

'Well,' Dr Thomas replies, stroking his beard, 'in that case the delivery will be long and difficult, and dangerous for both mother and child. We will certainly have to use forceps.'

Yes, she remembers these well, digging around inside of her during Maria's birth. But because Vincent shakes his head, the doctor explains that it is a tool much like tongs often used to help pull babies from the mother's birth canal. Vincent gulps, turning pale. She too shudders at the prospect of more meddling in that part of her body, a site of so many scars and battles.

'And the bleeding? Should she rest? Eat more meat?' Vincent asks, anxious.

'Look, it can sometimes happen after intercourse,' replies the doctor, eyeing them in turn. 'I will of course always recommend rest, a good diet. And yes, as much meat as you can afford, plenty of fresh air, you know that sort of –'

Vincent does not let him finish. 'Then we must do all that is necessary,' he says, palms smacking his knees.

The doctor, startled, nevertheless smiles approvingly. Removing his pince-nez, he addresses Sien again; this time his chin is lowered, his gaze stern. 'Well, Sien, it seems God has sent you a lifeline. A chance for you to turn your life around. I suggest you endeavour not to slide back into your old habits – I refer also to your drinking – and make every effort to look after yourself better. Do you understand?'

What can she do but reply with a deep nod, meeting his eyes for the briefest moment? Never before has he taken the trouble to give her this kind of advice, and, always a little afraid of him, she has never dawdled, taking leave of him as soon as she could. With Vincent by her side, everything is different.

The conversation between the men has turned to diets and bathing regimes.

'Oh yes,' Vincent is saying, 'I have heard about the health benefits of regular bathing. In England it's quite a common affair.'

'So you have lived in England? I have to say there's been much progress made in obstetrics there.'

And so Vincent and the doctor chat like old friends.

Before they leave, the doctor tells them the baby – five or six months into its term – is likely to be born in the middle of summer.

Vincent assures him that he will keep a close eye on Sien. Plenty of fresh air, a good diet and hygiene, strictly no jenever. 'Yes, mark my word, it will be done.' As Vincent bids the doctor farewell, he is so thrilled to be entrusted with Sien's care that he shakes not just the doctor's hand but his arm as well.

As they exit the building, Vincent babbles on. He boasts that he has never hesitated to put his trust in doctors; they have always impressed him with their knowledge of the human body. Moreover, he always enjoyed talking to them, for if pastors are the custodians of souls, then surely doctors were the body's equivalent, were they not?

Outside now, she manages to stride ahead of him despite her encumbered body, one hand lifting her skirt, her breath trapped in her chest. How she resents this sudden kindly interest in her just because Vincent is by her side. What do they know about a prostitute bearing another bastard child without a father's name, facing a blighted future? And what could be so sweet about it? *But oh, the grace of almighty God has blessed this poor, fallen woman with a gentleman. One who loves her despite her nameless children.*

How she would like to jump in the canal and free herself once and for all from her body and its vile swelling, giving herself over to whomever is waiting to judge her. Let it all be. Whatever her fate. Because why, after all these years, should she suddenly care about respectability when it could never compete with the business of survival? When her most enduring comfort has been the possibility of her suffering one day coming to an end? What good has this world, this body, this life done for her? Must she now also endure this shame?

Her boots slide on the gravel path, kicking up a storm of dust. Then, as she reaches the iron gates, she feels a kick inside her gut. The baby has started to move.

'Why are you in such a hurry?' Vincent calls out. 'Slow down, the train goes every half-hour.'

She leans against the post, her forehead pressing on the cold, hard stone. In vain she fights back tears. Then she remembers: around these months her emotions are always quick to surface. Sometimes there is a reason, other times not. Once, she found herself bawling at the sight of a grubby old woman in a dogcart who was not only peddling old pots, boots and brooms but buttons and dirty laces – anything she had managed to get her hands on. She can still recall the mangy hound brushing past her, and the wretched woman's gruff voice as she touted her shabby wares.

'Here, let's rest before we head back,' Vincent suggests, leading her to a bench facing the canal. As they sit side by side, Vincent drapes his arm around her shoulders but she shakes him off.

'Why do you insist on this – on these games?' she asks. It is a plea more than a question.

'What games?' He peers at her anxiously. 'It's far from a game. Do I need to tell you that I love you? That I am attached to you?'

'I'm a whore, Vincent. A *whore*. This' – she points to her belly – 'is my fourth. Why do you insist on your love for me? Did you not see the doctor's face?'

'Well, Sien, let me ask: why not you? Why not indeed? I'm happy to declare it should be you that I love more than any other.'

'But is it not my suffering that you love rather than me?'

'Can I not love both? The person and their life? If there's suffering, then all the better for me. How can I not love a woman who, despite her difficulties, can look into the heart of this poor artist with tenderness, one who must rely on his younger brother for bread.'

'Theo?'

'Yes, he sends me an allowance for the work I send him.'

Put like this, she can find little to say, his argument too weighty against her own meagre utterances. But more than that, his admission has made her angry heart relent. Her puffy body sagging deeper into the seat, the fight drains out of her, though she cannot entirely shake off her fears. Yes, she may have spent her life a presence barely noticed, but it also freed her from all obligations to worry about her fate. But now, to suddenly be witnessed in such light, she is forced to consider her life as something that has meaning.

His voice turning mellow, he continues, 'Sien, I only know what I feel. Remember what I said? I trust my heart more than my head. That's just the way it is for me. And my love for you does not care what you did to earn a living. If anything, my esteem for you has only grown because of it.'

'Yes, but you still had to run from your family on our way here,' she says, lifting her head. She does not doubt that he means everything he says, and the words that roll off his tongue soothe her like balm, yet still, she struggles to be convinced. 'But will it stand, Vincent, this business of the heart over the head, when your family learns of us?'

His tone is more amused than concerned as he replies, 'My family may be descended from royal bookbinders, they may own bookstores and fine galleries all over Europe, led a navy to battle, preach to the congregation – but they are not ready yet to understand because they do not know how to reckon with one's heart. But our bond is true and pure, so we have to be patient.'

She almost gulps. After all, his family has connections not only to the highest offices of the land, it seems, but to the royal court itself. She is torn between reason, sense and the swirl of her feelings. His nearness, his boldness, is like a magnet from which she cannot pull away.

'It may be so. But will time be enough? I can't see how they will forgive me. My past. I can't . . .'

He takes her chin gently between his finger and thumb and looks into her eyes. 'Why do you think you are unworthy of my love?'

'Don't you see? How could I expect or even dare to imagine this could happen to me? No one has seen me as a person before you. I've spent my life no more noticed than a crack in the pavement. Men don't see me; they see only pleasure. I live only to stop my family from going hungry. I am . . .' She stops herself, not wishing to say any more, afraid she may sound self-pitying.

'Well, then you must start to see yourself as I see you. Because why should you not be loved for what you have done and are still doing? How many of us could have done it, I ask you? Fending for her family as you did, walking the streets every night so they may eat. What's more, not once have you shown pity for yourself, despite what you've endured. And yet you insist on denying yourself. I tell you, I won't have it.'

It is no use, this effort to send him away. That he has been able to see her life with more clarity than she herself has calms the tumult inside her, his argument echoing a source more holy than common. Yet he is nothing like those preachers she has encountered on the streets. He does not admonish or pity; he only understands. After all her years on the street, she'd thought she knew everything there was to know about people, but she realises now how mistaken she was. Here is a man who seems to stand in defiance of all that she assumed mattered.

Even so, a stubborn part of her refuses to believe that a gentleman should feel love for her. She searches his face for signs of deceit, but his expression is as transparent as a sheet of glass. Is he really who he says he is? A gentleman capable of ignoring her past? Perhaps no one can know. But she finds her emotions swimming towards him, towards his every word – it seems they are buoys she must seize.

'I do not care whether the children are mine or not,' he says. 'They are simply children to me.' He sighs wearily. 'You will learn I do not care for many things that others deem to be important.'

The fight ebbs from her, the armour slips lower, and the tight knot inside her springs loose. As she dries her eyes, Sien notices they are in the hospital's garden, surrounded by a festival of spring flowers: the crocus and hyacinths are in full bloom.

During the next couple of weeks, Vincent is attentive to the point of being bothersome, making it clear he intends to adhere scrupulously to every one of Dr Thomas's prescriptions and more. Besides feeding her bacon and sausages, he brings her all sorts of concoctions – fortifying remedies – and urges her to drink them, prompting her to wonder if he is not falling victim to those jubilant nostrum peddlers who disappear from the streets just as quickly as they appeared.

She is served the greater portion of food. 'You need the strength for two,' he reasons. His unstinting generosity both quietens and staggers her, because never once does he make a show of being the one with the purse, as others in his position might have been tempted to do. Since their conversation in the hospital gardens, she has found herself yielding to him more and more, and yielding even to the child growing inside her; his awe at her changing body has persuaded her to think differently about this baby.

'It is the very presence of the holy,' he murmurs. Then, stroking her belly, he swears he can feel the blood churning, the new flesh stretching, the delicate bones knitting, and even the fluff of hair that must be shooting.

'I can only bear witness, so I must do what I can for it. After all, you are also occupied with an act of creation, different from mine, but just as worthy, if not more.'

It is apparent that, if he could, he would not hesitate to bear the child himself. Early on, she had every intention of telling him that this was not a life she wished to bring into the world, knowing only too well that the baby would always be her burden, and hers alone, with each one taking something from her so that afterwards less of her remained. But more and more, she is unable to be so candid. As well as the fear he may judge her harshly, his enthralment overpowers the misgivings she had with her other pregnancies, when, weak and hungry, she bitterly resented her condition. But now, perceiving her changing body through his eyes, she is able to regard it as a thing of wonder.

'I felt the boy kick,' he says, jumping back.

'How do you know it's a boy?'

'I can feel his pecker twitching,' he replies, laughing.

Then, as if the baby too is laughing, it begins to wriggle and contort, and her stomach comes alive. So much so that her waist seems to be dancing. Suddenly, from within, a potato-sized pummel – or is it elbow? – accompanied by a tight but graceful leap. There is synchronous stretching and contraction of flesh, a tug, a rise and fall.

'It's turning,' she mutters, gasping.

Still more snaking, followed by a stillness.

'A determined lad, is he not? Already preparing to leave his mother,' says Vincent, his astonished eyes still fixed on her stomach.

She can hardly believe this is her now. A woman who is care-free enough to chuckle. So, this was what it was like to be looked after by another. As the laughter leaves her, her insides seem flooded with light.

Seven

Spring is now well and truly underway. New verdant life is flourishing in the city's parks, and the streets are swarming with people, drawn to the outdoors by the irresistible pull of the warm sun. As if the season is a fever, Sien cannot help but catch its infectious, hopeful mood.

Vincent's campaign regarding her health continues unabated. One afternoon, it takes a new turn: he insists that she visit a bathhouse. 'You will not know yourself afterwards,' he tells her. She resists, disturbed by the idea of washing oneself in a place that isn't one's home, but Vincent is adamant. 'The therapeutic benefits of regular bathing have been proven in England, and it's bound to catch on here. It will make you stronger. You must go.'

He persists until she agrees.

Even before she has reached the entrance of the bathhouse,

she can feel the heat radiating from the bricks. In the women's second-class section, she is given towel and soap and shown to a small cubicle, where an enamelled tub – the largest she has seen – is filled with warm water. The attendant informs her briskly that it is not to be used for splashing her body, but that she should sit in it – in fact even try to lie in it.

She eyes the water, mesmerised by its volume. She has only ever sponge-bathed from a tub the size of a baby's crib, the water heated in pots and soon, after being shared with others, turned a dirty grey. But this deep trough of warm water, clean and clear, awaits only her, and invites her to steep her entire body in it. Gingerly she dips her toes in before slowly sliding her feet, ankles and the rest of her into the slippery warmth. Strangely her body, submerged, appears twice the size, almost fish-bloated. Her skin tingles and breaks out in goosebumps.

The sensation is unlike anything she has known before but too pleasant to forgo: she slips deeper. Every bit of her seems to untangle and loosen, and it is not hard for her to imagine herself as a leaf bobbing down a stream, free and untethered. Surrendering now to the weightlessness, she allows herself to sink even further, the soothing water lapping around her. She closes her eyes. Yes: when she could not see the light, when the weight of life seemed poised to crush her, she had often wondered about death. She thinks she would not mind it if it would be like this, a gentle drifting off into eternity.

The hiss and pinging of the pipes, the splash and slosh of water beyond her cubicle, reach her ears as nothing more than distant, charming echoes.

Stepping out of the tub, gravity seems to reassert its pull double-strength, and it takes all her effort to avoid dropping to the tiled floor. She becomes alarmed: what if the reason for the heavy feeling is the water? Has it seeped through her pores, into her? She shakes herself, half-expecting to spray the tiles. But no such thing occurs.

When she recounts her experience to Vincent, he chuckles. 'Trust me, water cannot enter you unless you drink it. How do you feel?' he asks.

'I feel different,' she admits. 'I feel as if reborn.'

He is pleased – she can tell by the way his eyes glint.

'It's no coincidence that we are baptised in water,' he says.

That night, the bed cradles her as if it were a cloud.

After following this regime for some weeks, she is not surprised to learn that he has completely run out of money. After all, has she not witnessed firsthand his poor skills in handling it? She is prepared to say careless, even extravagant. All those unproven health remedies, the money for the bathhouse, the smoked meats to give her strength; and though he no longer pays her a guilder for every sitting, it confirms her suspicions that she has been a burden on his finances.

Sheepishly, he reassures her that money is due any day from Paris. 'It could arrive with this morning's post. Theo never lets me down.'

But it does not come. In his pantry there is only a lump of crusty bread and just a thin smear of butter left, and she knows his rent is due. She fumbles in her purse. 'Here, I can give you this.' She returns to him her last guilder.

He frets. 'I cannot have you and the baby go hungry while you are working for me.'

'It's alright, I can manage.' And she means it. She has known hunger many times worse than this. Not on a few occasions, but often.

His tobacco pouch empty, he paces the length of the apartment, chewing the stem of his pipe as if it will provide him sustenance. Then he bites his fingernails until they are gnawed raw. Finally, he sits, trying to distract himself with his pile of magazines.

'Why don't you sell some of your work?' she asks, looking up from his socks that she is darning. 'Isn't your brother an art dealer?'

She thought it a reasonable question, but a flicker of fear she has not seen in him before flitters across his face. He does not answer her, turning the pages of the magazine in his hands quickly, noisily, while chewing the inside of his cheek. Then, almost leaping from his seat, he crosses the room to inspect his work. 'You see, I'm still learning. It takes time for these to obey me.' He holds up his hands. Then, turning them over, he examines them with suspicion, as if they are not his but someone else's.

He has come to art late, he explains. Before choosing this path, he tried his hand at many things.

'You see, I even sold art once. But the customers, well, they found me disagreeable and unfortunately I found them the same. I've preached at the Borinage, a coalmining district in Belgium.

I enjoyed the work but my style seemed to upset everyone, including the miners and their families. Apparently it was not acceptable for a man of my rank to live as poorly as they did.' He sighs. 'I also taught some fine boys at a boarding school in England, as well as selling books in Dordrecht. But I have come to realise it was my love for art that sustained me. And now I have just one ambition: I want to conquer drawing. And because I started so late, I am hell-bent on catching up.'

She nods, but she doesn't quite understand.

As if sensing this, he tries to explain. 'Don't you see? The line, it's the foundation of everything. Like a farmer who needs to understand his soil, drawing is the most fundamental thing there is in my work. For me it's the beginning of everything, of all art – though there'd be many who'd disagree with me. And if the line beguiles me so, well, I believe I must submit to it.'

His eyes burn with a determination far from ordinary; indeed, it almost frightens her. He looks like a man tormented, engaged in some internal battle. And though she can see the line is important to him, and that she must believe him, she still cannot fathom why he should suffer for it. How could she?

She is about to tell him so, her lips parting for a brief moment, but she changes her mind, worried it will only show up her ignorance. Yet her blank face must give her away, because he stands up impatiently, not bothering to try to explain himself further, and strides to the window. Gazing out, he rakes his hair as if trying to soothe a disturbance inside his head.

*

As she approaches the apartment the following afternoon, a lone figure in the distance catches her attention. He sits on the grass, near the ditch that runs past the Schenkweg. At first, she is unsure whether it is Vincent, but tracing the lean shape of his torso, his battered hat, she knows it cannot be anyone else. Yet, nearing him, she slows her pace. He is almost keeled over, legs tucked under him, and he is clenching the grass as if he means to turn the sod with his bare hands. She pauses, afraid but stirred by the sight of him huddled and alone. But hearing him sniffling she hurries to his side. Dropping her basket, she lowers herself to the ground next to him.

'What has happened?' she asks, a hand on his arm. Strangely, he is wearing what seems to be a newly cut suit from a cloth that reminds her of velvet.

He looks up but not at her, his wet eyes trained instead on the horizon.

'Imagine how simple life would be if one had wings, seeking shelter where one can find it, eating only what nature happens to provide,' he says wistfully.

She follows his gaze. A handful of swifts are gliding over the meadows.

'It's alright, I managed to get hold of some money,' he says, standing up and dusting off his trousers.

'Your brother?'

'No, I had to borrow it from someone, a man I used to work for. I'll pay him back when I have money from Theo.'

Astounded that he should have fallen into debt because of her, she bites her lower lip.

'There is still some bread in Geest, and it would have done me little harm to wait,' she ventures, but Vincent will not hear another word.

'No, no, no, you must eat while you are with me,' he insists, offering his hand to help her up.

'Well, what did he say to make you so upset?'

He sighs as he wipes his eyes. But as he tells her about the meeting with Tersteeg, who runs his uncle's art gallery, Goupil, on the Plaats, his expression hardens. 'I took some work with me to show him my progress, but his highness does not consider me an artist because I don't work with paints. Apparently, my work appears to have been done in an opium haze, and according to him I rely on drugs to deal with my fears about using paints. But his blockhead of highness seems to have trouble understanding that it's not because I can't, it's because I don't yet want to – not without first mastering drawing.' Then, after a sharp intake of breath, he continues, 'I told him I can't abide these so-called artists calling themselves painters when their canvases have nothing but feeble, unstable daubs of paint. But it seems Tersteeg has bricks for ears.'

Though she has heard him make this claim before, it is only when he attacks Tersteeg on another matter that the penny drops: the reason behind the men's strained relationship.

'In all likelihood it is because he is jealous. Not of me, necessarily, but my name. Deep down, I'm sure he wishes he were a Van Gogh. I mean, he is my uncle's right-hand man here in The Hague, and I'm sure he thinks if he had my name, he'd have a brighter future at Goupil. So it must vex him that fate should have bestowed on me a name I hardly seem to deserve.'

Jealousy – this, she understands. Nodding, she can't help but look over his suit, which is surprisingly well-cut, the rich fabric catching the light here and there, reflecting a dull sheen.

Noting her interest, he says, 'I had it made in Brussels last year. The fabric – they call it velveteen – was a bargain. Not that I should have bothered wearing a suit, for it made no difference. I could have worn a royal sash and Tersteeg would still have scoffed, I'm sure. He is nothing more than one of that accursed species, the petit bourgeois, with their petty preoccupations and smug respectability, lacking the noble qualities of even the simplest creature who is forced to find a bed on a cold night. Ha! Zola would have made a meal of him.'

Then, seemingly angry at himself for having attempted to please that man, he peels off his jacket with impatient fingers and rolls it tightly before tucking it under his arm. 'You wait, Sien, you wait. In time, I will show them all, do you hear?' He is almost shouting now. He picks up a rock and hurls it into the ditch. *Plonk.* Then, satisfied, he brushes the dirt from his hands before turning towards the Schenkweg.

She has no idea who Zola is, and though she is still reeling from having stumbled upon him in such throes, it is his admission about borrowing money – because of her – from a man he holds in little regard that continues to trouble her mind as she follows him.

Then a week later, despite her concern about the debt, she is left no choice but to admit the difference he has made to her wellbeing has been nothing short of remarkable. In these past few weeks, she has been unable to ignore the size of her flourishing body. Because the feeling is new, she has not been altogether convinced of it until one afternoon, in front of a hat store, Vincent stops and points to her reflection in the window. 'Have a look at yourself,' he says proudly.

He is right. Her face, almost plump, has become smooth. While her cheekbones have all but disappeared, her complexion glows peach-ruddy like they have been recently buffed, and her eyes, no longer dull, are as bright as marbles.

She stares, shocked. She can barely believe that it is her. When has she ever appeared this well, this radiant? She can't help but raise her chin just a bit higher.

But then she eyes her stomach, because it has never appeared this large. She may be glowing with health on the outside, but inside a darkening realisation begins to creep up on her: unlike the others, this baby is not only surviving but *thriving*. How else can she explain her girth? Only that morning, she noticed a lightning field of purple flowering across it, while the blood coursing through her feels as urgent as stormwater rushing down the drains.

As she turns away from the window, her old fears return, bracing and sobering. How had she managed to forget? How had she let herself be lulled by Vincent? His efforts are only making her body fertile for the baby, despite him knowing so little about bringing a child, precious or not, into the world. And what about those long, painful hours spent gasping for air, her body soaked with sweat as it expelled a thrashing creature, followed by the distressing realisation that she was expected to take the shrivelled thing home and keep it alive day and night when, after crawling into bed herself, she was unsure whether she would ever have the strength to leave it again? The men long gone, no one to help her but her contemptuous mother. It is little wonder some of the women in Geest have been driven to fling their newborns into the canal during the deep of night.

As they walk back to the Schenkweg, she is heavy not just in body but her mind. What can she do now? Any man from Geest, sympathetic to her plight, would have no trouble understanding her doubts and perhaps even try to help her. But not Vincent. No, there is no possibility of her confiding in him; if she did, she is convinced he would then have a good reason to abandon her. Just when she has finally found a man who is willing to take care of her.

Eight

Now that it is warm enough for them to do without the stove, Vincent has packed it up and put it away. But with the sunnier days, her body is not only large but has become bloated; and her ankles and feet, swollen, no longer fit her boots. After waking in her own bed one morning in Geest with cramps, she does not go to him for a couple of days. No doubt, if Vincent were to learn of her discomfort, he would insist they visit the hospital again.

When she does return to him, though it is midday, she finds him curled up in bed, wrapped in a blanket. He glances at her briefly, eyes strangely vacant. What is wrong with him? she wonders. Is he ill?

She deposits her basket on the table and searches the kitchen cupboards. There is no bread. No butter. No scent of coffee. He must have run out of money again. But there are just enough granules of coffee to make a half a pot, so she puts water on to boil. And by the time she returns with the cups, he is on his feet, eyes alert and body erect, and she wonders if what she just witnessed was a mistake on her part. Noticing his hole-ridden undergarments, she silently resolves to mend them.

'I . . . I don't have anything to offer you,' he says, swallowing hard, so his Adam's apple bobs.

It was just as she suspected.

'It's alright, I brought you some potatoes and beans,' she says, reaching for her basket. She now finds herself automatically putting aside any leftovers she can spare, for he is always in her thoughts when she is away from him.

He points to the letter on the table. 'I've just received word from Theo: there is money due in a day or so.'

While she warms the leftover vegetables, Vincent, seemingly spurred by the prospect of food and her company, dresses quickly. He almost swoops to the table, the wingspan of his arms hovering over the food. He eats ravenously, putting an entire potato in his mouth, his jaws clicking and twisting as his nostrils flare from the effort of breathing while chewing.

She notices a fresh drawing of an old woman, her back turned, hobbling with a stick, a chequered shawl around her head and shoulders.

'So, you had another model?'

'Oh, the old lady, you mean,' he says, swallowing. 'She was happy to pose for twenty-five cents.'

'You mean your *last* cents?'

He nods, cheeks bulging with food.

After they have eaten, he shows her the most unexpected thing: a black dress. 'It was in the window of a second-hand shop,' he tells her, as if this is the only explanation she needs.

She eyes it curiously. Why this dress? It looks like one of those worn by rich women in mourning.

'It was so reasonably priced.'

'Probably because it's a dress worn for the dead.'

He colours. 'Well, it's still beautiful don't you think?'

The fabric is shiny and smooth to the touch. The narrow sleeves, flounce-trimmed cuffs and collar, and triple-pleated skirt cause her to ponder the finger-stiffening time it would have taken a poor seamstress to sew them. Does he expect her to put it on? It is a dress so impractical that surely its only possible purpose is to adorn the body of a woman accustomed to never lifting a finger for herself other than to summon the maid.

'Can you . . . I would like to draw you wearing it,' he says, stroking his thighs briskly.

'Why?' she asks, holding it up at arm's length. 'Why spend the money on such a thing? It's useless. Where should I wear it? To the laundry?' She shakes her head, thinking of the bread it could have bought, the rent it could have covered.

'Look, artists like to draw their subjects in different costumes, so they can learn to draw all sorts of characters, if you like,' he says, avoiding her gaze and stroking his hair impatiently. She can see his cheek trembling, his tic starting up.

She is puzzled but also wary. His tendency to be particular, especially when it concerns his art, is hardly new to her. But why should he be so nervous? About a dress, of all things. A garment that is for her a ridiculous costume at best. And because he is behaving so oddly, she does not quite believe him, but nevertheless obliges and slips into the dress, which only just fits around her midriff.

He would like her to pose in the same manner as the first time he drew her, he explains – her feet resting on the foot-stove, wrist dangling on her knee, chin resting on her palm.

After only an hour, the pressure inside her becomes intolerable; she stands and begins to unbutton the dress.

Vincent glowers at her. 'No, I'm not finished yet. I need just a few minutes more.' His tone is noticeably terse and so, after a deep intake of air and a quick stretch of her limbs, she lowers herself to the seat again.

When the drawing is done, he is unusually hesitant, almost shy. Now more curious than ever, she insists on seeing it. 'I want to see how I look wearing a fancy dress.'

Reluctantly he shows her – and she realises immediately that the drawing is not of her, but someone else. Though she is dark-haired, the face he has drawn is much, much prettier. 'Who is she?' Sien asks, hands on her hips. Her mouth is so dry the words leave her as a whisper.

His cheeks flushed, he lowers his head. Unable to meet her eyes, he reaches for his pipe and fidgets with it, though there is no tobacco to speak of.

'Well, who is she?' Sien demands. 'It cannot just be the trickery of your hand.'

'She is my cousin Kee,' he admits, tossing the pipe back on the table. 'Last year, she broke my heart.' His voice is pinched, his disappointment clearly still fresh in him.

A broken heart, the most common malady going around anywhere. But the dress? She waits, crossing her arms.

He scowls and begins to pace the room, his fists planted deep in his pockets. Staring intently at the floorboards, he describes how he had fallen in love with his cousin the previous summer.

'She was recently widowed, you see. So you can imagine her fragile state. She came with her young son, to stay at my parents' parsonage in Etten. We spent many, many hours together walking in the copses. It was not just because she suffered such a loss, or because I was lonely; we . . . we grew very close. But when I finally found the courage to declare my feelings, she cut short her visit and returned to her parents' house in Amsterdam.'

Sien has little trouble picturing a sad widow wandering the countryside trailed by Vincent, who, stirred by her sorrow, waits at her elbow, ready to attend to her every need, but becoming more lovesick with each passing day. And she supposes only a woman from his world could afford to grieve in such a fine style.

'I went to Amsterdam to seek her out, to explain to her that my feelings were true, that I was sure she felt the same way about me,' he says. Then, his voice turning bitter, he continues, 'My parents, well, they showed me no sympathy. They were more worried about the family gossip than my feelings. But that's how they are. They even tried to dissuade me from going to see her. But when I turned up at her parents' house in Amsterdam, my uncle must have had wind of me coming, because he insisted Kee was not home. Now, I knew this was not true because I could see that a seat had been set for her at the table. So I refused to leave. Rashly, I put my hand over the flue of a lamp and threatened to keep it there until I was allowed to see her.' His voice quavers as he says, 'But my uncle turned down the flame and showed me the door.'

'And you are still in love with her. As for this dress – don't tell me it's hers.'

He shakes his head. 'No, no. But it's similar to the one she wore.' He winces as if in pain.

She gives him a level look. 'So, you decide a whore will be better for you. A cheaper replacement, I suppose.'

But why should she care? And yet, because she does, she is more annoyed with herself than with him. Yes, his heart has been broken, but whose has not? Yet who has the time and money to go to all this trouble to rub salt into his own wounds? A gentleman who does not have to count his coins because a postal order arrives regularly from a brother in Paris.

She steps out of the dress and flings it over a chair. The arms are turned inside out, the hem sags on the floor, the skirt slouches coquettishly. Her patience as frayed as her chemise, she steps clumsily into her skirt, almost losing her balance with the effort.

'You are using me to recover from your injured heart. I am not a fool, Vincent.'

He comes to her aid, one hand gripping her elbow, the other brusquely swiping the dress to the floor. 'Listen. Listen to me. I just lost my head for a short time, but I swear to you she means nothing to me – do you hear? Once I saw the dress, it seemed as if I became trapped in a dream.'

'Since you can always escape into a dream. Since you don't have to be part of the real world, I suppose. But you should be marrying your cousin, anyway, not a whore. You should just leave me alone and go back to her.' She searches for her bonnet.

'I don't have to be told what you are, Sien. But I see more than a whore. Why do you choose only to believe what others say about you? Why? Why does not my opinion of you matter? Is it easier for you to believe them because then you don't have to try to be different? Are you afraid of being with me?'

His question has the effect of a sharp jab to her head. She looks up. Is he playing mind games? How did this suddenly become about *her*, when it is he who has been caught out pining for his cousin? And yet his questions make her pause because what he says is not altogether untrue. Has she not also quietly worried whether she was really prepared to answer for herself this way? What it means not only to be with him, but to be so visible, so noticed?

'I know your heart is with your cousin,' she mumbles.

'It was with her, but now it is with you. You are the one who is prepared to roll up her sleeves and work alongside me. Don't you see? You are the one I love. I've never been happier than since meeting you. As I said, I don't care whether you are a whore.' His chin is lifted, arms crossed at his chest.

It is as if she is being split into two. One half of her is pushing her towards the door, urging her to walk out now and save herself the trouble, to make do until the baby comes then go back to how life was before. It is sheer nonsense that he should expect her to believe him. But the other half is rooted to this room, pinned by his unblinking, determined gaze, emboldened by his words. By the knowledge that he has come to know her better than any other. That he has been able to prise her heart open, when no one else had ever got close enough to hear it beat.

He draws her towards a chair. 'Sien, let me explain. It's simple. Because I do not earn two thousand guilders a year, because I am only a poor artist, I had as much chance of winning Kee as a streetsweeper trying to woo a princess.'

'I guess I am the streetsweeper wooing a prince,' she counters.

'Yes, this may be so,' he admits, chuckling. 'But it is also precisely why God would approve of our union even if others did not, and why those with priggish attitudes, always putting money first, will never understand anything about love. I will answer to God over those ignorant mortals. Besides, I am not interested in that kind of deceitful, false love.' He puts on a high, gossipy female voice. '*Oh, Vincent doesn't earn his own bread. He's nothing but a poor artist.*'

His mimicry is so convincing she can't help but burst into laughter. His tic stops, and his eyes glisten happily. But as her laughter wanes, something dark flits in her peripheral vision; something she cannot quite make out and which, even after a few blinks, refuses to disappear.

Nine

When she arrives at his apartment a few days later, even before Sien has put her basket down or taken off her bonnet, Vincent sweeps her up in his arms and attempts to waltz her around the room, despite her belly.

'I will have you know, I am a working artist now,' he says in a singsong voice.

'You sold your work?'

'No, not exactly, but I will soon be paid to do some.'

He releases her and sits, clasping his hands behind his head, pipe dangling from the corner of his mouth and feet propped on the edge of the table.

Surprised to find him like this, she joins him, eager to know more, warmed by the contentment radiating from this calm Vincent, who shows no trace of his usual skittish manner.

'My uncle Cor paid me a visit. One of my father's brothers.

He has commissioned me to do six cityscapes at two and a half guilders each.'

She does the calculation. Yes, a decent pay. More than a month's work for her on the streets.

'It's my first commission as an artist,' Vincent declares.

'Is he the one who owns Goupil?'

'No, that's uncle Cent, but uncle Cor also sells some art and deals in prints and books, so he knows his art. But it doesn't mean he and I see eye to eye about it. In fact, far from it, I can assure you. His idea of a beautiful painting is *Phryne Before the Areopagus* by Gérôme.'

She looks at him blankly. 'Who are they?'

He gives a quick, dismissive flick of his wrist. 'Gérôme is a French painter. Phryne was a prostitute from classical Greece. In the painting, she has no hair between her legs – in fact, she has not one single strand on her entire body. Her skin is purer than marble. You get the idea. My uncle and I argued about it a few years ago. He thought it the most exquisite painting, and he just couldn't understand why I disagreed with him. I thought the whole thing ridiculous and told him so.' Lighting his pipe, he takes a deep, slow puff. 'Anyway, he rifled through my folio, and I had hoped he would say something about the figures, but instead he liked the city views I had drawn. I shouldn't be surprised – my figures are hardly like Phryne, after all.'

'So he came today?'

'This morning, early. Like a man who had little time but many things to do. And as soon as he sat down he told me that

I should be earning my own bread instead of relying on my brother. This is all before I even offered him coffee.'

'But you said Theo was sending you a wage in return for all the drawings you send him.'

'Yes, but my uncle and Tersteeg do not seem to think that I deserve it because the work is not selling. Ha, but you see . . .' He springs from his seat and begins to pace the room. 'I told him that whether money came from one's pockets or another's, it has nothing to do with whether one deserved it or not. I told him that, like a farmer who toils on his land but is not able to reap the rewards of his labour for reasons beyond him, I too work damn hard – harder than most. With my hands, like any labourer. And I consider myself one of the most honest, hardworking men there is – and any man who strives deserves to eat.'

Absorbed in his recount, it seems to matter little whether she is listening or not. Like a man possessed he laughs aloud to himself.

'My argument was so clever, so right, I assure you it not only shut him up but made him blink like a fool who was seeing daylight for the first time. He looked rather sorry he mentioned it.' Vincent is sniggering now, his pacing gaining speed.

The earlier glow she felt inside her begins to dim. She turns away, tired from watching him, listening to him. She is getting a good picture of his family. An uncle who does not approve of Vincent being supported by his younger brother. And since Vincent is using Theo's money to help her, what are the chances they will approve of her? Of course, this fact has hovered in her mind from the beginning, but it now occurs to her that, despite

Vincent's heated words, he has no thought for the cold reality of how things really are. A pastor for a father, uncles who own art galleries not just in The Hague but all over Europe, an art dealer brother in Paris who is rich enough to send him money regularly. Had he not told her once that his mother's family were once bookbinders for the royal court? That one of his uncles was an admiral in the royal navy? Would they really allow one of their number to associate with a whore from the slums?

She shudders as if snow melt is trickling down her back. What in the world is she doing here? Picking up her basket, she heads towards the door.

'Where are you going Sien? We've got work to do.'

'It's no use, Vincent,' she replies, her eyes moist. 'Your family will never allow you to be with me.'

He wrests the basket from her and, slipping his arm around her waist, leads her back to her seat.

'Sit,' he instructs. 'As you know, my so-called family threw me out of home last Christmas. And apart from Theo, who has stuck by my side, they were glad to see the back of me. You know, not long ago my father attempted to have me sent to the madhouse in Geel, all because of a misunderstanding, a disagreement. But I got wind of his plans just in time. You see what he is like? Can you imagine a more devious plan for one's child?'

She shakes her head. A most harsh measure for anyone, she supposes. For all of Vincent's oddities, she cannot see how he should belong there. Whenever she happened to pass the madhouse in Geest, the thought of all the poor souls stuck behind its walls always made her heart heavy. How could anyone stand the constant screaming, the shouting, the moaning day and night? Surely the place would send you mad if you weren't already.

'It was not I who saved you that night we met, Sien – it was you who saved me. Meeting you made me forget my despair. I would not be surprised if God himself delivered you in my path.'

She stares at him, disbelieving. Is he trying to deceive her? Is this false kindness?

But he is looking past her, gazing at some faraway place over her shoulder. 'Were it not for you, I would certainly have gone under; my friends, my family had all forsaken me. Even Theo wrote a terse letter, scolding me. And' – he pauses, swallows – 'and that night I was . . . well, I was at the end of my tether. But then to see you struggling gave me strength, took me out of my despair.' When his eyes meet hers at last, she notices he is blinking back tears.

She had simply thought him lonely, and her rescue the act of a good Samaritan. But now his zealous efforts to win her over are beginning to make sense. He too was caught in the scramble of trying to save himself, to retreat from the edge of the precipice. Does she not know that feeling well? She feels herself softening, the tension leaving her. So, they had saved one another. It seems that despite the vast difference in their social and financial standing, he had been in a situation not too different from hers that night. Did that explain the immediate sense of intimacy between them? she wonders.

He takes out his handkerchief and quickly wipes his eyes and nose.

'If only I could see my parents' faces when they learn of this commission,' he says, sniffling and sneering all at once. 'My uncle is not the indulgent type, they know that. They will now have no choice but to admit my career is well and truly underway.'

'Would they not be happy for you?'

He snorts. 'They will be suspicious at first. Of course, anything that Theo does causes them to stick out their chests like a proud pair of pigeons and coo approvingly.' She can see the hurt on his face. Though the brothers may be close, it seems there is a rivalry between them nevertheless.

'And I suppose, they cannot know anything about me,' she says, fixing his eyes with hers.

Because they flash-startle with panic, she thinks at first she has backed him into a corner. But he returns a stare even more defiant, almost confrontational. 'It makes little difference. In fact, none, because I am nothing like Theo, you see. Unlike him, I will stand up to them. Indeed, this is the perfect test for my family.' He is smirking now. 'Let's see if they are who they claim to be. Let's see if they know the true meaning of Christian duty. Instead of just delivering sermons, let's see if they can put them into practice. Yes, it would give me great satisfaction to –'

'So, you are using me to punish your parents? Is that it?'

His mouth drops open, as if such a thought had never crossed his mind. 'No, no, that's not true. How could any man worth his salt turn his back on a woman who is poorly, especially one with a child? You tell me. What is the point of writing sermon after sermon only to then walk past another in need?'

He is prepared to defy them. For her. She fears God himself is demanding something of her: have faith in this man. *Have I not shown you proof of my compassion?* But more than anything, it is Vincent's stubborn audacity that leaves her speechless – and moved. Though it will cause a scandal for his family, he appears unafraid, determined not to bend. Looking into those unflinching, steady eyes, she can feel her own heart growing bold. After all, who else would have done what he did for her? Certainly, not those on street corners waving their Bibles, urging her to lead a sin-free life without ever reaching into their pockets to buy her a meal. Doesn't she too hold in contempt those who invoke God's name only when it suits them?

'Still,' she points out, 'wishing for your family to accept me may be like wishing for the sun to never set.'

'Sien, you don't know what I'm capable of,' he says coolly. 'Yes, it will upset them, but if I am to be with you, I have no choice. And believe me, I intend to marry you – as soon as you have had the baby and are well again. Just you wait and see.'

At his mention of marriage, her earlier doubts come flooding back. She stands and walks to the window. She purses her lips, trying to stem the tears welling in her eyes. She is almost certain that, on learning of her, the Van Goghs will arrive at the Schenkweg to claim him while she will be banished back to Geest, where she belongs, and where her own people will be waiting: *Well, what did you expect?*

Perhaps she is a fool to remain here. But then what other life is there for her? Nights walking the streets searching for men, and a future as dead and bleak as the cold ash in the stove. But it's too late in any case, for she does not know how to undo this heart of hers, which she never had cause to think about as much as she has in these past weeks. It occurs to her that it is not Vincent who has been backed into a corner: it's her.

He comes to her and, as if he understands his words are not enough, he kisses her. As her doubts flee and the helter-skelter of her emotions calm, she realises she *must believe him*. She must believe that he is as different in this way as he has shown himself to be in everything else so far.

Ten

It has become different, the screwing. She would not have believed it possible, but in recent days it has become more tender in feeling. He still has the intensity of an animal on heat but, no longer clumsy, he has become a gentle and deft partner, so they are not just screwing but making love, something that is entirely new to her. Slowly, gradually, she finds herself accompanying him to new depths. Even the smell of him, and the blaze of hair that covers him, are cause for moments of small pleasure.

Always now, he is quieter afterwards. It is like lying next to another man. He is as still as a pond at dawn. His lightning-crackling nerves calmed, his wound-up body unspooled, his breath smooth and steady. They do not speak. She forgets time, the moment stretched so long that she is ready to believe there has been no other, and there will not be another – only this. But, as always, he is the first to break the silence.

'What better balm is there? It's like a tonic,' he says, fingers drumming playfully on his bare chest.

Talking as if to himself, he wonders why people – including his parents, uncles and aunts, who at one time or another must have also felt this undeniable calling of the body, the most natural of inclinations – insist on considering it an unfortunate affliction, when really it is one of the most fundamental conditions of being alive.

Then, seemingly pleased with this insight, he turns to smile at her. 'You are just like one of Landelle's angels. Your profile, I mean.'

She sighs and rolls her eyes. 'Angels, the Virgin Mary – who will I look like next? God?' she asks, only half-joking. She does not enjoy this nonsense talk of his. She has never been told that she is pretty, not even as a young girl, and certainly never likened to an angel.

But he just laughs and says, 'Well, I wouldn't dismiss the possibility.'

She rises from the bed to use the pot. These days the growing baby presses more urgently against her bladder than before. She squats, naked, to empty it, and the noise she makes sounds as if a dyke has burst.

He props on one elbow to watch her. Again with those eyes that seem to want to peel back a layer of her skin. She shoots back a frown.

'It's the line, Sien: you are an unbroken line,' he explains.

Then, hastily pulling on his undergarments, he insists on drawing her.

'Without my clothes?' she asks, perturbed by his request.

She may have screwed many men but to be drawn naked for the world to see . . . well . . . she may as well undress herself in the middle of the Spui and stand there naked. Where would the drawing end up? Hung on somebody's wall, someone she doesn't know, for countless pairs of eyes to gawk at?

She shakes her head.

Ignoring her, he fetches the foot-stove and, throwing a towel over it, asks her to squat as she did earlier on the pot.

'No, let me get dressed. I should take the pot down to the privy.'

'Leave it, I'll empty it in the morning. Just do as I say.' He holds her by the elbow as she lowers herself onto the brick-high seat. Then, standing back, he tips his head to one side and takes her in from head to toe. What is he seeing? What is he looking for? He seems to appraise her, examining her as would a farmer at a livestock auction. She is not cold but goosebumps cover her arms. Vincent's gaze makes her feel as if she is lost in the woods with not a single thread on her body.

'I want to at least put my drawers and chemise on,' she insists.

'Are you cold? I can unpack the stove.'

'No,' she almost shouts, turning to him with eyes as big as she can make them.

'You must understand, artists' models must be prepared to pose nude. All the great artists have painted nude women – even Rembrandt.' He comes to her. 'An artist must learn to draw the human body, as God made us.' Seeing that she remains unconvinced, he takes her face between his hands and pleads with her. 'Do it for our future. If I am to earn a living as an artist, this is a skill I must learn.'

He is speaking of them as if they are one. She hesitates, still apprehensive but drawn to the vision of their shared life.

Sensing her softening, he presses his advantage. 'This is only possible because of the way I feel about you. I have not been moved before to do it. All those artists sitting in front of a model at the art club to draw a body they do not know, for which they have little feeling, is not for me.' A kiss. 'What if I keep your face hidden?'

So, she relents. He allows her to look at the floor between her feet, fold her arms across her knees and rest her head there. He plays with her hair, arranging tendrils over her shoulder. She can just make out the dark thatch peeking out below the curve of her belly as the sour odour of her feet and body fill her nose.

Unusually, this drawing doesn't seem to take long.

'Here, finally, my first nude,' he says, lifting it off the easel.

To her relief, her face cannot be seen. No one will know it is her. He has drawn her from the side, her limbs, torso, traced in a thick black curve. That line he keeps fussing about: it is there, from her head to her toe, a single, solid thread. With her hair loose, she could be mistaken for a girl of sixteen, not a woman of two and thirty. But the breasts give the story away, for they hang udder-heavy, almost cradled by her swollen belly. The portrait is too ugly. And yet it is utterly real, and she can't help but admire his skill, that his hand should have rendered her so. Despite her earlier reservations, she is glad that her posing proved so useful, that the drawing is a success. Still, who would want to look at such a picture? Of a creature so pitiful? Surely no one would find it attractive enough to buy, let alone put up on their wall.

'It is the best one yet,' he murmurs excitedly. In the lamp's glow, his face gleams like polished brass. He fetches fresh paper. He wants to make copies. He will trace it.

She climbs into bed and props herself on her elbow – her turn to watch him. It is remarkable, she thinks. How he seems to lose himself entirely when he holds a pencil, his hand steadier than a bird gliding through the air. A man who normally hums and sparks with energy is suddenly nothing but concentration and stillness.

Next morning, he is up early, writing a letter to his brother. He will send the drawing to Theo at once. 'Because it is nothing short of a breakthrough.'

'Does he have to see it? It's just an ugly whore.' Now clear-headed after sleep, and once more self-conscious, she tears her gaze from the image.

He raises his head to look at her, eyes wide with surprise. Putting his pen down, he says, 'Is that really what you think?'

'Look at the spindly thing; it's a stick with a pillow for belly.'

'There is beauty in sorrow, there is beauty in a stick,' he replies, grinning mischievously.

'What would he think? This whore of yours. He will cut you off for sure.'

'Ah, no, my brother is not like the others. He will appreciate it as a fine drawing, I am sure of it. It will be the most convincing evidence of the improvement I have made in my work. Besides, I have yet to tell him about you. But don't worry, I will – soon.

As I will also inform him that I could not have undertaken this drawing without a regular model.'

In the light of day, she can't help but be filled with doubt. She frets, frowning and twisting the ties of her drawers around her fingers. 'What will he say?' she asks, collapsing onto a chair. 'He will tell you to go to hell – with me.'

He laughs. 'Well, as long as we are there together, why not?'

He returns to his letter, and just like in his drawing sessions, when he seems to disappear into his work, as if merging with the task, there is only the writing and nothing else. Hushed and bewitched by his ability to write, she can only watch him, her concerns forgotten. Page after page he fills with neat, tiny script, his arm, hand, wrist rolling across the paper without lifting once. It is a mystery to her that someone should write so tirelessly, so gracefully. Read she can, a little, but write, no.

Not long after, following one particularly unbridled bout of lovemaking, he dashes off another nude of her, this time from the waist up, his wrist almost flying off the paper, his strokes neat, broad and sure.

But glimpsing it she wonders if it is a joke. She looks almost mad with her eyes half-shut, unsightly bust and teats prominent, making her appear no different from a cow. But she is wearing a spontaneous smile, and she appears content, even happy. A strange sight and yet it captures exactly how she feels. How did he know? Do his eyes have special powers?

Vincent, chuckling, tells her that it is a rare privilege for him to draw a figure caught in an unguarded moment – one that he could never have captured at Pulchri where, in the stuffy, stifling atmosphere of their life-drawing classes, he found his hand seizing up so much that he dropped his pencil, causing the other artists to turn and look – he was at the back – all wearing the same withering frown. Even his pencil worked against him, rolling further away from him as he scrambled after it. Then, after he managed to retrieve it, he broke out in such a sweat it became impossible for him to resume.

She nods, chortling. Yes, it is not difficult for her to picture him there, uncomfortable, nervous. She is beginning to understand why this studio on the Schenkweg matters so much to him; why he must recruit his own models.

'Now, if only those artists could see what a few assured lines, done in hare-footed time, can achieve.'

He sits at the table and packs tobacco into the bowl of his pipe with visible glee, glancing at his work as if he has ensnared a prize catch. The drawing mattering less to her, she is simply pleased to see him happy.

Eleven

It is now almost summer. Vincent ventures outdoors in search of streetscapes for his uncle's commission. His enthusiasm infectious, she finds herself accompanying him into the streets, sometimes posing against a backdrop as a figure.

They establish themselves on a bench near the Mauritshuis. He is no longer shy about what he is up to, but the prying crowd has no qualms about interrupting him, making it difficult for him to work. Some of them peer over his shoulder to boldly offer their opinions, often scoffing, as if they, despite their threadbare clothes and wooden shoes, know something about art. She can hardly blame Vincent when he stands up and blusters to an elderly man, 'What business is it of yours? Are you an artist? Or a failed one who thinks he can do better with his mouth?' As Sien chuckles, the man scuttles away, shouting over his shoulder, 'My eyes may be old, but they know an artist when they see one, and *you* are no artist!'

Eventually, Vincent decides it will be easier for him to work at dawn, when the streets are quiet. But once the drawings are sent to his uncle he is beset with worry when he does not hear from him straight away. Then, when his uncle finally sends a word, Vincent is still not satisfied. 'How can he not tell me what he thought of the work? Whether he liked them, or whether he thought them poor, good. Not a word of encouragement.' Yet he has given Vincent a commission for six more drawings.

'See? He must have liked them otherwise he wouldn't be asking for more,' Sien says, confounded that she should have to point this out to him.

'Yes, yes, Theo has also said as much,' he mumbles, sounding only half-convinced. 'Now, I have to find more streetscapes.'

Where is his previous excitement? Another lot of drawings, another payment, yet he broods, fiddles with his pipe. When she complains to him about the frenetic activity in front of her house, of workers digging up the street to lay sewage pipes, his expression finally brightens, his eyes flashing keen. 'I would like to see it. It's a streetscape, after all, with busy workers.'

On their way to Geest, they pass a house under repair. Above them a sudden loud noise, like thunderclap, shatters the sky. Though they duck their heads, it is too late. Broken mortar and clouds of dust rain down upon them, followed by a raucous bellow of laughter. Sien's throat swells, her chest heaves. She knows this was no accident. The jeers of the workers above confirm it: 'There goes that whore and that bothersome artist.'

She waves her fist at them, shouting, 'You cowards, safe up

there in your little nest. Why don't you come down here and say it to my face, and see where that gets you?'

Vincent does not bat an eyelid. He has already dusted off his clothes and tries to do the same for her. She is seething but he looks at her with admiring eyes.

'Your temper, it is magnificent,' he says, taking her arm and leading her away. 'You know, my mother and sisters would have scurried away as quickly as mice.'

In front of her house, Vincent is thrilled to find the street torn up. 'I have come just at the right time,' he says, delighted by the hustle and bustle. The pavers have been lifted and a sizable trench – into which the pipes will be laid – has been half-dug by the hefty workers, their garb splattered with mud. A gentle, hazy rain drifts lazily from heaven, a damp veil.

Vincent tucks himself into the corner of an alley and begins to draw.

While he works, Sien goes to the grocery store to buy coffee. Outside, she encounters Lena, who greets her with a manner too gushing, so affected that Sien immediately draws back. 'How well you look for someone carrying,' Lena says, her nostrils flaring as if she has detected an unpleasant smell. A good few years younger than Sien, she also walks the streets but is sprightly and youthful, giving the impression her job is no more than taking evening strolls through the city. And as if she does not believe herself bound by the same rules as everybody else, she does not don a bonnet, but wears her feathery blonde hair pinned up in a small crown, while a smattering of freckles decorates her pert nose, helping to enhance her carefree look and attract a steady supply of men.

Sien nods and, though she tries to refrain, she can't resist an envious glance at Lena's supple waist. Since Lena has so far, miraculously, escaped bearing a child, Sien supposes she can afford to be cheerful and untroubled. There are rumours that Lena drinks a special concoction that stops the men from impregnating her, but Sien suspects that Lena has been blessed with a body that refuses to bear children.

'Let me see,' Lena says, cocking her head to one side thoughtfully, 'it's your third, right?'

Sien shakes her head. 'No, my fourth,' she replies, her chin lifted. 'I'm hoping this time it's a boy, since I already have a girl.'

Lena pretends not to hear her, waving instead at someone across the street, before turning back to Sien. 'I have not seen you around here lately; where are you working now?'

She is sure that Lena, like everyone else, would have heard about Vincent, for news travels through the alleys and streets of Geest more swiftly than a spark in a haystack.

Sien puts on a small smile and, playing the game, answers in a bright tone, 'I'm working on the other side of the city, over the train line.'

'Are the streets busy there?' Lena asks, eyes wide.

'I'm working for an artist. Posing.'

'There was an odd fellow around here,' Lena says, twirling a coil of hair just above her ear. 'A red-haired man, if I remember, hassling people to –'

'His name is Vincent,' Sien says, cutting her off.

Lena raises her brows. 'Oh, it's him, isn't it? You're working for that . . .?'

'Yes. And he pays better than any man you can find on the street,' Sien replies, turning her back and heading into the store.

Inside, waiting her turn, embarrassed and confused by her tactless display of one-upmanship – so unlike her – she wonders what is happening to her. In the past, she would have avoided the likes of Lena, crossing the street if she had to, preferring to mind her own business. Or, more truthfully, she would have been too intimidated by the younger woman to do anything more than offer a passing nod. Instead, as when she rescued Rika, this new Sien is unafraid to speak in a different voice, one brassy, almost righteous even. Puzzled by this woman who is happy to indulge Lena in a conversation merely so that she may have the last word, she walks back to her house briskly, her head down.

As they are drinking coffee, her brother Karel arrives. It is not even midday, yet he reeks of beer. It is clear he has been out all night, drinking and fighting, for there is a fresh bruise on his cheek. Unlike Pieter, Sien's other brother, who found a trade making chairs, Karel has a knack for finding trouble. Yet he always seems to have more money than anyone else. For a time, pretending to be a nightwatchman in the rich suburbs of The Hague, he managed to earn a living more profitable than all of them combined, getting a generous cut of the robberies' proceeds.

His smile is wily as he takes in the gathering, his eyes dancing over those seated around the table. When his gaze comes to rest on Vincent, his grin becomes livelier, almost devilish. Sien can feel her stomach knotting. Though she may have raised her fist at those builders, here she knows her place.

As if his entrance has cast a spell over everyone in the room, they sit in uneasy silence, each unwilling to speak first. But it seems Karel is in no mood for conversation; he leans his mouth into Sien's ear and whispers sweetly that he would like a word with her in the bedroom. There, with a hand squeezing her neck, he slams her against the wall. Her gasp is smothered by the pressure on her throat.

'What do you think you are doing?' he hisses.

Tears spring up in her eyes. Though younger than Sien, he has always frightened her, even when they were children. 'Let me be,' she splutters, pushing him off her. She dashes for the door, but he grasps her wrist and pulls her back.

'So, you think you are too good for us now? I hear that some nights you don't bother to come home. How lucky for us that we are graced with your presence today.'

'It's not what you think,' she says, swallowing. 'The work is just as hard as screwing, if not harder. It goes on and on, sometimes for hours.'

'He's got money then,' he says, squeezing her wrist tighter. 'Enough to dole it out for those who do nothing but sit on their dumb arses.'

She shakes her head. 'No. His brother sometimes sends him money, but his father's a poor pastor in the country. And there's never enough bread.'

'Oh, so you are doing it out of charity, are you?'

'He says we . . .' She is about to blurt out his promise of marriage, but changes her mind. He will think her crazy.

But it is too late.

'So then, is he going to marry you? Is he? He's told you that he loves you, has he? And I suppose you believe him?'

She shuts her eyes.

'Or do you think the bonus sex that he gets with the posing may have something to do with it?' The sly smile has returned to his lips. 'You're mad if you think his family will allow it. You're just wasting your time.'

'He has taken me in a cab, he has fed me meat, he bought me a dress. No one,' she says, wiping her eyes, 'ever bought me anything before.' She immediately regrets her words. Where had this self-pity come from? Besides, it is only likely to invite Karel's contempt, his ridicule.

And so it proves.

'Oh, poor Sien. A dress, is that all it took? Well, you will have something to wear when he introduces you to his family, I suppose.' He puts on a mock-serious face. 'You won't forget to tell me the date of the wedding so I can have a suit made in time, will you?' And then, roaring with laughter, he leaves the room.

After the episode with Karel, Sien does not wish to spend the night in Geest and decides to accompany Vincent back to the Schenkweg. Shops are shuttered and the gas lamps flare like giant stars against the dusky sky. Vincent, inspired by his productive day, wants to make a stop at the Plaats. The Goupil gallery's window display, gas-lit, dazzles them.

'Ah, here is the temple of art and its holy relics,' Vincent says, snorting. 'It resembles a theatre set. It's hard to tell whether they are selling the gilded frames or the art.' But then, leaning into the window, he eyes the paintings hungrily, his face so close that his breath leaves a damp patch on the glass.

'Ah, Jozef,' he murmurs, focusing on a portrait of an old fisherman in a sou'wester. 'Isn't it marvellous?'

She agrees. 'Yes, it's so life-like.' The old man's craggy face has an almost hypnotic effect. His skin, after years of working in salty spray, is thick and cracked like old hides. A pipe is clamped between his lips, and his formidable chin rests in the crook of his neck, his eyes gazing into the middle distance. What is he thinking about? she wonders. What has he seen? Unable to take her eyes off him herself, she can see why Vincent is so entranced by the painting.

'This fisherman's head is so Rembrandt-like it is as if it has been painted by the great master himself,' Vincent says.

She has not heard of Jozef, but like any Dutch woman with ears, she has heard of Rembrandt.

'I must draw my own fisherman soon, with a sou'wester and all. I doubt there is a more interesting subject type than a fisherman. Cast out into the unpredictable elements, making a living pitted against the most volatile of nature's forces,' Vincent raves.

'Will you be able to sell your work here too?' Sien asks.

The spell is broken. He turns his back on the painting as if it is now unbearable to him.

'Perhaps, but it won't be any time soon.'

He walks away, so she follows him. Catching up to him, she presses, 'But doesn't your uncle own this gallery? Doesn't your brother work for them too?'

He stops and glowers at her. 'I told you, remember? I'm still learning. Yes, maybe, one day, if I can become as good as Jozef, but . . .'

'Well then, if your work improves, I can't see why not. I mean . . .'

Without waiting for her to finish, he turns and marches impatiently towards the Spui. Then, crossing the street carelessly, he ignores the shouts of time-pressed drivers whose carriages have no choice but to swerve around him.

Watching him, she realises, while she may have become intimate with his body, his struggles with his work will always remain a mystery to her.

Twelve

With summer just around the corner, the temperature begins to climb, and Sien's body feels like treacle, heavy and lazy. Vincent's, on the other hand, is more charged than ever. He is restless to see the sea. He has mentioned the painting of the fisherman in the Goupil window not once but a few times. He now wants to draw the water, the sky, the fishing boats, the fish-drying barns, the dunes.

She packs ground coffee, bread, and they catch the tram to Scheveningen. She has not been there since she was a young girl, and she is as excited as he is. The tram is full, and though she has a seat, Vincent, like an itinerant peddler, stands on the footplate and hangs on the side, his easel dangling from his back, one hand planted on the crown of his hat so it does not fly off with the wind. He smiles in the way of someone who does not have a care in the world. The other passengers glance at him disapprovingly, appearing to be offended in some way. But Vincent remains oblivious, his expression exuberant, and she can't help but admire and envy him. If not for the baby, she would happily have joined him.

At the seaside, they leave the narrow boardwalk and trudge over the dunes; Vincent has taken off his boots and has persuaded her to do the same. 'We must feel the sand between our toes,' he tells her.

Above them, the seagulls squawk, seeming to protest at something. The wind brushes her skin, and she breathes it in, gladly filling her lungs with the fresh, bracing air. The sea surprises her, the immensity of it, the way it moves like a single vast creature, alive, frothing and lapping the shore, frightening and wild.

They set up camp near the fish-drying barns. Vincent wants to draw these gale-beaten buildings for his uncle's commission. 'Aren't they charming? Look at their brine-worn timber, the fish baskets planted with flowers and the crooked pickets.' Everything about them he finds irresistible. 'Most artists who come here are only interested in painting that palace up there,' he says, pointing with his chin at the grand bathhouse this coastal village is famous for. 'That's where their wealthy patrons like to holiday, so I suppose they are guaranteed to sell pictures of it. *Oh, what a delightful painting of the Scheveningen baths. We holiday there every summer.*' His exaggerated posh voice makes her laugh. How she enjoys hearing him mock his people. That he should see them with the eyes of her own tribe reassures her that he does not quite belong to them.

While Vincent draws, she slips into her boots and heads into the village to buy hot water for the coffee. She finds a sombre-faced old woman in front of a little shack, selling hot water and coal. Her clothes appear to have been stitched from ragged sails. After filling the coffee pot, the woman opens her palm for the money without a glance or a word, as if she has no tongue. Sien is sure these fishing families who are subject to the whims of the sea have it even harder than the families in Geest.

On her return to the dunes, she describes the woman to Vincent. 'A widow probably, who lost her husband at sea. And brothers, even sons, who knows?'

Vincent's eyes light up. He would like to see the woman. So, he wanders off to refill the pot. When he returns, he is pleased. 'Yes, I saw her. You were right: a most hardened soul. You could almost read her life in her face, as if it were the weather. She did not look up once. And when I thanked her, she just turned her back on me and disappeared into her house. And did you see her apron, how it was like the pelt of a Holstein? From hauling the coal, no doubt. She would make a wonderful subject, but I doubt she'd bother to hear me out.'

They huddle together on the sand, eating their bread while the gulls hover overhead, alert for any stray crumb. She feels like the young girl she was the last time she came here with her father and brothers. Was she ten? No, perhaps a bit older. They had waded in the shallows, feet bare, clothes wet to their knees. A rare happy memory from childhood . . .

When she recounts it for Vincent, he stands and extends a hand to help her up. 'Come,' he commands. He seems to be brimming with excitement.

He leads her towards the shoreline. But, impatient with her

waddling, he releases her hand and breaks into a run. Reaching the wet sand, he throws his arms out and begins to spin. Slowing, he pulls her into his orbit. Water splashes around their ankles, and though she picks up the hem of her skirt, it's too late, for it is already dark from the sea's spray. Now out of breath, she retreats to dry sand and watches in amusement as he runs through the wavelets, not bothering to save the cuffs of his trousers from the splash. Suddenly, as the wind travels through her head, entering one ear and flying out the other, it leaves behind a surprising thought: she has not a care in the world, and she is convinced she can make herself forget everything, make herself believe that there will never be another worry ever again.

In the afternoon, Vincent completes another drawing of the fish-drying barn. This time he wants to put a figure near the picket fence, so she poses there. When the sun begins to wane, they reluctantly pack up their camp to take the tram back to the city. As they climb over the dunes, Vincent continues to chat excitedly. 'We could live here – perhaps it will be cheaper. And by the sea too,' he says, catching her by the elbow as the sand gives way beneath her feet.

Back on the boardwalk, a man approaches from the other direction. He wears a light-coloured suit, a shade so similar to the dunes that, for a second, she thinks the sand is moving. Just ahead of her, Vincent walks jauntily, his feet still bare, his boots, laces tied together, slung over his shoulder. As the man nears, Vincent comes to a sudden halt, standing as if frozen, while the man speeds up, walking quickly towards them. His face now within her sightline, she draws back because his expression is not just stern, it is angry. So, the two men know each other. The man looks Vincent up and down, then her.

Sien steps back, her arms folding protectively across her belly before realising how silly she must appear, thinking it was possible for her to hide it.

'So then, Vincent,' the man says, his jaw clenched. 'I'd hoped the rumours weren't true, but alas.'

'What are you doing here, Mauve?' Vincent demands.

'What am *I* doing here?' retorts Mauve, furrowing his brows. 'I should be asking *you* this very question.'

'I've . . . I've been drawing . . . working over there,' Vincent says, waving a hand towards the beach. 'I'd like to show them to you some time. After all you did to help me, I feel I owe . . .' Vincent's voice trails off because the growing hostility in Mauve's face is impossible to ignore.

Then Vincent's manner changes. As if he is about to draw a sword, he stands tall and erect. 'Well, Mauve, I have a regular model now,' he says, half-turning towards Sien.

When Mauve turns to Sien again, his expression is one of undisguised contempt. Vincent, amused, says brightly, 'You've probably heard about Sien. And now that you have seen her for yourself, you can inform everyone that the rumours are indeed true. But I should think everyone would be pleased. If not for me, what would the Van Goghs write about in their letters and discuss in their sitting rooms?'

The other man does not appear to share Vincent's amusement.

'After all I did to help you, this is how you show your gratitude? First you refuse to work with my plaster casts, and now you decide to take up with . . . with this . . .' Mauve does not say the word, nor look at her, as if both are beneath him.

Ha, Sien thinks: she knows the likes of him all too well. She's had her share of them, and she has found them to be the worst type of man: panting like sick dogs one minute, then afterwards unable to look at her, acting cold and imperious, pretending nothing had happened between them. And then, afraid of being caught in her company, slipping away quickly, pulling their hats so low only their chins can be seen. Now, raising her head, she takes a step forward to stand beside Vincent.

'Mauve, I cannot see how my personal life should change things between us, nor what, if anything, it has got to do with my becoming an artist,' Vincent says.

Mauve snorts, shaking his head. His expression has become more pitying than angry. 'Why? Why would you besmirch your family's good name like this, and throw away every chance that has been offered to you?'

'Tell me, Mauve, how should a man live?' Vincent responds, his tone softer. 'How should a man know or learn anything about life, or art, without love?'

But Mauve does not seem to be listening. Letting out a heavy sigh, he says, 'Vincent, this time . . . this time you have gone too far.'

'If you could only see how Sien helps me,' Vincent replies. 'And the work I've been doing. If you could see the progress I've made since winter, you would –'

'You just don't get it, do you? It's over. We are done.'

'Listen! Listen to me, Mauve. It's still *me*. The same Vincent you were kind enough to help a few months ago. I haven't changed.' Vincent is leaning towards him, imploring. '*I am still the same Vincent.*' His eyes are pleading; Sien's own begin to sting.

'It's too late,' Mauve says matter-of-factly.

'So, you choose to be like the others, wanting only to work against me,' Vincent says, his voice turning bitter. 'I'd hoped that you, more than anyone, would have been sympathetic. I assumed that, like your work, your soul was filled with something generous and wonderful – but I see that I was mistaken.'

Mauve sets off again but not before having the last word. 'Well, I am sorry that I was not able to see what a vicious character you are much earlier.'

As Mauve disappears around a bend, Vincent drops to his knees and – to her horror – he begins to yank at his hair like he is trying to tear it from his scalp. She swallows, her mouth as dry as the sand, and feels a sob building in her chest. She bends to help him up, but he does not budge. It is clear to her now how much he has given up in order to be with her.

She turns to glance back at the dune where they had set up camp. Those carefree hours now seem to belong to some distant past. On the water, fishing boats are coming in with their catch as the men's families gather on the beach, ready to welcome them onto dry land. She is beginning to suspect that Vincent's future, her future, is just as precarious as those who ply their trade on the seas.

Thirteen

Back at the apartment, he explains that Mauve is his cousin-in-law. 'A great painter, who paints large paintings that are very, very good, and very, very expensive.' Over winter, he learnt a great deal from Mauve at his studio, but their relationship ended abruptly because Vincent refused to work with Mauve's plaster casts – those human body parts concocted from lifeless powder – preferring instead to draw real people. Prior to their falling-out, though, the artist had loaned Vincent money to help him set up the studio on the Schenkweg.

Smiling wryly Vincent says, 'Alright, I admit I was ruffled by Mauve. He . . . he is someone I admire greatly, but still, he has no right – no right to spurn me like that. Why should he judge me? Just because I am with you.' He tries to be jovial – 'Well, anyway, it's good to know where I stand with them all' – but his voice is too thin, too sour to disguise his hurt.

It was true, he had not backed down in the face of Mauve's condemnation, but despite his gallantry, she cannot help but worry. If he can be reduced that swiftly, that tellingly, can he continue to hold his nerve against his family? But, more than apprehension, it is woe that sweeps over her, because it is useless to be asking this question now – it is too late. Did she not stand shoulder to shoulder with him against Mauve's attack? Was she not proud of Vincent who, though a gentleman who hails from the same world as Mauve, is nothing like him? And was she not humbled that he defended *her*, defended *them*? That he was prepared to suffer anguish doing so? Trying to be the man that Michelet described: a man who is a woman's strength.

'Well,' Sien says, 'you said your brother knows nothing about me, but he is bound to find out now and . . .'

'Cut me off?' he finishes. He sighs. 'You're right. Quite right. It's time I told Theo myself,' he says, reaching for his pipe.

'What will you write him?'

'That I intend to marry you as soon as you have had the baby,' he replies, his face breaking into a grin. 'But remember, Sien, you will be living with a poor artist.'

'I too am poor, so how can I refuse you for that?'

His chest seems to swell with pride and his smile dazzles like the summer sun. Something passes between them, as if for a brief moment they have managed to step into each other's bodies.

'When I explain everything, he will understand it would have been impossible for me to have forsaken you. I'll tell him that we are devoted to each other. That I cannot live without you and that he must accept you otherwise he may as well cut off not only our allowance but our heads.' Still smiling, he slides his finger across his neck.

'Still, if he . . . how will we manage?'

'Let's not be like other couples, carping about money when the only thing that matters is what is in here,' he says, pressing a hand to his chest.

'So, we are going to live on your heart? Eat that, I suppose?'

'Come now, listen to yourself. You have suddenly turned into a nagging wife, and we are not yet married. Anyway, perhaps we *can* live on my heart. It's big and strong, after all.'

An absurd suggestion, yet she suspects he is only half-joking.

Well, it is done now. The letter has been written. Theo will learn of her. Vincent puts his pen down, pensive, but also restless. Unable to sit, he gets up and charges around the apartment like a bull in a pen, puffing hard on his pipe, tobacco smoke swirling around him like storm clouds. Whatever Vincent says about Theo, she has difficulty picturing this well-to-do brother, no matter how kind his heart, giving his blessing to Vincent for taking up with a whore.

His anxiety as he waits for Theo's reply has made Vincent not just agitated but ill. It has been two days without a word from Paris, so he sends another letter before taking to his bed, where he shivers, sweat trickling from head to toe. She does not doubt his will, but what of his constitution? It seems too weak to keep pace with his uncompromising nature, or the demands of his fierce determination. For whatever he may say, whatever he may believe, his nerves seem to have their own ideas; she wonders if perhaps they speak for him more accurately than his words.

His suffering, though disquieting, also serves to raise her spirits. That he wants to be with her enough to write that letter to his brother, that he cares enough to put himself through this ordeal, is undeniable proof of his love, of his commitment to her, to them. She can feel their fates becoming ever more entwined, more braided, and that it should feel increasingly natural and inevitable tells her they are indeed in love.

She fetches a glass of water and offers it to him. He sits bolt upright, drinks it, then, flinging aside the sheets, he mumbles that he is fine, that he must get to work at once, since she is here. That he must not waste any more time. Then he begins to search for his clothes, raking his hair, rubbing his eyes like a man who has overslept and is in danger of missing a train. As he dresses, she puts the kettle on the stove to brew coffee. She too hardly slept, aware that her fate, their fate, hinges on this man in Paris. Many times she has felt Theo's presence not far away in another country but nearby, a ghost hovering in the apartment, for every other day Vincent is either writing him a letter or receiving one from him.

She pauses because her hand, grinding the coffee, is shaking. This is all so new to her: this business of living with hope, but also with uncertainty, fear. Before Vincent, having never been in a position to contemplate nor plan for the future, she never bothered to squander her energy on possibilities, fully occupied by the daily task of feeding herself and her family, and keeping a dry roof over their heads.

This letter will change everything.

She begins to pour the water then puts the kettle down abruptly, making the lid clatter. The trembling in her hand is echoed by a fluttering in her chest. She may as well be awaiting the judgement of God himself.

Then a couple of days later, it arrives. Vincent tears the envelope open and begins to read.

'What does he say?' Sien asks, looking up from her sewing. The muscles in her neck are so tight, the question comes out as a croak.

His frown deepens, his face reddens. When he crumples the letter into a ball and flings it across the room, her heart sinks.

'They can all go to hell,' he mutters angrily.

'I suppose he says he will not send any more, because of me.'

'No, no, that's not it,' he says. 'Something far, far worse.' He is so wound up, she is afraid he will snap like a thread pulled too tight. 'Theo thinks my family will try to have me locked up in an asylum, which as you know is something they have tried to do in the past.' He clutches his head as if he would like to crush it.

'But how can they do that?'

He looks up at her, his eyes glistening. 'My parents will claim that I'm unfit to make sound decisions about my life,' he says.

'Because you have chosen me as your woman,' Sien says heavily.

He nods. 'That, and because I am unable to manage money.'

'And before, when last they tried . . .'

'Oh, just as silly a reason,' he says, flicking his hand in irritation. He tells the story, pacing, barely looking at her. 'I told you about my preaching in Belgium, among miners and their families. Their poverty was unlike anything I had seen. And so, yes, I found myself sharing my bread with them, and yes, I gave away my belongings. One day my father turned up unannounced and, seeing that I was sleeping on a sack on the dirt floor, he thought I had lost my mind. I ask you, how could they have deemed my actions as sufficient grounds for incarceration? If I thought my bed more useful to a rickety-boned old widow, what harm had I caused in providing a modicum of comfort to her, a woman with very little time left to her, when I myself was strong enough to endure the cold, bare earth?'

She knows she is supposed to agree with him, but his excessive generosity unsettles her. How far should a person go to help another?

'But I made sure they didn't get their way,' he says, holding up a finger. Then, halting his pacing, he turns to her and declares, 'And this time, too, they will fail.'

'But why give up your bed?' she asks, still struggling to understand. 'At least you could have found a pallet for yourself. So, when do you stop then? Until you are left with nothing? If they were bare-bottomed, would you offer . . .' But she falls silent. That he should have given up his bed for that elderly widow should not surprise her. After all, was he not the only one who stopped for her that night? While the whole city rushed past as she sat on the cold stone? For him, the sharing of his money, his possessions, is natural if another has need of them. Indeed, how many would willingly give to others in such a way?

'What does it matter? If I am in a position to help, then isn't it up to me to decide whether or not to do so? Surely, it cannot be cause enough to have one locked up.'

'Vincent, why not go on just as we are? Why go to the trouble of getting married if it will cause such trouble with your family?'

'If I want to marry you, why shouldn't I be allowed to do so? No, no. I have to show them they can't have their way with me. I am a man of thirty. Besides, wherever we are, we will always be at the very least a source of gossip, if not persecution.'

'Then why don't you find another job, so that you are not dependent on them for money?'

'Another job?' he asks, looking offended. 'But I already have one. I work for my brother. Besides, he makes no mention of withdrawing his help, which shows that he still believes in me, in my efforts.' His eyes burn as steadily as the flame of the lamp on the table.

'I understand, but . . . you know . . . just until your work begins to sell.'

'Are *you* losing faith in me, Sien? Have *you* already decided to write me off as an artist?' His gaze has turned cold, suspicious.

'I just meant that . . .' She trails off. How had this again become about *her*? How can she be accused of losing faith in his art when she knows so little about it? But she knows better than to challenge him in this belligerent mood of his. In a matter of minutes, he has become the volatile man of the night they met. Flinty temper at the ready. A man who, she is beginning to realise, takes offence easily, quickly. Pity the person, whether his uncle or anybody else, who does not see things from his point of view.

'As I said, Sien, I will sell my work, and we will be free of them. *Do you hear?*' He is nearly shouting now, glaring at her.

She nods, afraid that if she were to utter anything else, it would only prove her ignorance. After all, she can't possibly know more than he does about the business of art.

Fourteen

One morning, he tells her the apartment next door has become available. A bigger home, only just recently renovated.

'I have already spoken to the landlord. After you have the baby, we will move in there. We will need more space anyway, with the children. And besides, my work will improve even more quickly if I have a proper studio.'

She is not sure she has understood him correctly. 'You want all of us to come and live with you?'

'Yes, why not? You are here enough already,' he replies.

'With Maria and the baby?'

'Yes, we will make a family, don't you see?' He is smiling. 'Do you know what Michelet said? *Alone, one is sure to perish; only with another can one be saved.*'

She should breathe a sigh of relief, she should feel grateful, but it is disbelief that strikes a more powerful note in her. This home he wants to set up, has it become a kind of a dare? To his brother, his family? Then, because it seems too good to be true, as if her elation cannot be borne and must be brought to heel, she hears the naysayer in her head asking, *Live with a gentleman? You? A whore from Geest?*

'Why are you like this?' he demands. 'Do you not want to be with me?'

'Of course I do!' she exclaims. 'It's just that . . . What will Theo say? What will *everyone* say? Are we not being rash? Should we not wait until we are married?'

He waves away her concerns. Well, since they plan to marry as soon as she has recovered from the baby, what does it matter? 'It's only time, that's all.'

Working, posing for him – and, yes, screwing him – is one thing, but living together before they are married will certainly signal to the world that they have lost their minds. It will invite not just ridicule but damnation, since they will be living in sin and declaring their contempt for the holy institution of marriage. Furthermore, though they may marry after the baby is born, she is certain, given her experience with her other pregnancies, it will be many, many weeks before she will be well enough to be a bride.

And, too, the rent will be higher. 'Did you not tell me you were nearly evicted not long ago? Could we not remain here until your work starts selling?'

Since Theo has made no mention of denying him his support, they will not want for money, he assures her.

Her body getting heavier, her brain soft and cloudy, she is unable to continue her protest.

In any case, her misgivings are of little interest to him. He has made up his mind. A couple of nights ago a storm had smashed the studio's window – 'See? It wasn't even strong enough to withstand the wind' – and he was forced to nail a blanket over the opening. But, even before the storm wrought its damage he had been thinking of finding somewhere else, so when the landlord brought his attention to the newly refurbished apartment right next door it seemed the obvious solution – and the rent is not that much more, only a little over three guilders a week. But, he adds, after the baby is born, because she will not have the strength to do very much, especially the tiring work of posing, he will have no choice but to find other models and therefore he will not be able to give her as much money.

'But my mother . . .'

'Don't worry, I'll take care of her, though she will have to find somewhere cheaper to live.'

'Are you sure? How can you afford . . .'

But he has already left her side and is busy with his trunk, as if preparing to undertake the move straight away.

Her mother, as Sien feared, is far from happy with the news.

'You are mad to go along with his scheme. All of you moving into a larger apartment together?' Wilhelmina stares at her daughter in consternation.

'He would like us to be a family, he wants the children,' Sien replies, her gaze sliding to the window.

'A family? What ridiculous talk. And what's more, this talk of marriage too.' She throws her hands in the air 'Wake up, Sien! Open your eyes and stop pretending that all of this is normal.'

Sien turns back to search her mother's face. Had she not always done whatever her mother asked? Smudge kohl around her eyes and rouge on her cheeks and open her legs for the men in the neighbourhood? Has she not done everything she could to save them from destitution? But now, with her body worn out, her mother cannot possibly expect her to pass up this chance to escape Geest. Escape the streets. Though she can see her mother's disappointment and hurt, she does not waver, pursing her lips tight.

Maria runs inside and clambers onto Sien's lap, ignoring her mother's bulging belly. Sien is sure that the girl has become heavier. It seems the regular meals have made a difference.

'But . . . but this is not proper, Sien,' mutters Wilhelmina. 'I don't see why you can't keep posing and earning, and I'll look after Maria, as I've been doing, and the baby too.'

Surely, the rules of what was proper had ceased to apply to them a long time ago – if they ever had. When were they ever in a position to influence their fate? As if Wilhelmina has been struck by a similar thought, she lowers her head and stares down at her clenched hands on her lap.

'He is offering a roof over our heads, so how can I refuse him?' Sien says. 'And besides, he insists he is serious about marrying me.' Her cheeks are no doubt red, for they feel as hot as if she has a fever.

Wilhelmina raises her head and gives her daughter a sharp

look. 'Don't tell me – you've gone and done a stupid thing, haven't you? You've fallen in love with him.' She shakes her head. 'Him, as your husband? As my son-in-law? I may as well wish for the Prince of Orange to turn up here in his carriage to whisk us all away.'

'No one – *no one* – has ever looked after me the way he has. And no one has ever offered me their hand, other than while they are poking me. What's more, he is the only one who knows me,' she cries, pointing at her chest.

'*Knows* you?'

'Yes. It's the first time someone has been able to see what's inside me. I feel like . . . like I count . . . that I matter as a person.'

'Is that really the best you can come up with? Is that all there is?' her mother asks, thrusting her chin forward.

Sien narrows her gaze. 'He sees me as more than just a whore who is only good for earning. Do you know how that feels for me? You had Pa, before the children. And he worked until it killed him.'

'You dare to mention your father while we are talking about that artist of yours? A man who knows nothing about real work?'

Aware of Maria's weight now pressing down too heavily on her legs, Sien attempts to push the girl off her. But the girl turns and, baring her teeth like a wildcat, bites her mother's wrist.

Sien yelps and gives the girl a slap across her face. Maria howls and bursts into tears.

How Sien has relished her frequent absences from this household, and especially the demands of a small child. But now, stirred by Maria's crying, she bends down and hugs the girl, fearing for this daughter of hers, growing up in this neighbourhood without a father's name, without a future to speak of.

She holds the girl's face in her hands and looks into her eyes. 'You must be good, Maria. We are to go and live with Vincent in a new house, and you must behave.'

As Sien wipes away her daughter's tears, the girl nods. After receiving a kiss on the temple, she wriggles free and disappears outside.

Sien turns back to her mother, sure more than ever of her decision. 'Besides, the children need a father's name, and this is my chance to give them one. How will they have a proper future otherwise?'

'Do you really think that fancy brother of his will let him marry you and give his name to your bastard children? Now, you listen to me, Sien . . .' Wilhelmina leans forward and takes a firm hold of her daughter's chin. 'You know very well they are not our people. They look down on the likes of us as no better than rats that run down the sewers. Surely you must know this.'

Sien twists away from her mother's grasp and tells her, 'He says that when he gets his own income we can do what we like. And he is so different from all the rest – how can you be so sure about him?' Her voice does not falter, nor her gaze.

'Huh, different, you say? Well, let's see how different he is when his brother stops sending the money. Can he afford to be so different then? And if you think he will stick around to raise children that are not his, you are out of your mind.'

'You're just upset because he won't be able to pay the same

as before. You'll just have to find somewhere cheaper – maybe a courtyard place at the back.'

Her mother looks aghast. 'Live in one of those vermin-infested boxes? Oh no. I've always had a house that faced the street proper, and I don't intend to –'

Sien cuts her off. 'Ha, only because you put me to work on the street.' Then, gripping the back of her chair with one hand and her belly with the other, she stands slowly to deliver the last word. 'Well, this time you will just have to.'

A few days later, the arrival of a visitor at the studio further strengthens Sien's resolve. To Sien's relief, this friend of Vincent's, also an artist, is quite unlike Vincent's cousin-in-law, Mauve. When Vincent ushers his friend inside, the man enters the apartment without recoiling at the sight of her, only smiling because he has expected to find her there all along. His tone and manners are composed, and open in the way of a man comfortable not only with himself but with his place in the world. As he and Vincent shake hands, Vincent pulls his friend towards him in a half-embrace to which the friend submits happily, demonstrating that such shows of affection are customary between them.

Rappard, as Vincent calls him, has closely cropped dark hair and a broad face with handsome features, though his eyes – which appear to be almost crossed at times – carry a hint of sadness. As he and Vincent talk, he glances at Sien now and then, seemingly more out of curiosity than any wish to cast judgement. He appears younger than Vincent, and if Vincent is all quicksilver movement, his energy a coiled spring, Rappard is as steadfast as the prow of a ship in calm waters. It is clear he genuinely admires and respects Vincent.

'Rappard, look at this,' Vincent says, pointing. 'See, when the black shines too much, you can add a bit of milk to dull it. Then you can also touch it up with a pen – you know, highlight certain bits, make it sing.' Vincent almost talks over Rappard, barely able to contain his excitement. They drink coffee, talk ceaselessly about the work hanging on the walls, from the type of pencil Vincent favours ('I prefer carpenter's pencils to those fine Fabers') – to the difficulties of perspective – Rappard admiring the perspective frame that Vincent had had made by the carpenter and blacksmith.

Rappard listens more than he speaks, though he does not defer to Vincent on everything. 'No, I understand the sitter is most important. But often I prefer to give the subjects more space, something of their surroundings. I think you would do better to try it.'

Vincent's shoulders stiffen and his brows twitch for a brief moment. Sien flinches, afraid that Vincent will ruin the congenial mood with his temper. So, she is relieved to see Vincent, though clearly feeling slighted by Rappard's comment, nonetheless land a friendly palm on the other man's back, as if to reassure himself as much as Rappard that he will not allow any difference of opinion or disagreement to mar their friendship.

'Like this one here, of the woman in front of her house,' Rappard continues, pointing to Wilhelmina in the courtyard of the Noordstraat house.

'Ah, yes, that is of Sien's mother,' Vincent replies, delighted.

Rappard is mostly generous about Vincent's work, encouraging and praising his friend's efforts. He does not doubt Vincent's uncle will be pleased with his commission. When Rappard points to a tear in one drawing, and Vincent replies that he intends to have it repaired once he has some money, Rappard immediately offers him a loan of two and a half guilders, so that it can be attended to straight away.

'No, no, I can't possibly take it, Rappard – I mean, you are probably in need of it yourself.'

'For the moment, I can do without it. You can pay me back when you are able. And if you need extra . . .'

Vincent refuses the extra, but gratefully accepts the amount needed for the drawing to be fixed and she can tell that he does so not only because he would like to see the work restored, but because he is touched by Rappard's gesture. Warmed by the fact that he has a friend, a very good friend, who will not hesitate to put his hand in his pocket to help him. A friend who understands how important his work is to him.

They spend another couple of hours leafing through the pages of woodcuts in Vincent's collection of magazines, talking about the artists who did them with such familiarity Sien assumes they know them all personally. They also talk about books. English and French authors are mentioned almost in one breath – Dickens, Eliot, Edmond and Jules de Goncourt, and Zola – especially Zola – whom Vincent urges Rappard to read. As always, when he speaks about art, literature, he becomes someone else, so assured, so fluent, that it seems to take no more effort than sipping coffee or smoking his pipe. What a rare and wonderful thing it is for her to observe him like this. Transformed by Rappard's company, he is radiant, possessed of an easy charm. It occurs to her that Vincent must feel a certain loneliness being with her, unable to share with her these passions of his.

Before Rappard takes his leave, Vincent presses on him a drawing. It is the one of Sien naked. 'It is my finest to date, Rappard, so I insist you have it.'

Rappard thanks him then, blushing a little, glances warmly at her one last time. Quickly she turns away, heat rising in her cheeks too, reminding herself that her face is hidden, that even if Rappard may guess the drawing is of her, he cannot see her.

Fifteen

She recognises the symptoms before he does. The tip of his penis is red and swollen, discharging a sickly, yellow pus. When he is peeing at the pot, which is often, he winces not from relief but burning pain. She has seen it before, and though she has managed to avoid the symptoms, Vincent has not been so lucky.

There is no doubt it is her doing. Yet just when she was beginning to think he could not surprise her any more, she is taken aback by his good-humoured, almost jovial response. 'Why not share everything? If the clap is one of those things I must bear to be with you, then so it shall be,' he says with a shrug, showing no trace of the annoyance that she, at the very least, expected from him.

She finds his cheerful but anguished face discomfiting. How could he possibly view it in such a romantic light? Of course she is touched by his refusal to cast blame, since she did not have an inkling of it, but the gesture seems excessively gallant. Then again, only Vincent would consider bearing an illness to be a demonstration of love.

Though the clap is common enough, his condition soon worsens. The pus becomes thicker, the burning, accompanied by spasms of pain, more intense. Almost delirious from fever and poor sleep, he is unable to summon his usual energy. Ashen-faced with exhaustion at the end of the day, he appears like a man who has had his blood drawn from him. It is her turn to persuade him to see a doctor.

At the hospital on Brouwersgracht, he is given a bed in the fourth-class ward. But the long room is not unpleasant. Summer light spills into it through a bank of windows, from which there is a picturesque view of a canal and a handsome row of houses with bell-curved gables and well-tended gardens. After he gives her a few guilders to see her through his absence, he has just enough to pay the ten and a half guilders for the two-week treatment.

Vincent begs the doctor to shorten it, declaring he would rather work than spend time lying on his back, but Dr Molenaar stands firm. 'You may have to stay longer. We will see how you are in a fortnight. In the meantime, you must follow the course of treatment and rest.'

Vincent sighs resignedly. But then in the next breath he becomes lively, likening his confinement to a sea voyage through treacherous weather. 'How dull the adventure if one sailed only through the calm. How insipid the view. Besides, my illness will remind me of what you will soon be facing. While my suffering will no way mirror yours, it will be in sympathy, so I must bear it in the right spirit.'

She shakes her head, smiling. If nothing else, the man is exhaustingly relentless, unassailable.

Whatever he may say, she is certain it will be difficult for him to stay in bed without much to do, and as if afraid of this very thing he tells her, 'You must bring me my perspective books and my novels, and pen and ink, writing paper. And, of course, any letters from Theo.'

The next day, when she brings the things he asked for, she finds him weaker but nevertheless still upbeat.

'All of us are more or less in the same boat,' he tells her, looking around the ward. They are nearly all men, withdrawn and downcast, suffering quietly, very likely from the same ailment. Soon she too will be in a ward very much like this one, the air fetid with the clammy smell of bedridden bodies and overflowing bedpans.

'Have they given you something?' she asks, dropping into the chair next to his bed, glad to be off her feet.

'Yes, quinine tablets. And they like to stick a tube into my bladder, you know, to flush things out. It needs to be done quite a number of times, and the tubes will get bigger, I'm told. But I intend to keep busy reading and, if I can, drawing as well.' His head falls back on the pillow, the effort of keeping it raised seeming to be beyond his strength.

His sketchbook already has quite a few drawings of the other patients, and the houses across the canal. He complains about the strict nurses who have threatened to confiscate his drawing materials, forcing him to sketch under the covers, out of their view. But sometimes he has been able to sneak to the window and take a peek outside.

'The doctor said you must rest,' she reminds him, frowning at his grey complexion.

'Yes, yes, but the effort of resting is more disagreeable to me than the treatment,' he grumbles. 'It is my groin that hurts, but my hands have not lost their appetite to draw. If anything, they're hungrier.' His fingers clasp the sheets, claw-like. 'But you shouldn't be worrying about me,' he adds, glancing sidelong at her stomach. 'It's you we should be . . . because . . .' His face crumples and, too distraught to speak, his head falls back onto his pillow once more.

In recent days, as her departure for Leiden looms, it has been Vincent, not her, who has been racked with anxiety, and she finds that it is she who must reassure him.

'I've done it before, I know what's coming – all will be well.' But looking down at her belly, dumbfounded at the size, she thinks there's a good chance this baby will tear her to shreds as it leaves her. Perhaps, she thinks, with a pang of dread, it will even outlive her.

As if divining her thoughts, Vincent says, 'But . . . what if you don't pull through?' His hands twist the thin blanket, the tic in his cheek pulsing. What a state he is in.

But touched by his concern, she reaches across to him and tells him, 'I'm stronger now than when you met me, remember?'

By way of answer, he squeezes her wrist so tightly she loses all feeling in it.

*

Sien is cleaning the apartment, stripping the sheets and straightening the studio for Vincent's return, when a parcel arrives from his parents. He made it clear she should open anything addressed to him and so she does now. There are men's underclothes, ten guilders, a letter, even cigars. Despite what he says about his parents, she can see that he holds a place deep enough in their hearts never to be forsaken by them. Now she better understands his cavalier attitude towards his family; he can afford to be cavalier, because he knows they will always be there for him. How she envies him.

Not for the first time she asks herself what she, who has nothing, has to offer him. Her life of suffering? Her children?

Seeking relief from her tangled thoughts, she wanders to the window. The meadows are green now, the sky a deeper blue, the clouds wisp-thin. Her wrought nerves instantly let up. Then, wishing to hear his voice, his bold, undaunted words, she looks over her shoulder, expecting him to be bent over his easel. Then she realises it is not just the apartment that is lifeless and empty without him there, but her heart.

She leaves for the hospital at once, taking the letter and the money with her.

Vincent is more interested in the letter than the gifts. She assumes he is eager to learn whether they have heard anything about her yet. As he reads, the tension in his expression lifts. 'So, it seems they make no mention of Geel or . . .' He carefully refolds the letter without finishing his sentence.

'Or me, I suppose?' she says, opening her basket and unwrapping the food she has brought him – bread and smoked meat.

He does not answer.

'Well?' she persists. 'Has Theo told them yet?'

He shakes his head and picks at the food. 'There's no hurry with my parents, is there? As long as Theo knows, and as long as he still sends my allowance.'

'For now,' she mumbles.

'Believe me, neither he nor my family could bear to have me wandering the streets. They will do what's necessary to ensure I am clothed and fed and have a roof over my head. That is their way. Appearances matter to them, you see.'

'Whatever you say about your family, at least they are determined to keep you off the streets – unlike mine.'

She takes the sheets and towels to Gerda, the laundrywoman behind the apartment, in whose company she is more at ease than even her neighbours in Geest. While the people of the Schenkweg are not unfriendly, she has found it easier to keep to herself because many regard Vincent not only as an outsider, but one who rouses their worst suspicions. *Stream of strangers going in and out of their apartment at any time of day and night. And she and he are not even married.* Though Vincent told the landlord's son who collects the rent that they are intending to marry soon, it has made little difference, serving only to confirm the sinful nature of their union. She is grateful Gerda seems to care as little about their living arrangements as about Vincent's work. As their friendship grows over the weeks, Sien has found herself confiding in the other woman more and more.

'Ah, a snake who has swallowed a mouse,' Gerda says now, chuckling and pointing her chin at Sien's belly. Gerda's limbs are as thick as tree trunks, her back as broad as the washboards propped in the tubs of water next to her. She is wringing wet towels and sheets, turning the handle with a sure, practised grip. Beneath the rolled-up sleeves, her hands and wrists are permanently pink, in that way of new skin. Her face, framed by a white cap, is also pink but milky.

Gerda lays the damp washing aside and stretches her back, her hands on her ample hips. Picking up a corner of her apron, she dries her hands.

Sien likes Gerda's unflappable demeanour. But more than that, she envies her friend's strength, her sturdy body. She is sure even the strongest of winds would have trouble making Gerda sway. The life that she has lived, and continues to live, seems hardly to have left a mark on her. How is that possible, with a husband long dead, a son lost in Java and a crippled daughter at home?

As Sien perches on a stool, Gerda boils water on the small stove she has set up on the long, narrow table below the window.

'You will be leaving for Leiden any day, I suppose?' she says, now reaching for her pipe.

'Day after tomorrow.'

'Is Vincent still at the hospital?'

She nods. 'But he should be back before me, I think. He is in a worse fix than a fisherman's wife watching her husband go to sea.'

'Well, it is the first time for him, so I can't be surprised,' Gerda says, packing her pipe. Then she adds, 'But I am surprised that he should be so when the baby is not his.'

'He's keener than the other fathers who keep drinking in the tavern after learning they've begotten another. But it's because he doesn't know what he's in for.' It's true. How will his nerves cope with a baby crying day and night?

As Gerda pours coffee, the steam from the kettle condenses on the small window, blocking the view of the drying lines. Gerda hands Sien a cup before fetching a stool for herself. Then, sitting in the open doorway facing the courtyard, she lights her pipe.

Unable to contain her worries, Sien blurts out, 'His brother knows about me, but his parents don't yet.'

Gerda merely lifts her brows, taking a good gulp of her hot drink before puffing on her pipe. What is she thinking? Sien wonders. Though she hadn't planned to, she finds herself telling Gerda about the stern father who threw Vincent out the previous Christmas, and the family's plan to lock Vincent up in an asylum in Geel two years earlier.

'And the brother: who knows if he will continue to support us? It's just as likely that we'll end up on the street tomorrow.'

'You, maybe, but not Vincent,' Gerda says, shaking her head. 'Whatever happens, they will make sure he is looked after.'

Yes, how many times has she said the very same thing? And yet hearing it from Gerda's lips, she is embarrassed to have suggested otherwise. Her cheeks flushed with colour, Sien can only look down at her hands.

The older woman, draining the last of her drink, mutters, 'Blood is thicker than water, thicker than love.'

Sien realises how easy it was for her to believe Vincent while ensconced in their apartment eyrie, away from the world, but here in Gerda's laundry, surrounded by tin wash tubs, dented and rust-edged, sloshing with grey suds, the wet dripping clothes and the mounds of dirty ones, and Gerda's plain speak, Vincent's reassurances ring hollow. She feels as if she has just been shaken awake from a vivid dream. She stands to leave but, disorientated, has to reach for the wall to steady herself.

Back at the apartment, reassured by Vincent's art materials, his bed and the clothes that still carry the scent of him, she wants to rush back to Gerda and tell her she is wrong. This man will not abandon her but protect her: he has told her he would not just once but repeatedly. And she has no trouble believing him, because he is a man quite unlike any other. A man she only has to think of in order to feel his love.

Before leaving for Leiden, she visits Vincent one last time. But Vincent already has a visitor, a silver-haired man in a dark suit. She is sure it is the father; his profile is just like Vincent's. She turns on her heel, her heart thumping with such force it threatens to burst from her chest. Downstairs, though no less calm, she finds a bench and waits.

A few minutes later, the father appears at the stairs, clutching his black hat. Dour-faced, erect-postured and his frame broad and solid – just like his morals, no doubt – he exudes that unmistakable air of authority so common to men in his position. As he passes her, she quickly lowers her eyes, beset with such nerves she forgets to breathe.

In the ward, she finds Vincent chewing his bottom lip, distracted. He is brooding so intently, he does not seem to notice at first that she has arrived. The chair is still warm from the father. She can only assume they argued.

'Didn't the doctor tell you to rest?' she asks, unable to ignore his sunken chest, his hollowed-out cheeks, suggesting the treatment is beginning to take its toll on him.

Only half-listening, he picks up his sketchbook, which is now filled with drawings of fellow patients, houses, canals and barges, rooftops. 'All this useless lying around, waiting, it's impossible for me, Sien. I . . . I can't just *rest*.'

What can she say to help him?

'I saw the landlord,' she tells him, 'and he said to tell you the new apartment will be ready as soon as you leave here.'

Her news has the desired effect, as he cheers up instantly. 'Oh, that's wonderful – I must get the new studio set up for your return.' But his face darkens as he adds in a whisper, '*If* you return.'

'Just make sure you get better, so you can visit me in Leiden,' she says briskly.

'Don't worry – whatever the doctors tell me, I will come.'

She waits for him to tell her about his visitor, but when he makes no mention of him, she says, 'I saw your father.'

His colour deepens. 'If you must know, he didn't speak of you,' he says, sitting up. 'But when I thanked him for sending the money, the old man demanded to know by what means did I learn of the package when I have been confined here all this time. He thought he was being clever, tripping me up, but I told him that my regular model has been keeping an eye on the studio. Well then, he said, why would you allow your model to open it? Can this person be trusted?' Then he sighs, his head dropping onto his pillow. 'It seems Pa's mind is still as sharp as a blade.'

He turns to the bedside table, reaching for his glass of water. She passes it to him. As he sips, his brows are knitted. 'Here I am, unwell, and the only thing he can say is, *Remember to be grateful, don't spurn those who want to help you.* As if I am only worthy because others have taken a special interest in me. Then he reminded me of Uncle Cor's commission. Most generous. And –' here Vincent deepens his voice – '*Don't forget Tersteeg and Mauve. You know they have your best interests at heart.* When I replied that they have mounted a campaign to deny me Theo's support, he was quick to point out that even Christ kept an open heart for those who did not understand him.' Vincent, almost breathless from his outburst, tries to cool himself with another sip of water. 'But I set him straight. *You would not dare say that to me if you knew the truth*, I told him. Then Pa looked at me as if I were the Devil himself.' Then, his voice turning surly, he says, 'He did not mention my illness once.'

She is about to tell him that his father must know, without the need to ask, how he came to be ill. But the hurt from his father's visit is still too raw; she doubts she can get a word in edgewise, for he seems barely aware of her presence, his complaints seemingly uttered more for his own ears than hers.

'Can you believe that? *Be grateful.*' He shakes his head. 'It was like he was delivering a sermon instead of visiting his sick son. What's more, he didn't ask or say anything about my work, my studio. He only spoke of all those who are bending over backwards, apparently, to help me. Nor did he apologise for throwing me out at Christmas.'

'Your father is a pastor,' Sien reminds him. 'How could you refuse to attend church on such a holy day, and while you happen to be living under his roof?'

He groans. 'Not you too, Sien,' he murmurs, raising himself on his elbows. 'He used his might to throw me out. Even a lame dog would have received more sympathy than I did over my broken heart. How could I hope to please the Lord if I were to attend church under such duress?'

You may have deserved his fury, she thinks, but does not say aloud.

'Look, perhaps I deliberately provoked him because of Kee, but he hauled me up by my collar as if I were no more than a sack of bones,' he complains. 'You know nothing about his coldness. When I was twelve, I ran away from a boarding school I was sent to against my wishes, twice. Each time he took me back to that prison by force, though I begged him not to.'

More than fifteen years ago, she calculates. That he should still be smarting over this incident from his childhood after all this time astounds her. Has he kept an account of all his hurts over the years? Undeterred, she points out, 'They also sent the money, the package, remember?'

'I'd rather they took some interest in my work,' he says, sighing.

She sits back and folds her arms. When had she ever received anything from her own family?

'Perhaps I am expecting too much of them,' he concedes. 'And, of course, undergarments are always useful.' Then he turns and picks up a small muslin-wrapped parcel from the bedside table. 'Here, Pa also brought some pressed tongue from home. I saved some for you.'

She accepts the offering but is amused to see him like this; for all his chivalrous actions, his wilfulness, he is turned into a sullen, disappointed child after only a brief reunion with his father. And despite his passionate talk of the value of struggle, it seems he feels entitled to be treated well by his family.

On her way home, she recalls the father with the proud carriage. In his black suit and hat, he cut a formidable, almost severe, figure. Though his hooded eyes were not unkind, they were serious enough, so too his mouth – thin and firm. One fleeting glimpse was enough. Was Vincent really prepared to defy this man? If Vincent is strong-willed, then it follows the father will also be too: apples rarely fell far from their tree.

Whatever Vincent thinks, Sien is sure his father knows about her.

She stops and leans against a lamppost. A queasy sensation has settled into the pit of her stomach as if she had swallowed something disagreeable. What would she possibly say to this elder Van Gogh if she were to meet him? A passing glance was enough to seize her with terror. And now that he is bound to know that she is the one who made Vincent ill, what standing can she possibly have with him? Would she be able to look at him in the eye? The cordial meeting with Rappard had left her filled with an optimism, but after this fleeting glimpse of the father she suffers a fresh wave of doubt, prompting the question, can she dare to even think they could stand eye to eye? The father is a man whose life has been guided by the strictest of morals, and though he may be disposed to kindness towards his congregation, how would he react to one of his own flesh and blood becoming intimate with a whore?

She knows the answer, but she has no time to dwell on it, for, feeling a cramp in her belly, she turns towards home.

Sixteen

She waits. The jabs of pain have started. They are erratic for now but will no doubt soon become regular. In the ward, her bed is the one with the best view of the summer that is in full swing outside. Through the window, she can see trees, their abundant foliage sparkling in the rich, golden light while birds perch on the branches, chirping incessantly.

The nurse told her that it was the doctor who assigned this bed to her.

So this is what it's like to be attached to a gentleman: special favours are granted automatically.

As she lies there with little to do, she is filled with remorse for having criticised him. Perhaps she should have visited him the morning she left for Leiden. What if his fears come to pass, and she does not pull through? It would be just her rotten luck to die now, when for the first time in her life she has a man willing to look after her.

She begs the head nurse to help her write a letter to him, implying that he is the father of her child. *You see,* is the unspoken subtext, *he's a gentleman. I'm not like the other women here.* I *have a gentleman waiting at home.* Between contractions, she mutters messages: she hopes he is recovering well; the baby, if it turns out to be a boy, will be named Willem, which is Vincent's second name; and, most importantly, she will see him again – soon.

Even through the thick fog of her increasing pain, she can recall Vincent and the apartment on the Schenkweg. She can hear his sure voice, smell his musky tobacco scent, feel his jittery energy, and she wonders whether he has managed to slip under her very skin, absorbed into her body's memory.

The baby is stuck. It is too healthy, too strong, and it's going to undo her, she thinks. She has been given gas and, though heavy-headed, she cannot escape the pain. At times, she fears the entire length of her may be in danger of being split down the middle. Voices swirl around her. Doctors and nurses come and go, peering between her legs as if she is one of those circus freaks. Too weak to keep pushing, she lies back, rivers of sweat pouring down her temples, cheeks and neck.

She curses the baby's size and vows never to let another man touch her again. She curses Vincent and that health regime of his which appears to have helped the baby more than her. The first time, she tore, but the others that followed slipped out as easily as if they were no more than frogs. But this one is taking its time. For hours she pushes and pushes. Exhausted, she does not have the energy even to moan. Then finally its crown appears. Enough that the forceps can seize hold of the baby's head. She lets out a gasp and then her spent body surrenders to blackness.

Vincent was right. A baby boy lies next to her. He is scrunched but perfect. He has survived, and so has she. Tender all over, but alive. Miraculously, she did not tear. It seems God has willed her to go on.

She gazes at this little thing beside her. There is certainly more flesh on him than there had been on the others. Almost puffy, like rolled dough, he is covered in a fine down, and his lips, like petals turned out, give the impression he is smiling while he sleeps. He is so unlike the others, it's difficult for her to believe that he is in fact hers. In the first hours, she almost expects the nurses to take him away, explaining there has been a mistake, that he belongs to someone else.

Though her body is like a punctured balloon, though her swollen genitals throb, her milk is flowing, and the nurses are being unusually kind. But, used up, she is all easy emotion. She can barely hold her tears in check, they are ready to gush at any moment, while the edges of her seem to be blurring. Bewildered but moved by the sight of this newborn, the hope now piercing her heart is sharper, keener. What would Vincent say if he were here? *A miracle from God, Sien.* She yearns to hear his voice, the fearless talk that always shores up her spirits.

In a state between sleep and wakefulness, she is in and out of dreams, her mind visited by all sorts of ghostly imaginings. In one, she is back at the Schenkweg studio, posing next to the warm stove. Next, her father appears, beckoning her kindly with worn and blackened hands. Another time, she lies shivering in the bare, cheerless orphanage in which she and her brothers lived at various times.

She wants to write to Vincent again. What if, in her absence, he has taken on another model, another woman? How will she find the strength to make a fresh start? She sits up, overcome by a desire to see him.

They arrive. Vincent, her mother, Maria. Vincent, spotting her, almost sprints to her bedside. Maria scurries after him, squealing. He is not merely weeping but crying openly. Even her mother's eyes are moist.

'When the nurse said we may see you, I knew then you pulled through,' he murmurs. Then, collapsing by her side, he rests his head on her shoulder. She can taste his tears, sweet and salty, and feel his heart pounding against hers, and all her misgivings about his family and the future evaporate.

'We'll get back to work, won't we? I'll return to posing as soon as I leave here.'

He lifts his head and wipes his eyes; his tears have left a dark stain on her chemise. 'Yes, yes, this will be a new beginning – not just for the baby, but for us all.'

Maria, having climbed onto the bed, now sits swinging her

legs over the side. To Sien's surprise, the girl is no longer wearing clogs, her feet now clad in boots.

'Mama, look,' the girl says, kicking one leg high in the air.

'Boots?' she asks, looking at Vincent inquiringly. It must have been him; she knows her mother would never have bought them.

He nods, telling her about his discovery of a large crack in Maria's clogs, and how he could not pass up this bargain pair of boots at the cobbler, scuffed at the toe but hardly worn. Yes, she thinks, but they will not see the child's quick-growing feet through summer, let alone winter. She merely smiles, though, and glances at the baby in Wilhelmina's arms. Sien's mother has always preferred boys. Vincent peers over Wilhelmina's shoulder, beaming, and no one watching could possibly consider him as anyone other than the delighted father.

Wilhelmina hands Vincent the warm bundle; he accepts it eagerly but tentatively, his shoulders hunched and arms drawn around the child as if he must protect the newborn from some invisible threat. Then, cradling him, he studies the child intently. He will scare the baby, Sien thinks. But Willem does not stir. Vincent, tender-faced, seems to have fallen completely under the baby's spell. He gazes with his mouth open in awe, speech beyond him.

But, of course, Vincent's silence cannot last long. 'Willem,' he whispers, his eyes now dewy. Lightly, he strokes the baby's little cheek. 'Why, it is smaller than my finger, and softer than a feather. There is not a follicle of hair out of place. And his husk is as unsullied as the first snow.'

Maria, impatient now, jumps up and down at Vincent's side.

'I want to see the baby. I want to see the baby.' Vincent leans down towards the girl, who frowns at this little brother of hers before giving him a small tap on the head.

Dr Thomas appears and greets Vincent warmly. The two men have a murmured conversation, then Sien hears Vincent exclaim, 'He was stuck for nearly five hours? And five others attended to her? Why, that is truly remarkable.' He glances at her with such pride, she can't help but blush.

They are all looking at her, Sien Hoornik, now – even the other patients have turned to stare. *How did the likes of her end up with a gentleman?* they seem to be asking. Instead of the baby, it seems Vincent is her big prize.

In the days following, the nurses are even kinder than before. Then, just before Vincent arrives to collect her, the doctor comes to see her.

'So, it seems your gentleman has remained devoted to you,' he says, his manner avuncular but strict. 'I would advise you to devote yourself to him in turn. Do you understand my meaning?'

'Yes,' she replies, her cheeks scalding-hot.

He then advises her on her diet – no vinegar, no mustard or pepper, meat once or twice a week, bitters. Also, plenty of fresh air and walks. And regular washes down there with brandy and water, and a weekly bath if it can be managed. No lifting of heavy items, nor strenuous tasks like scrubbing floors and the like. In addition, she should do her best to avoid taxing emotions like anxiety and tension.

When Vincent arrives, even the head nurse makes an appearance to wish them well.

On the train, she recounts her bedside chat with the doctor, and together they chuckle quietly while peering at the baby fast asleep in Vincent's arms.

She has not given the prospect of their new home much thought. It's enough that she does not have to worry about the rent. As long as it's warm and dry, she would have been happy in a barn.

When Vincent removes his hands from her eyes, she becomes slack-jawed as she glances around the room. She could not have wished for such a place, because she simply could not have imagined it. All the surfaces gleam, and the scent of raw timber, glue and varnish still lingers. The floorboards are scrubbed; fresh muslin drapes the windows; the alcove kitchen is equipped with utensils and crockery; and there's furniture she has not seen before. And a special chair, a wicker one with arms, is positioned next to the window so she can nurse the baby comfortably while admiring the meadows and the pink and red geraniums he has thoughtfully planted in the window box. It seems as if every nook and cranny has been attended to. What did he tell her once? That every task must be undertaken with love. Dazzled but confused, she wonders if she has not stumbled into someone else's home. Surely all this could not possibly be meant for her.

She turns to him, trying to express with her look the gratitude she is too overcome to voice, and he beams at her.

On the newly papered walls, he has already hung his drawings and pictures. But he also points to a couple of new ones: *Christus Consolator*, that he may bestow a serene, hopeful mood throughout this new home; a print of Millet's sower and diggers, to remind them of the hard work at the centre of all endeavours, even family life.

Then he moves to stand before an iron crib in the corner as if it were a shrine. 'For Willem,' he murmurs, voice cracking with emotion. 'Now, anyone who walks in here will know this is a nest for a growing family, not a room for a lonely bachelor.'

She lowers the sleeping baby into it.

Up a small ladder, in an attic bedroom, there is a large bedstead with a newly stuffed mattress. Maria has been given his old one. Impressed by the timber-panelled ceiling, she is immediately drawn to the room's cosy warmth. It is nothing like the draughty attic she shared with her brothers as a young girl, where the roof tiles may have kept out the rain but not the wind.

'And you won't find a mattress more comfortable than this one,' he says, almost bouncing on the large bed. 'Your mother helped me to stuff it. Besides straw, there's eelgrass.'

'You've gone to such trouble,' she says. 'How did you manage to move all your belongings, and the furniture?'

'The workers from the carpenter's yard helped me.'

'But you were supposed to be at the hospital.'

'I convinced the doctor to grant me a short leave, explaining that it would serve the same purpose as the recuperative exercises he ordered me to take in the hospital's garden. Besides, I gave him my word that I'd return if there were problems, but I've been fine, everything is working again.' He gives her a wink.

He helps her back down the ladder. Downstairs again, he shows her another small room for storing his art-making tools and materials as well as Maria's mattress; the girl for once will have her own little bedroom. Then he swans about the studio, arms spread wide. 'It's a home, Sien, a real home for a family. With a studio large enough that I have the space to look at my work from a proper distance.'

The more he shows her, the more she becomes frightened by his unnecessary extravagance. The sheen begins to dull, tarnished by that inevitable question: how much has he spent? So many things they could have done without. Must the crib be made of iron, when a simple weaved one would have done? Her earlier elation is gone. She can't help but question his need to create this . . . this fancy. Though it may have been carried out with love, it seems more the result of him indulging a picture in his head, whatever the cost.

'How much . . .?' she begins, but because he blenches, she stops, realising that her question may appear graceless.

'I thought . . . are you not happy?' he asks, expression wounded.

His question catches her off guard. *Happy.* It's a word she rarely hears, rarely gives any thought to. She does not have to try to remember the last time someone wanted to make her happy because it has never happened before. But this man only wanted to make her happy, of all things. She immediately regrets her mention of money.

'It's a home, Sien,' he reminds her, his voice pleading. 'A real family home. And a proper studio. There's bound to be additional expenses.'

There is nothing she can do but nod and smile, for is it not already done?

His earlier jubilance restored, he busies himself in the alcove kitchen. He has bought smoked pork, and potatoes to be fried in its fat, because the doctor has said the meat would help her to regain her strength and produce good milk for the baby.

When her mother arrives with Maria, Wilhelmina's astonishment, so satisfying for Sien to observe, quickly banishes her dread about the expense. Maria notices little more than the food on the table.

Sien tends to the girl, wiping her hands and face before she is allowed to eat, murmuring, 'Look, Maria, this is our new house. Your and Willem's new home, here with me and Vincent.'

Sien explains to her that she must be good, because Vincent has gone to a lot of trouble, but the girl nods without listening, her eyes following Vincent as he serves the food.

'The faster your recovery, the faster you can return to posing,' he says, heaping Sien's plate with the potatoes. He is all business, his movements brisk and sure. Her pulse quickens as she watches him, and she can feel herself being energised by his very presence.

Seventeen

Straight away, Sien knows she does not like him. At first, she thinks he is the brother, and her heart almost leaps from her chest. But Vincent blurts out the name Tersteeg and she remembers. The man who works at the uncle's gallery on the Plaats. Holding the door open, Vincent greets the man with a crooked smile. 'Well, well, what brings you all the way here?'

Without replying, Tersteeg pushes past Vincent, forcing him to step aside quickly. As if he has some claim to the place, he stands in the middle of the studio, eyeing the baby, her, Maria without bothering to remove his hat, which is so plump and smart she suspects it must have cost more than several weeks rent for them. His grey suit likely several months. She shudders because he makes no effort to conceal his disgust. Even Maria drops her dolls and runs to her mother's side.

'What is the meaning of this?' Tersteeg demands, looking at Sien.

She lowers her head, the heat rising in her cheeks. What had her mother said? *They look down on the likes of us as no better than rats that run down the sewer.* This man is looking at her as if she were less than a rat; as if she were actually sewage.

'Why, it is a newborn being fed at the breast. Have you not seen a mother provide her milk this way before?' Vincent asks. Strangely his demeanour is unruffled. But his tone, too bright, rings false and hollow. She can see that he is struggling to keep his temper at bay because the veins at his temples are throbbing as if near to bursting, and his tic is fluttering in his cheek.

'You mean to tell me that with Theo's money you are supporting this . . . this whore *and* her children?' A sudden fit of laughter overtakes him, and he makes a show of taking out his handkerchief to wipe his eyes. A band of gold flashes on his pinky: a signet ring.

She can feel little else but the scorched temperature of her face. Willem, squirming, spits out her nipple and begins to cry. She hoists him over her shoulder and pats his back, causing him to release a small burp. She turns to Vincent, eyes imploring him not to be baited.

Ignoring her, he folds his arms across his chest and regards Tersteeg with an indulgent smile, as if he is merely obliging a difficult guest. 'So, now you can report that everything is true. And since you are here, don't be shy. Say everything that's on your mind, would you? Is there anything else you wish to tell us?'

'Does your father know about this?'

'That you should mention my father is rather interesting.

Theo understands perfectly well my arrangement with Sien here, who poses for me – and, yes, her children too. Because unlike many of your so-called artists, I will only draw from life.'

'So then, you dare to call this art?' he says, not even bothering to point to the drawings adorning the walls, only giving them a disparaging glance. 'One must use paint, my dear Vincent. These are mere doodlings of a hapless amateur, wouldn't you agree?'

'I assure you, I will pick up a brush one day – but only when I am ready,' replies Vincent, rocking back and forth on his heels, 'or when Theo deems me ready, and not a second before. Do you hear?'

Tersteeg arches one brow, and lets out a snort.

'And I don't mind telling you that a few of your so-called artists could certainly do with more practice at their drawing boards and the use of a regular model. I myself could not have found a better model than Sien.'

'So you say. But one would have to be mad to call this a proper studio. When your esteemed family asked me to look in on you, I certainly did not expect to find a scene such as this.'

'You just don't get it, do you?' Vincent nearly shouts. 'If art is to truly stir another's soul, it can only do so if the artist has experienced love for himself. So I make no apologies.'

'This gives me no pleasure, Vincent, I want to make that clear. What you are doing here is . . . it's absolutely unforgivable. I mean, just who do you think you are? A hero from one of those French novels?'

Tersteeg's question is like a burning match thrown onto dry tinder.

Vincent has stopped his rocking and now leaps towards Tersteeg. Sien braces herself for what's to come.

'Get out!' Vincent orders, his face just an inch from Tersteeg's, the white heat of his anger shimmering around him.

Tersteeg is unmoved. 'You will come to regret your actions, Vincent,' he says coolly. 'And sadly, my friend, this little studio of yours will end in the same way as all your previous ventures. Failure. And the woman over there? You will leave her in the lurch. Mark my words.'

'How dare you? You . . . you *scoundrel*,' Vincent cries, seizing Tersteeg by the collar. 'How can you be so . . . so heartless?'

Tersteeg only smiles smugly, appearing pleased he has finally achieved his aim – to see Vincent rattled, reduced. Sien would not mind if Vincent were to pummel him, but to her disappointment Vincent instead lets go of the man's collar and stumbles backwards, falling into a chair.

Tersteeg's smile vanishes, replaced by an expression of mock sympathy. Now a chill runs down the length of her spine. Without thinking, she rises from her seat, the baby still in her arms. Moving to stand beside Vincent, she glares at Tersteeg, intending to demand he leave at once. But the words dry up before she can utter them as she is pierced by his knife-sharp gaze.

He then has the hide to pat down his jacket; it seems he fears his pocket may have been picked. Then daintily tugging the brim of his hat he heads for the door.

Good riddance, she thinks. But watching him disappear, she is punctured by a realisation: Tersteeg has made known the truth of their standing in the eyes of the world.

She tucks Willem, now asleep, in his crib. Maria has run after Tersteeg, peering down at him from the landing. Vincent tries to pack the bowl of his pipe but his hands are unsteady and most of the tobacco scatters on the table. She relieves him of the task, gathering the loose shavings, her cheeks tear-stained, her heart heavy.

When she returns from the landing, Maria climbs onto her mother's lap, seeking the comfort of her embrace. Sien strokes the girl's crown.

Vincent does not touch his pipe but reaches for a sheet of paper and begins to sketch. He sees her but he does not seem to notice her tears. How can he dare to ignore what just happened? She pushes the girl off her lap and charges at him. Snatching the paper, she rips it in half. He looks up, stunned, then frowns at the damage.

'But it's the Ingres paper from Paris,' he protests.

'Well, you now have two pieces of your precious paper, don't you?'

Hearing Willem stir at the sound of their raised voices, she climbs the ladder to their bedroom. He follows her, and it is there they have their first big, serious fight. She is surprised at herself, that she should have the nerve to corner him like this. That she has suddenly come to care what the world thinks of her when before she cared nothing for it, and cared little for her own survival.

'How could you let that man barge into our home and say and do anything he likes?' she shouts. Had Vincent not seen the contempt on the man's face? He hardly needed to use a weapon to cut them down. 'Do we need to hide, to run from them?

But where can we go? Tell me, Vincent. Are we not crazy to even try to make a life together?'

Vincent lowers himself wearily on the bed and leans forward with elbows on his knees. Looking up, he asks, 'Are you quite finished?'

She stops her pacing though it has far from calmed her; shame hotter than any she had endured while walking the streets still burns through her. She does not belong here in the clean air, with the pretty view. She is like a fish out of water. Perhaps it is only in the soot and grime of Geest that she can truly feel at home. No: she cannot remain here. And nor should he expect her to after this.

She sits next to him. 'I will leave,' she mutters, staring at the floor. 'I'll return to Geest.'

Vincent scoffs at her words. 'Do you think I give any weight to Tersteeg's opinions? Yes, he came and belittled us. But it is because he is a little man himself. A man who is jealous of me and who earns his self-regard by making others feel worthless.'

'That might be the case,' she counters, 'but do you not think he is simply stating what everyone else is saying about us? Doesn't that bother you at all?'

Vincent shrugs. 'Yes, I admit he upset me. But I will never allow him to get the better of me or crush my spirit. I will always hold my truth over his. And you too, Sien, must find the courage to stand against petty-minded scoundrels like him. If you cannot, then you are simply not fit to be with me.' He stands and looks down at her.

Sudden anger bubbles inside her, red, hot like lava. How had this become about *her* again?

'Why must it be about me,' she demands, 'when I cannot help any of it?'

'Ha, that's where you are wrong. They can't help being the scoundrels that they are. It is up to us not to stoop to their level but to hold to our own ideals, as difficult as it is. Do you not see that?'

She throws up her hands. 'It's easy for someone like you to say so. But with my past, I have no standing, no say. Oh, why, did I have to cross paths with you? I'd rather have died on the streets. Death should have been my saviour, not you. But I've never had any luck with life, even trying to escape it.' Even as the words leave her lips, she wishes she could take them back, fearing she has gone too far. But it's too late.

He glares at her as if she has just blasphemed. 'No! No, you are never to give in to despair. *Never.*' Leaning down, he seizes her shoulders. 'Never, do you hear?' She has not seen him this angry before; he appears like a man about to lose his mind with his rage. When she does not reply, he shakes her, hissing, '*Do you hear?*'

Never mind her despair, his explosive reaction makes it impossible for her to think, let alone form words. Rising, she slaps his cheek, hard.

For a moment, he is too shocked to respond, but then he quickly releases her and clambers down the ladder. A moment later, she hears the apartment door slam behind him, and a moment after that, Willem's long wail.

*

It is late. She is relieved to hear him come in. As if the door clicking open gives her permission to breathe again, she lets out a long sigh. Willem who sleeps next to her during the night does not stir. After Vincent left, as she grappled with his question – was she prepared to weather the storm to be with him? – she discovered that their argument had caused her greater distress even than Tersteeg's visit, for what remained was an ache in her trembling heart from the slap she gave him, the bitterness of their words. But then again, she was staggered that her wish for her own end had met with such a vehement reply, when he himself had admitted to feeling a similar ambivalence towards life on the night they'd met. It is as if she had touched his rawest nerve, and she suspects his sensitivity to the topic is likely bound up with his own fears. And yet she cannot help but draw strength from his defiance, his determination to fight against this weakness, his refusal to let it get the better of him; before now, no one has ever made her believe that her life was worth fighting for.

She lights a match and holds it to the wick of the candle stub next to the bed. He comes up the ladder, his shadow cast giant-large against the panelled ceiling. He does not look at her but undresses quietly and climbs into bed. She can smell the fresh scent of the night's air, feel the cool of the meadow on him. He had most likely been walking there.

Quietly, without disturbing the baby, he runs his hand down her side then, hungrily, his mouth seeks out her breasts. As he suckles, her milk begins to flow. Below he is hardening. But she keeps her thighs closed, for she is still too ginger, too chafed.

But it has also been some time, so she reaches down and, taking hold of him, ministers with her hand until his back arches, and he shudders.

Part Two

Eighteen

Theo shifts restlessly in the seat of his second-class carriage, struggling to arrange his legs in a comfortable position. He crosses and re-crosses them several times, attracting the displeasure of the man facing him, whose frown above the newspaper he is holding prompts Theo to offer a tight, apologetic smile. The late summer heat has well and truly penetrated this iron-wrapped compartment, and despite the half-open window, the air is stifling. Tucking his finger inside his starch-stiff collar, Theo attempts to loosen it.

As the train nears The Hague, it is no ordinary sense of foreboding that begins to gather inside him. Again, he will be visiting his brother under onerous circumstances, as he did in the Borinage, where he found a near-destitute and half-starved ghost of a man – but one who nevertheless possessed the will to declare his artistic ambitions.

In that bleak, coalmining village, the matter of extricating his brother required no more than packing up a dilapidated timber shack, his belongings so scant a small trunk was all that was needed. Now, thinking of this regrettable nonsense about marrying a woman of the street, who could very well have conjured some sexual spell over his brother in order to wheedle funds from him – *his* funds – his heart feels heavy enough to sink below its chamber. Who else but Vincent could induce in him such nerve-shredding anxiety? Then again, who else but Vincent could provide him with the rich, keen insights about art, about life, that over the years have become nothing less than the very fuel he needs for his own internal combustion? In short, he has come to realise over the years that Vincent completes him.

While Vincent's uncompromising nature sets him constantly at odds with the world, Theo has found, to his surprise, that it relieves him of his own anxieties and worries. That in witnessing Vincent's struggles, he is afforded not only a glimpse of one ruled by passions but reminded afresh of his duty to avoid the same fate, saving their parents from the burden of two errant sons. Have they not suffered enough because of their oldest? That persistently troubled child, who so far has proved himself incapable in matters both personal and professional. How many times did he find the parsonage in a state of disquiet because of Vincent's presence? It continues to both confound and irritate him that Vincent had so few qualms about turning his back on his family.

But perhaps it is only right that Vincent should possess such conviction for if one is to pit oneself against the world, then one must also be prepared to fight it. As for himself, no, he'd always choose the smoother path. Why upset those you love? It would not be wrong to say his parents are almost at their wits' end. Even though far from them, he can feel their anxiety so palpably they may as well be sitting beside him.

There is little doubt in his mind the day will be a long one. There are meetings with both Tersteeg and Mauve, who will no doubt offer their opinions on Vincent whether he asks for them or not. And though he relishes Vincent's correspondence, he is sure the company of the scribe himself will be an entirely different affair. It will require not only infinite patience but his most artful skills as salesman and negotiator. He is, however, under no illusion that his brother will so easily be influenced as his well-heeled but impressionable customers at Goupil; money they may have, but Vincent has an iron will.

At the rumble of iron drawing into the station, and the hiss and sigh of the engine coming to rest, Theo sits taller, releases a long-withheld breath.

A commotion on the platform draws his attention. Turning to look out the window, he immediately spots his brother, the lone figure in a punctured hat and crumpled jacket, busily sketching as the crowd swerves around him. The object of his brother's transfixion is a stooped old man, shuffling along with the aid of a walking stick. Theo slumps in his seat and watches Vincent for a few moments, his finger and thumb stroking his moustache, wondering how Vincent has the temerity to step out in such shabby garb. Though they have not seen each other since the previous summer, and despite the excitement Vincent expressed in his recent letters at the prospect of their reunion, that he should have been distracted by this opportunity for a portrait surprises Theo not at all. Doesn't Vincent always live stubbornly in the moment? Art is now his obsession – no, his addiction. Sighing, Theo rises to his feet, retrieves his valise, disembarks and joins the throng on the platform.

'Vincent,' he says, about to tap his brother's shoulder from behind.

Vincent, turning too swiftly, knocks Theo's hand away.

Suddenly face to face, they stare at each other open-mouthed, too startled to speak. When Vincent offers him a wide smile, Theo remains hesitant, aloof. He may have arrived in body, but a part of him is still on the train, hostage to prickly thoughts continuing to seesaw in his mind. Before he has fully adjusted to his brother's presence, Vincent is not only squeezing his hand but has thrown an affectionate arm around his shoulder.

'At last, my dear Theo,' Vincent exclaims. 'I can shake your hand in person rather than through the postal service.'

He is immediately overpowered by Vincent's exuberance. Finally breaking into a grin, Theo admits, 'Yes, it is good to see you.'

It is indeed good to see him, this older brother of his, and at this moment his resentment over the vexed matter of Sien, which has made his head and heart smart in recent weeks, seems as of little consequence as the last wisp of steam vanishing into the air.

Vincent's eyes glisten as they roam eagerly over Theo's face, and his lips tremble as if words, at this moment, fail him. Theo smiles – *Yes, I am here* – and gives his brother a small nod. Becoming reacquainted with Vincent's presence, the very nearness of him, has a deeply stirring effect on him too. Is he still not in thrall to his memories of waking with Vincent beside him, sharing as they did the same pillow for many years? This brother who, four years Theo's senior, was never lost for what to do. Inexhaustible, always searching the woods surrounding their home in Zundert for nature's pleasures, with Theo following behind. Reading, drawing, hunting insects, preoccupied by one thing or another. But Theo is not yet ready. Not quite ready for Vincent's emotions to gush. So he turns away to follow the bustle.

After arranging for Theo's valise to be delivered to his lodgings, they leave the station, Theo unable to ignore Vincent's firm, steady hand on the small of his back.

'You've breakfasted?' Vincent asks, leaning into him.

'Yes, early.'

'Shall we find a cafe?' Vincent is scanning the coffee houses near the station.

It has been mere minutes since he stepped off the train but already Theo is reminded that, despite his reputation at Goupil and his professional achievements there, in Vincent's company he will forever remain the younger brother. The weight of the day begins to press on him as dampness gathers near his temples. Suddenly, he misses Paris and the delicious freedom of his bachelor life there.

But Vincent, peering through the mullioned window of one establishment, is disconcerted to find it not well patronised. 'Perhaps because it's not that good,' he muses.

For all his propensity to dismiss many finer points of decorum, Theo's brother can be very particular about the most unexpected things. 'Come, Vincent, this will do,' he says, not bothering to hide his irritation as he heads inside, leaving Vincent no choice but to follow him.

When the brothers enter, two older women wearing high-necked blouses and haughty expressions, seated at the back, glance long at them, eyes shifting from one man to the other. Theo has no trouble reading their thoughts, for the marked difference in the men's sartorial habits has no doubt piqued their interest. He, in his spotless bowler hat and well-cut suit, can justifiably invite comparisons to a dove, while Vincent, in his sorry jacket and misshapen hat, is a tufted bird of the sea.

As if sharing an understanding, they both head instinctively for the table near the window, out of the women's earshot, and order coffees and pastries.

Vincent, his face lighting up, immediately suggests a trip to Scheveningen.

Theo quickly agrees. 'Yes, it would be good to see the sea again. It's been some time.'

Theo has not had a chance to study his brother properly and, doing so now, he is astonished to find Vincent looking well. In fact, even better than well. When has he seen his brother glow with such health? It is clear he has gained weight, enough to round out his sharp edges and soften his flesh, suggesting that for once he is finding life agreeable. It is a gratifying contrast to the emaciated man he found in the Borinage.

His brother is pleased by Theo's acquiescence. 'That's settled then,' Vincent says, slapping a palm on the table before leaning back and folding his arms across his chest.

But in the next moment, the hair at the back of Theo's neck stands to attention. Even before Theo is aware of it, his body has apprehended a shift in the atmosphere, brought on by the sudden change in Vincent's gaze, which is now narrow. 'I say, things must be good in Paris. I take it the city is still agreeing with you?' There is a discernible tightness in Vincent's voice as his eyes appraise Theo's dapper suit coolly

Theo stiffens, detecting a veiled attack on Paris. It is clear Vincent is still smarting from his time there – or, more precisely, from his forced departure from the City of Light following his dismissal from its Goupil branch. That Paris should, for Vincent, be forever associated with a professional failure does not surprise him. Therefore, wisely, Theo chooses not to tell Vincent how much he loves that city, nor how grateful he is for the distance separating him from the rest of their family. Nor does he confide how much he relishes his professional life as well as the one of a bachelor and flâneur who has on more than one occasion found himself attracting the admiration of the city's many pretty young women. 'It's an exciting time,' he says, merely offering a little shrug.

'Tell me, are they still buying that rubbish by Gérôme?' Vincent asks, leaning forward to plant his elbows on the table.

Vincent's sneering tone, though it rankles, fails to provoke

Theo. Shrugging again, he replies, 'You know he always sells. But his art appeals to the –'

'To the well-heeled and easily swayed,' his brother interrupts.

'That's a matter of opinion,' Theo counters. Though Vincent's appearance may have softened, it's clear his strong views about art have not. If anything, they seem to have become even more pointed now that he has become an artist himself. Moreover, Theo was right not to have been fooled by those long, eloquent letters Vincent wrote him, for, just as he suspected would be the case, in person his brother is the same irascible, opinionated man Theo has come to know in recent years.

Theo's reply seems only to shore up his brother's position. 'How do they justify their obsession with that silly, lifeless academic style? Where's the human soul? Such paintings leave me more frigid than the canals in winter.'

Theo sighs. 'Some of us admire a work of art for its obvious beauty,' he reminds Vincent. Aware that he has dealt a blow but also keen to make another – for rarely does he have the opportunity to do so – he tells Vincent that unless he is willing to make amends with the world, unless he is prepared to smooth out his rough edges, those around him will use his uncouth manners as a reason to dismiss him altogether.

Vincent cranes his neck, impatient to defend himself. 'It may be so, but I can only tell you what I feel. And what moves me here' – he thumps his chest with his fist – 'are not those flawless pictures.'

It occurs to Theo that the cause of Vincent's aggrievement is not just the celebrated style of Gérôme and the academic school but Theo's success at Goupil: it should be him, the older brother, doling out advice; he who should have climbed the ranks at Goupil; and he who should be sending money to the younger man.

Fortunately, the arrival of their refreshments distracts Vincent sufficiently to ease the tension between them.

Theo seizes this pause to steer the conversation to the time they'd spent together once before in The Hague. One of Vincent's favourite memories – his brother always brings it up when they are reunited after a long separation – it has become a touchstone for their relationship.

'Why, it's been nearly ten years,' Vincent exclaims, happily taking up the subject. He proceeds to recall their walk along the canal near Rijswijk in the summer of 1873, when Theo, then fifteen, stayed with him for a few days.

'Remember the beautiful weather?' Vincent asks, eyes lighting up.

'Yes, I remember,' Theo replies, smiling, unable to forget the powerful current of emotions he'd felt that day, when his very soul seemed to merge with Vincent's. Back then, he was apprehensive about visiting his brother because it was around this time he first had an inkling of their parents' worry about him. But those few days had not only rekindled their childhood ties but forever cemented their fraternal bond, sparking their regular, frequent correspondence.

And the highlight of his stay was that walk.

On that day, as they ventured away from the bustle of the city, Vincent was more animated than usual, sharing with Theo his impressions about his work at Goupil, the art he was allowed to see and touch every day, and his hopes for financial independence. Perhaps it was the open countryside, perhaps the fresh air, perhaps the sun, but Theo felt his heart and mind fill with Vincent's words: so frank and ardent it seemed as though a part of him had always been awaiting them.

A pang of regret now rises in him; his earlier remarks were perhaps too harsh. So now, as he listens to Vincent's recollections of that day, he smiles encouragingly.

'And the eel and milk we bought from the windmill's owner,' Vincent reminds. 'He had those ferocious brows, like thistle.'

'You can remember that?' Theo asks, eyes wide. He is always astonished by Vincent's power of recall.

'I can still see him now, leaning out of his window to offer the cups of warm milk.' Chuckling, Vincent continues, 'And he had the animal that had only just been relieved of its swollen teat tied up nearby.'

On that journey to Rijswijk Theo was so reassured by Vincent's confidence and optimism he did not have cause to doubt his older brother's success – in fact, if anything, Theo became inspired to emulate him. But now he struggles to recognise that former version of Vincent, for it seems as if that man were someone else entirely.

After their rest at the windmill, the brothers had walked back to the city, hushed by the deep connection they'd forged. At their parting, they attempted to bid each other a jovial adieu, but it was undercut by Vincent's quiet melancholy, and Theo understood that Vincent would miss him, and that, despite everything he'd said about Goupil and the future, he was deeply lonely.

'Whatever obstacles, whatever trials we may face, we . . . we must never forget the generous spirit of kinship that held us that day,' Vincent says, sniffling. Then, tipping his head to one side, he gives Theo a wan smile.

Theo nods, but he does not wish to dwell on that day, nor is he willing to indulge his brother's maudlin nature. Quickly changing the subject, he blurts out, 'I should tell you, I think your work is showing much improvement.' Then, having succeeded in diverting Vincent's attention, he continues eagerly, 'Your control of the line is becoming so assured, I think it is time you started to use paints.'

His words achieve their intended effect, for Vincent's expression flares briefly like a lit match. 'Are you sure? I mean, do you really think I'm ready?'

'Yes, I do, Vincent,' Theo replies. Then, knowing that Vincent will be worried by the cost, he adds, 'We'll buy a paintbox for you.'

At this reassurance, Vincent sits taller. 'Yes, yes, I suppose it's probably time.' Then, his posture dropping, he adds, 'But you know how wary I am of artists who slop on paint before they can handle them properly.'

'You must make a start,' Theo says firmly.

'Well, I've been drawing so much in the last few months . . . So, if you really think I am ready, then I must be,' Vincent says.

'If your drawings can improve, then it follows your paintings will too.'

'Yes, you are quite right. I need to make things that will sell. After all, I can't expect you to . . . what I mean is, I must be able to support Sien and the children before we marry,' Vincent says, glancing distractedly around the cafe.

Though he has been anticipating – and dreading – this moment for some weeks, now that it has arrived, Theo finds that he must take a few moments to gather himself. For want of something to do with his clammy hands, which are gripped by a nearly overwhelming desire to shake his brother by the shoulders as well as to embrace him, he picks up his coffee cup, though it contains only the dregs. As these conflicting impulses retreat, he decides this is the moment he should utter the words he began to rehearse back in Paris, words he is duty-bound to deliver not just for his sake, but on behalf of their entire family.

In his coolest, calmest voice, the one he likes to adopt at delicate moments in certain business negotiations, he says, 'Vincent, this marriage is out of the question, whether you earn a living or not.' Then, putting his cup down so serenely it comes to rest on the saucer without the slightest noise, he repeats, 'It is no use, whether you sell or not.'

As if Theo's words, cold and precise, may have been delivered with a scythe, Vincent slumps into the back of his chair.

'I . . . I thought you understood,' Vincent mutters. 'You made no mention of . . . I believed you were sympathetic to . . .'

It is true that, despite his shock upon learning of Sien, Theo had said nothing to disparage the match, making up his mind to bide his time until he had the opportunity to deliver his message in person. The matter was too important and of too intimate a nature to commit to paper. What's more, he did not possess the energy nor appetite for an epistolary argument with Vincent about Sien, for he was sure Vincent would not hesitate to mount an exhausting, unrelenting offensive through the postal service.

But witnessing his brother's anguish, he regrets not only his directive but this whole sorry affair with Sien. Why, *why*, must his brother become caught in such barbs? What else is it, this absurd desire to marry a whore? Has he not yet learnt to give such nonsense a wide berth? Tempering his tone, he says, 'I understand she helps you, Vincent, but surely you cannot mean marriage.'

'But . . . but she's devoted to me, and I to her,' says Vincent, voice thin and high. He explains the indispensable role she has played in his artistic progress. 'She's a tireless model, exceptionally patient. But it's not just that . . .' He looks down at his hands, now twitching on the tabletop. 'I simply cannot do without her. Yes, there is art, but its magnificence cannot be realised without life, without love. If I do not know what it is to love a woman, if I have never felt the blood rushing to my groin, my body shuddering from her kiss, the shape of her breasts, then what am I? I might be able to hold a pen or brush but I would not be capable of investing my work with *feeling*.'

Though Theo is not unmoved, he is nevertheless undeterred. 'But is love grounds enough for a marriage, when there are so many other things to consider?' Then, afraid he may have gone too far, he removes his arms from the table and sits back.

But it is too late. Vincent taps his fingers on the table with a rapid, impatient tempo. 'Besides love, what other foundation should there be for a marriage?' he demands. 'I hope you're not becoming one of those who values everything else *but* love. I hope I've taught you better than that.'

But this accusation only spurs Theo to mount a formidable campaign of his own, reminding Vincent that there is always more to consider besides love where marriage is involved. It cannot be compared to any ordinary arrangement – love or no love – for there are also obligations towards one's family, reputation, career, future, even the welfare of the children who may arrive.

Vincent listens, his expression pensive, but he shows little sign of yielding. 'Do you think I am not aware of these things? And, as always, I will insist on love first. Yes, of course one must earn bread, but one can find those means when one has love, don't you see?'

'This is precisely why marriage is of the least importance. Your career should come first. Was it not only a few months ago you said, "Kee and no other"? And yet suddenly you insist on . . . on this . . . woman.' Theo finds himself unable to utter Sien's name.

At Theo's mention of Kee, Vincent's expression darkens. 'Do you know how cruelly I was betrayed by those who had nothing to do with either her or me?' He shakes his head. 'By those who would not hesitate to tread on a new shoot.'

Theo knows better than to share with him Kee's version: that she never encouraged Vincent's infatuation with her, gave no indication of similar feelings, having felt for him only the affection one might for a like-minded cousin. He knows Vincent only too well; if he is to succeed in his mission, he will have to be prepared to show tact, but, more importantly, he must arouse his brother's sympathy – make him *feel* the logic of his argument rather than urge him to consider his duty and responsibility, for such considerations were only likely to invite his brother's scorn and encourage him to dig his heels in further.

'Come, Vincent, let's take a walk in Scheveningen.' Theo stands and picks up his hat, not waiting for Vincent's reply.

Nineteen

On the tram to Scheveningen, they are forced to sit apart, a portly gentleman between them. Vincent, impatient for Theo's ear, asks the man if they might swap their seats. The man declares he is quite comfortable, so he'd rather not. When Theo notices Vincent is about to rebuke him, he quickly cautions his brother with a tight frown. Vincent, sighing resignedly, sits back. Theo, reminded afresh of his brother's inclination to flex his temper, is relieved to be spared his company for the short journey to the sea.

When they reach the picturesque fishing village, they immediately head towards the water, lured by the band of blue shimmering on the horizon. After removing their shoes and socks they climb the dunes, just as they had ten years earlier. An occasional wind lifts the sand, sending fine granules in their direction, but it bothers them little, taken as they are by the novelty of the setting and being together again.

Vincent shares with Theo his wish that their parents would visit the seaside once in a while. 'They could come here, for example,' he says, waving his arms to take in their surrounds. 'Surely their flock could do without them for a few days a year.'

Theo, irritated by his brother's impractical suggestion, shakes his head, reminding Vincent that they have only just moved to Nuenen. 'So, you can imagine how busy they will be now, getting to know everybody, settling in.'

'No, I suppose a seaside visit for leisure purposes is unlikely to entice them. Unless, of course, Pa was asked to write and deliver sermons, or Ma was asked to run embroidering or knitting classes for the bored girls.'

'Well, perhaps the well-to-do holiday crowds would find such sobering lessons welcome after overindulging in their pleasures,' Theo jokes.

After Vincent's heated departure at Christmas the previous year, he is relieved to hear Vincent speak almost fondly of their parents. Is it because he is in love? Theo wonders. Because a woman is always warming his bed? He mentions how pleased the elder Van Goghs were to hear about Uncle Cor's commissions.

'Though one would think a word or two could've been sent along with the money,' Vincent grumbles, sliding back, unable to secure his balance on the dune.

'You know how they can be. You should take the fact he paid you as a sign of highest praise. He would never have done it out of charity – or duty, for that matter.'

Vincent is nevertheless grim-faced. Theo guesses he is probably still harbouring some grudge against their uncle, likely the result of some disagreement about art long forgotten by Cor but still vivid to Vincent.

'As soon as your career is on its way and you begin to sell,' Theo consoles him, 'then everything will be in the past, and you'll see none of it will matter.'

'Yes, yes,' Vincent replies dismissively, before turning to conquer the dune behind him. As he struggles for footing in the sand, he blurts out, 'Does it occur to you that you may be squandering your talents by spending your days selling art? I mean, is Goupil the best place for you?'

Theo should give up the world of commerce, he continues in the next breath, and join him in pursuing an artist's path so that they may take on the art world together. That Theo should remain chained to Goupil when he too has an artist's eye seems to Vincent a great pity, for he is convinced there are great paintings inside Theo that should be realised on canvas. In a recent letter, did Theo not provide the most painterly description of Paris at night, an image he is sure even the finest artists would have struggled to convey with paint?

Theo, standing a few feet below Vincent, pretends not to hear him, having previously been subjected to this pointless line of thought. What's more, he can see through Vincent's act: though he does not doubt the veracity of Vincent's claim about his own artistic eye, his brother's suggestion is likely also motivated by a desire to cut him down in size and put them on an equal footing, engaged in the same romantic struggle. Yes, Vincent would no doubt welcome him as an accomplice, so they might stand united in defiance of the rest of their family;

but Vincent must know that, as much as Theo will always remain his loyal brother, his pride and love for their family would never allow him to act against their wishes. Besides, does Vincent not realise how much Theo enjoys the cachet that comes with their family's name? The deep satisfaction of his working life? The cut and thrust of commerce? To have the means to enjoy restaurants, the theatre, the nocturnal delights of Paris? To have a berth in the Parisian art world? No, Vincent is unlikely to approve of the comforts afforded by professional success and ambition, just as he is unlikely to understand the need for putting family before art.

But more than that, if he were to join Vincent, who would support the two foolish brothers in their joint endeavour? Hardly their hardworking but pinched parents who also rely on Theo to supplement their income.

'I mean, do you really think it's the best career for you?' Vincent persists.

This time, frustrated and exasperated by Vincent's tenacity, Theo replies, 'If I joined you to take up art, who'd pay the bills? Since the oldest son cannot be counted upon, what am I to do? Can Ma and Pa afford to have two indigent sons? I urge you to stop worrying about me and worry instead about making good work – worry about painting,' he almost shouts as the sea crashes and the gulls squawk. Then, displaying a mountain climber's energy, he turns his attention to the ascent of the dune, overtaking Vincent, stumbling, feet digging and sliding. Upon reaching the crest, out of breath, his chest rises and falls in time with the beat of the waves upon the shore. As he takes a large gulp of the salty air, he is comforted by nature's relentless, timeless charge, obstinately indifferent to his dilemmas and that of his family.

By the time they are on the tram back to the city, they have resumed their tender manner towards each other – for they do not know when they will see each other again after this day. Their discussions return to art, and Vincent enthusiastically tries to restore their camaraderie, talking Theo's ear off, pushing his ideas about drawing. Theo mentions the avant-garde scene in Paris, suggesting that perhaps Vincent might like to come and see it for himself, but Vincent cuts him off impatiently. 'Yes, yes, in time, when I'm ready. You know I started so late, and there is still much to do.'

Then, to Theo's inquiries about Pulchri Studio, the city's esteemed art society, Vincent lets out a contemptuous laugh before telling him about artists who, either embarrassed by the poor state of his jacket or something else he can't even begin to suspect, glance distractedly over his shoulder as they greet him.

'Then, it always ends with, "Will you excuse me." All I can do is turn around and watch as they approach someone else with a warm handshake and hearty slap on the shoulder, while I'm left standing there, muttering to myself.' Vincent catches his breath before lowering his voice. 'I can't bear it, Theo. It is better not to go. I may be a Van Gogh, but to them I am simply an inconvenient presence.'

Vincent tells him that, since meeting Sien, and having a model always at his disposal, he has not needed Pulchri's drawing classes. Then, as if afraid of disappointing his brother, he reassures him, 'I tried, Theo, but so many are lacking the fundamentals of drawing and yet they don't seem to care.' His voice now inflected with amusement as well as consternation, he describes his peers' blighted opinions, and their desire to please each other above any honest appraisals of the art.

It is not difficult for Theo to imagine these scenes. And though he wishes Vincent would dress better and conduct himself with a modicum of grace and charm, he also understands these skills escape his brother not in any small way but entirely. In the business of selling art, Theo has learnt the art of bluff can be just as important as a discerning eye. But Vincent, according to those who worked with him, was baffled by such tactical manoeuvrings. Too often, he put customers in awkward situations, offering them art they did not want but dismissing the works they liked.

'Don't pay them any heed, Vincent,' Theo advises. 'Look, if you have Weissenbruch and Breitner to occasionally call upon, then let it be that way. Just keep going and try your hand at the paints.' Theo cannot help but worry for Vincent's future if art-making were to come to nothing, like his other endeavours. So his hope for Vincent's success is as fragile and uncertain as a bud caught in late frost.

Vincent speaks animatedly of the Schenkweg and his new studio as they make their way there. 'The rent is very reasonable,' he reminds Theo. 'When you consider its size, and the quality of the building.' Though Theo would have preferred to skip the visit to the Schenkweg, this is impossible since Vincent's work is stored there. And he is sure that if he refuses to meet Sien, Vincent will think him as cold-hearted as Tersteeg and Mauve. Moreover, he reminds himself, if he is to persuade Vincent to change his position regarding Sien, he must do it in stealth, allowing Vincent to feel he is making the decision for himself and not because he is yielding to flimsy arguments about maintaining appearances.

So, with time running short, Theo is prepared to indulge his brother, driven by that single goal for which he has come to The Hague.

They climb the stairs, Vincent's voice rising excitedly as he describes the number of drawings filling his folio, due in no small part to Sien and the children.

As Theo follows Vincent into the apartment, the woman and two children inside seem barely aware of their entrance, caught in a drama of their own. Both children are crying: the baby appears as if he has just woken while the girl sits on the floor weeping and nursing her cheek, having no doubt suffered the force of her mother's palm over some misdemeanour.

He has no trouble recognising Sien. After all, he feels as if he has already met her from all the drawings Vincent sent him and the stories Vincent wrote him. Busy consoling the baby in her arms, she glances up at them, looking as stricken as a cornered animal.

If she is struggling in his presence, Theo is contending with a fresh burst of outrage that threatens to undo him. And though he promised himself he would resist venting his feelings, he is only just able to contain them. That Vincent should have put him in this position – asking him to consider this woman as his intended now seems more a cruel joke than a romantic folly.

Managing to conceal his disdain, he offers her a curt nod. After removing his hat and hanging it on a hook next to Vincent's, he turns back and steals glances at Sien, trying to reconcile this first impression of her with the woman his brother had written about so lovingly. All Theo can see is a haggard woman who appears much older than her years. There is not only the lifeless, greying hair and the stoop in her shoulders, but a face and body made gaunt by a life he imagines she could no more have wished for than the two bastard children she bore.

He is certainly unable to see any resemblance to Landelle's angels, as Vincent insisted, nor Delaroche's Mater Dolorosa, nor Ary Scheffer's portraits. This woman would be invisible to Theo were they to pass each other in the street. And though he is not unmoved – as Vincent mentioned, it is clear that life has not merely been unkind to her; it has given her a good drubbing – he can't help but wonder: why her? Is the city not awash with such women? Yes, he can understand that Vincent would have wanted to save her, as he tried with the miners in the Borinage, but he cannot see how Vincent can be in love with her, as he claims. There is so little coquetry or beguiling charm about her that he has trouble picturing her as a prostitute – but then, recalling that she is one of those forced to ply her trade on the streets, he should not be surprised.

And nevertheless, here she is: his brother's beloved. And whether she loves Vincent in return is of little consequence to

Theo, because he is convinced this business with Sien is only likely to land his brother in hot water. It is like the Borinage all over again.

By this time, the little girl has picked herself up off the floor and run to Vincent's side, fastening her arms around his leg.

'Ah, Maria, have you disturbed your brother again,' Vincent chides good-humouredly as he hoists her small frame into the air, eliciting a squeal of delight that makes it clear their acrobatic act is a well-loved ritual.

To Theo, this scene is nothing short of bewildering, revealing a side to his brother that is new and unexpected: a paternal figure, surrounded by those who regard him with the kind of affection typical of any family. How at home he appears, how at ease. It is clear Vincent relishes the role of father, carrying Maria across his shoulder and lowering her into a chair before giving her nose a little squeeze. Then, pointing to the baby in Sien's arm, he announces, 'And that roaring lion over there is the mighty Willem.' The pride in his voice makes Theo wince – a tribe of them living off the allowance he sends to Vincent, the allowance he sends punctually three times a month. Theo slips his finger into his collar, for breathing has suddenly become difficult, the inside of him filling with too much heat. 'And, of course, Sien,' Vincent says softly, turning to her. But Sien is too busy trying to soothe Willem to acknowledge Theo properly, imparting only a glance before turning away to nurse the baby.

As the din ceases, Vincent fetches his folio and eagerly shows Theo the black-and-white world he has been so busy creating.

'See, this one has been washed in milk, to give it a softer look.

And this is the trick from Weissenbruch I told you about: soaking the charcoal in linseed oil to achieve an un-burred look.'

Though Theo tries to keep his attention on Vincent's work, he is too distracted by Vincent's new family to parse the drawings with his normally critical eye. And noticing that the work is not dissimilar to that he has already seen, he makes do with nods of encouragement rather than trusting himself to speak, because the seething resentment he felt in Paris at Vincent taking on a whore and her family at his expense is now threatening to turn into a vast wave of rage inside him. The distance between Paris and The Hague may have buffered him from his brother's foolishness, but witnessing him thriving in this domestic milieu, he wonders if this bonhomie is not being performed merely for his benefit.

But then, upon glimpsing Vincent scrutinising the drawing in front of him with his brows knit tight, Theo quickly dispels this notion, overcome instead by a different and far more discomfiting realisation: that Vincent should consider this arrangement with Sien and her family perfectly acceptable to all. His astonishment ebbs as his eyes begin to sting. That his brother – with such a distinguished name, and hailing from a respectable family – should have chosen this woman for himself speaks so resoundingly of the sad turn his life has taken. How could he so emphatically reject all the advantages of his background? That he can be happy and satisfied with this . . . this . . . when he was destined for so much more, deserved so much more, and should have expected so much more.

'Theo, I want to show you this portrait of Sien,' Vincent says, reaching for yet another drawing of the woman. 'I still consider *Sorrow* to be my best drawing, but this one too has a quality I'm proud of.'

Blinking, Theo returns his attention to Vincent's work. Picking up the drawing of Sien seated on a chair, Theo agrees. 'I'm impressed with your progress – and, as I said, I think painting is the next step.' Contemplating Sien here, he is startled to see her anew, as if through a stronger, more powerful lens; a woman rendered so lovingly that, despite her forlorn countenance, she manages to radiate a quiet strength. Her dark, formidable features, worn and tired as they are, have somehow become more striking on paper than in life.

'She is a veritable Mater Dolorosa. It's uncanny, I tell you.' Vincent is peering over Theo's shoulder.

Theo appreciates that in this drawing there may be a fleeting resemblance to the subject of Delaroche's work, but he remains steadfastly puzzled by the comparison. Then again, he is not the one who is smitten with Sien. There is no doubt in Theo's mind that Vincent, like many artists he knows, has wrought a very personal interpretation of his subject, finding in her an agent who can convey his particular creative urges. In this way, she suits Vincent very well, he thinks. Then, flipping through the folio, it is clear to him that while Vincent's draughtsmanship is beginning to demonstrate a certain confidence, his drawings, besides lacking refinement, and though moving enough, have an unsettling dreariness to them. Their rustic, authentic character is all very well, but finding an audience who would be willing to pay for them is quite a different matter. One thing he has learnt from the salesroom at Goupil is that buyers like to hang works that are pleasing and charming to the eye. If workers or the poor are depicted, they should at least be placed against the bucolic settings of harvest time, reaping golden wheat while the even more golden sun throws its last rays across the resplendent sky. But Vincent's subjects, untethered to a narrative or a backdrop, float on white space alone, brought to life by lines perhaps too thick and vigorous for most buyers' tastes.

'Vincent, you must start to put these figures within a scene. Alone, they will not do. I know they are studies of types, but they must belong somewhere,' he advises gently.

'Yes, eventually I will work them up.' Vincent replies, a little impatient but not without enthusiasm. 'Especially when I can do groups, which I am keen to do. You know, a scene with multiple figures, like those you see in *The Graphic*.'

Sien, having finally succeeded in settling the baby to sleep, and after providing Maria with a tattered magazine in the corner, slips into the alcove kitchen. Soon the room fills with the scent of coffee brewing, and not long after she joins them at the table, and they are left with little choice but to grapple with each other's company. While Theo and Sien remain subdued, Vincent's legs, propelled by what seems both excitement and nerves, shake and shudder. Theo is not surprised that Sien keeps her eyes lowered, her hand gripping her cup so firmly the knuckles of her hand shine white. As for himself, he has barely taken a sip of his coffee, all his energy and concentration taken up by his effort to remain outwardly calm. But his brother seems determined to single-handedly thaw the awkward, frigid atmosphere with his incessant chatter while Theo, only too glad to remain his audience, returns small nods.

The neighbourhood, Vincent says, is full of hardworking couples and young families, eager to get on in the world, just like he and Sien. The grocer has offered him credit, and the baker too. Then, eyes twinkling with amusement, he says, 'I am sure they are under the impression that we are a long-married couple with two children. And there is no harm to let them believe so, because it will become the case in time.'

Theo steals a sideways glance at Sien. Her face is flushed crimson. He is not unsympathetic towards this pitiful soul; after all, she has simply been ensnared in Vincent's longings. What choice did she have? Why should Vincent drag this woman from the gutter in an attempt to rehabilitate her, when clearly he will fail? It perplexes Theo that Vincent cannot see none of this will come to any good – especially for Sien. That she should have been rescued from the streets and made to entertain notions of becoming betrothed to a man of Vincent's rank seems to him rather cruel than worthy.

So, again, his headstrong brother is bent on living out his whimsical fancies with little regard for the consequences; chasing an impossible dream, not only to the detriment of their family but to this woman, whose only fault was to catch his brother's eye. His resentment wanes, overtaken by a quiet anger. It then occurs to him that everyone in Vincent's world plays a role. He, the brother who provides his bread; the parents and family he must rail against to seek his truth; and the woman who will help him fulfil his wish to be a particular artist and man.

Now he feels truly sorry for her.

Vincent, undeterred, is extolling the virtues of his home. 'But really, it's better than anything in Geest or the old part of the city, and I'm grateful that I have the space here for a proper studio. One cannot underestimate these small advantages.'

No longer able to stand this . . . this charade, Theo stands abruptly as if he has remembered a pressing engagement. 'I'd better return to my rooms,' he announces, glancing at his pocket watch.

'Already?' Vincent murmurs, rising.

Theo ignores him, heading for the door and plucking his hat from its hook.

Vincent offers to walk with him. 'It's hard to say when our next meeting will be,' he says, already wistful.

Aware that he will not see Sien again, Theo addresses her directly as he bids her goodbye. He cannot deny that a small part of his heart has been made soft by this encounter. She is hardly the conniving type; he can be sure of this now. No doubt Vincent is also drawn to her for this very reason. Still, nothing about this arrangement bodes well for the parties involved. And even if Vincent may come to earn his own bread in time, he is convinced this relationship will not last. It serves his brother well to play the paterfamilias and fulfil his yearning to be the type of man Michelet lauds – for now – but Theo doubts Vincent will be able to withstand the grinding pressures of raising a family over the longer term, nor of continuing to love a woman simply for her past suffering.

And now, about to take leave of this studio, he is glad he did not forgo the opportunity to observe this intimate tableau with his own eyes; now he can report to their family, reassure them confidently that it is all just another of Vincent's passing vagaries, and that they shouldn't worry too much. It will be over in a matter of months, he predicts.

As they approach the door, Vincent manoeuvres himself through it first. Theo detects a change in him. Now nourished and revived by Theo's company, his brother almost skips down the stairs like an excited child. Outside, the warm evening air seems to match Vincent's ebullient mood. Soon Theo's steps fall in time with his brother's and the synchronous rhythm of their feet seem to speak of their bond more accurately than any words. He is not surprised when they stop and turn towards each other at the same time.

Vincent places a hand on Theo's shoulder as he tells him, 'Brother, I cannot promise anything other than to work harder, so let's not discuss this matter of marriage for the time being.'

Hearing these words, Theo feels as if he might become airborne. He was right. In his company, Vincent has been prompted to remember the world he hails from. Yet he knows better than to express his relief, merely muttering, 'My commitment is to your career foremost, you must understand.'

But Vincent, to indicate his admission must not be interpreted as a concession, lifts his finger and says firmly, 'But know this: I am happy with her. As you have seen, she is no Kee. She's had a life you and I can no more imagine than being a man with wings.' Then, his voice turning whisper-soft, he declares, 'But I love her. I may have rescued her from the streets, but she rescued me from my despair, my loneliness.' Theo is pinned by the intensity of his gaze.

But the voices of his elders echo unrelenting in his mind, reminding him not to be dissuaded from his mission.

'Then you must promise me one thing,' Theo says, returning a gaze just as steely. 'I will continue to support you, but from hereon there will be no further mention of Sien. I will not hear of her or the children in our letters. I am only prepared to discuss your work.'

Vincent hesitates, lips parted. Then, searching Theo's face, he mutters ruefully, 'You reminded me of Uncle Cent just then. All of you are more interested in upholding the Van Gogh name than thinking of my happiness.'

Theo turns away, coughing into his hand as he does so. Though he knows Vincent is right, he wonders what, if anything, Vincent thinks can be done about it. Is he himself not proof that one can still be a good son, capable of honouring one's family's name, while seeking one's own path? Given there is so much at stake – not just the reputation of the living Van Goghs but that of their illustrious forebears who worked hard to ensure their distinguished legacy – do they also not deserve to be shown some respect?

He clears his throat again, dispelling the tension. He will not be drawn into this argument; it is one unlikely to be resolved here and now – if ever.

He will of course not withdraw his support, despite Sien. As if his brother is also reminded of this, he simply lowers his head, disappointed but nevertheless also relieved. 'When I sell, everything will be taken care of,' he mumbles, walking ahead.

As Theo's eyes follow this figure lost inside his own head,

sorrow rises quietly but unmistakably until it almost chokes him. Swallowing hard, he is again reminded how Vincent, like a full moon hanging low in the sky, can seem both so near and yet so far away; familiar but also inscrutable.

And now, at this day's end, in the waning light, he understands his earlier elation at his success in thwarting his brother's plans was foolish, a mistake; none of this was ever about winning or losing. How naive of him to have thought in such black-and-white terms. What has he learnt in these past few hours if not that the affairs of the heart, whether involving family or a lover, are always fraught? Then again, are they ever capable of being straightforward or simple? He thinks not.

When he catches up to his brother, he thrusts guilders into Vincent's hand. 'You must take this. You will need it to buy the paints.'

Now that they are about to part, Vincent is overcome. Fighting back tears, he accepts the money, but taking hold of Theo's hand with a tight grip he leans into Theo's ear and whispers, 'Remember that you have a second home here in The Hague, for the apartment on the Schenkweg is as much yours as it is Sien's and mine.'

Theo cannot help but draw back at the suggestion he would ever seek out their apartment. It is so like Vincent to think he might. He returns a hasty nod and pats his brother's back before making his way briskly towards his lodgings, relishing the prospect of the silence he will find there, for he feels emptied out. As always, a day in Vincent's company is equivalent to weeks with any other.

Part Three

Twenty

The future has dimmed in just an hour.

After the men have left, Sien seeks refuge in her wicker chair, glad to be alone. The cramp in her chest that she has not been able to shift since the brother walked in begins to ease. How tired she is of these men's unforgiving scrutiny, their arrogance. Well, he was no different to Tersteeg. Just as dapperly dressed and unmistakably proud. While Tersteeg did not hold back in speaking his mind, the brother, wisely, remained silent. But though he may not have uttered his thoughts aloud, his eyes and expression spoke for him. That he would never let Vincent marry her was now as certain as night arriving.

But how can she blame the brother? Beneath that cool exterior, she felt him squirm, cringe with dismay, much as she herself did. That his older brother should put him through such an ordeal. After all, this was Vincent's doing. Because of him, they had endured the awkwardness, pretending as if their introduction should be considered no more unusual than one arranged between prospective in-laws, making a long-wished-for acquaintance.

The comfortable apartment is suddenly intolerable. She would like to smash all the crockery, pull his pictures off the walls, throw the bedding out the window. She should simply pack up and leave at once for her mother's house in Geest. No longer does this studio appear as a home but a display set up to trick her, with no meaning beyond its walls, and just like the steam of a passing train, it would evaporate at any moment like it had never really existed in the first place.

She goes so far as to fetch one of Vincent's cases, but as she walks around the apartment gathering the baby's linen, Maria's clothes, her own clothes, her resolve gradually deserts her. How will she pay the rent? How will she pay for bread? For anything? She is still too weak from childbirth to return to the streets, and there is also that awful, foul discharge that dribbles from her as if from an open wound. Who will have her? Who will want her? But even more worryingly, after these months of being looked after by a man, the prospect of selling her body seizes her with a horror she would not have thought possible.

How she resents this tattered husk she has become. This suit of pathetic flesh that traps her – one that she would not hesitate to discard if given a chance. For what good has it served her? In her experience, whether for screwing or bearing children, it would seem it was only put on this earth to serve the men, being of the least use to her. And all the effort to feed it, keep it alive, so that it may suffer more seems as futile as trying to keep dry on a leaky boat. At times like these, she feels as if she no longer has the strength to keep her head above those currents that are always threatening to pull her below, and she is overcome with a desire to surrender to their power.

The brother surely will have made his case to Vincent. She supposes at least now there will be no more need for pretence.

When Vincent reappears, Maria is sitting quietly at the table, and Sien is slicing the dark bread for their supper, dishing up warm potatoes.

But Vincent, approaching her from behind, puts his arms around her waist and nuzzles his face into her neck. 'Everything will work out, you wait and see,' he whispers.

She frees herself from his grasp and steps back. She turns to study him, incredulous. Is he really that simple, for all his learning?

'What's the matter?' he asks, frowning.

'You really think your brother will continue to help you, now that he has seen me and the children?'

'Yes, he has promised as much,' Vincent says, shrugging and picking up a slice of bread. 'Don't you see? He wants me to start painting so I can sell. He's given me extra money to buy the paints, which aren't cheap, I can assure you. That's how much he believes in my work. And us.'

'You did not see what I saw in his eyes.'

'Don't mistake Theo for another Tersteeg,' he warns. 'He is only looking after our interests. Besides, how can we marry when we are dependent on him?'

'It was no different when you asked me,' she points out, one brow raised.

Vincent recoils as if stung. His face twitching, he says, 'I . . . I do intend to marry you, but I must . . . I must have my own income.'

Yes, it is as she thought. Vincent has changed his tune, because of the brother. She is a fool, she thinks. A silly fool.

'Don't you see?' she asks him. 'I am nothing to your family. In the end, you'll leave me for them, and you'll be no different to the others.'

'No, no,' he mutters, shaking his head, eyes filled with hurt. 'You must not . . . you must not say that. It cannot be true. You cannot – no, you *must not* accuse me of such a thing. I am nothing like my family . . . I am not like those men who abandoned you. I *cannot* be like them.'

'You carp on about the truth, well, you should learn to stomach it then.'

His hands wrestle with his hair as he paces the room, trying to make her understand. 'We will be free to do what we like. My work will soon sell, and we will be free,' he repeats over and over again.

Watching him, the satisfaction she felt a moment ago at seeing him shaken is followed swiftly by regret. Why should they pit themselves against the world like this? Why should they put themselves through such a trial when, as he insists, living with a loving companion by one's side is the most important thing?

Her hands on his shoulders, she halts him. They are eye to eye.

'I heard that a man next door who works at the gas factory earns nearly eight guilders a week, and his brood of four live on it just fine – and they have a boy who eats double what Maria does.'

He pushes her away and smothers his ears.

Exasperated, her tongue sharpens. 'Why are you so reluctant to become a worker? Are you not always praising them? Telling me how much you admire them?'

He sighs and sits. 'I admit there are some days I would have liked nothing better. Nothing better than to wake up without a single thought in my head other than I must dig a hole, shovel coke, haul bags of sand, push drays over the bridge. Yes, I have yearned to be able to do those simple things, but I also know they could never do for me.' A pause as he examines his hands, turning them over and back again. 'If you only knew what it's like. What it's like to live with these hands. And this heart, these eyes. They don't make it easy for me. I . . . I don't know how else to be. And sometimes I wish it were not so.'

She studies him; his face is so open and frank that she cannot help but be drawn to his case and, yes, sympathise with his plight. For it simply did not occur to her. Is this why he is so enraptured by those poor workers? Envy for their plain and modest life? Yet, glancing at those graceful hands of his, she cannot picture them holding anything but a pen, a pencil, sticks of black, books. And they probably have never held a broom, a shovel. After all, how can they forget? He is a gentleman. It is she who looks away first.

'Besides,' he continues, 'we should not be fighting each other. We have to fight *them*, don't you see? The world out there. Prove them wrong. Make art that will sell and shut them up.'

She nods. He hardly needs to remind her. She knows what it is to fight, having spent a lifetime doing so. For bread, for coins, for survival. Perhaps they are well suited to each other after all, familiar as they both are with the strife; a gentleman who does not fit into his world, and she, a prostitute who will never have the means to claim a proper place on earth, or in heaven.

The storm inside her begins to quieten. Perhaps he is right; perhaps that is the only fight worth engaging in, the only one worth their time and energy. For now, there is this roof over her head, there are potatoes in the pantry, bread on the table. And there is this man to whom her heart has not only become tethered but enmeshed, as if she were the warp to his weft.

Twenty-one

The next morning, Vincent heads off early to purchase the paints and the brushes, returning with a shiny new wooden box tucked under his arm. He examines the plump tubes and the neat, handsome box with the kind of delight that reminds her of children gifted new toys. It is English made, he explains, with a clever, folding lid that has been designed to also serve as a palette. He had enough left over to buy her smoked meat. 'You have to build up your strength so we can work,' he tells her.

He then explains that since she is still not well enough to pose for him, he intends to try his hand at the paints, and there is now little reason to delay, since Theo, who has more to say about his career than anyone, has deemed him ready.

But strangely, the following day he does not venture out straight away as she expected he would but stays inside, sullen and pensive. What was stopping him? she wonders, as she changes the baby's linen. Had he not claimed only the day before that he was more than ready?

He stands at the window, puffing his pipe, the smoke leaving his mouth in short, quick bursts. Then he begins to pace, talking to himself, half-mocking, half-serious. 'Well, no single figures, no matter how well drawn, Vincent. You must put them somewhere. Like pretty sateen-upholstered parlours or ripened fields at harvest time.' Then, voice turning sour, he mutters, 'Why should I try to please others' dull, predictable tastes? How can they not appreciate the infinite beauty of the simple line, the ordinary figure? Perhaps their eyes should be examined before they can be deemed an audience worthy of my work.'

Eventually, he bites down so hard on his pipe that the stem cracks. He removes the tiny shards of enamel and timber from his mouth and nurses his jaw. Then, she catches him glancing suspiciously at the paintbox as if it has somehow spooked him.

The night before, he had slept fitfully, heart palpitating, covered in sweat from crown to heel. Eventually she'd heard him rise in the darkness and descend the ladder to light the lamp in the studio. He would have tried to calm his nerves, sitting up all night reading and smoking, for his side of the bed was still empty when that reliable timekeeper, the rooster crowed.

Now, he finally confesses to her the reason: his dream – no, more a nightmare. In it, there was a room stacked to the rafters with his work, dust-covered, flaking like the paper that walled old, abandoned houses. His models, including Sien, were floating mournfully around the room, ghosts forever trapped, denied the world beyond. All his labour forgotten, cast into worthless oblivion, like the human flesh. It was perhaps a premonition, he admits with a sigh, shoulders hanging limply.

'It was clearly a warning: *make only saleable works*,' he says, eyeing the paintbox warily.

Just as sleep-deprived as Vincent, the baby suckling yet again at her breast, she has not the energy to reassure him nor even pity him. Though the baby is a good sleeper, unlike Maria at the same age, he still wakes every couple of hours to be fed. As long as his small belly is full of milk, he nods off without too much trouble. A contented child, it seems. But with her nipples constantly raw and red, she cannot fathom how art can be the cause of such torment. That it should be the reason he loses sleep, bites his nails, and why his nerves suffer so. Despite what he says, would he not be better off delivering hot water, or digging a ditch, like those broad-backed workers he admires so much? In the end, she knows he will not be able to help himself. That it is just a matter of time before his itchy hands will find the contents of the box too tempting to leave alone.

And so it proves. The next morning, though the sun's red crown is only just peeking above the meadows, he cannot rise quick enough. He pulls on his thick, workman's trousers and painting jacket and boots sturdy enough to climb a rocky peak and sets off like a soldier leaving for war. When she points at the window, indicating the thick band of dark clouds in the distance, he waves away her concern, telling her he is off to Scheveningen, walking there so he can pass through the woods on foot; if it is only nature he has to contend with, however ferocious, it is still preferable to people.

He returns in the evening in a state of disarray but jubilant. His face and hair are streaked with sand and paint, so too his clothes. He tells her of the roiling sea, the leaden slurry of the clouds, like old snow, and the angry gale that whipped up quite a scene, reminding him of something from the Old Testament.

'You should've seen it,' he exclaims. 'Everything was flapping, dancing wildly. And the ocean was nothing short of a monster: foaming, churning, covering everything in a briny spray.'

He finds that he is always consoled by a storm, he tells her: by nature at the height of her fury, a force more untamed and impassioned even than him. When his ears fill with the howl of the wind and the roar of the sea, he is becalmed, soothed. Bewitched by the scene before him, and protected by a dune, he managed to work through the rain and the wind before eventually taking refuge in a nearby inn so he could finish the painting in peace.

'Look: you can see the grains of sand still stuck there,' he says with glee, pointing to a corner of the oil study. 'I have caught the mood of a perfectly nasty storm, don't you think?' But he is not interested in her answer. 'One must wage a war with paint, wrestle with it, if one is to make it submit to one's will, one's eye,' he rattles on happily as he hangs his effort in the studio before standing back to admire it.

For her part, she tries her best to see what he sees, but she is unsure. Though there are fishing boats and small figures dotted on the beach, mostly she sees globs and drips of paint. But not wanting to dent his enthusiasm, she tells him she likes the sky and the water. Surely, they are the best bits, swirling and tumbling as they do in life. Smiling, he nods.

Now, seized with an unshakeable resolve, he heads out each morning battle-ready, his brush and paints his weapons. She envies him, and all those who are able to just walk out, leaving behind the screaming, hungry children, the dirty linen, in pursuit of something else, an altogether different purpose beyond the domestic chaos.

But she is also relieved to hear the door shut behind him. Left with only the children, her wicker chair beckons. There she remains for hours, mustering just enough energy to rise when the hungry children summon her. Then, overcome once more by the same listlessness that has overwhelmed her since Willem's birth, she returns once more to her seat. Then it is only when the last of the day's light begins to fade, signalling Vincent's return, that she stirs.

Though she has returned from Leiden alive, she is beset by a mood so dark the inside of her is a ceaseless night. Even her vocal power has been smothered to a series of grunts and sighs while her body feels corseted from head to toe, and her movements as laboured as if she were living at the bottom of the sea.

One morning, the racket Vincent makes as he prepares to head out wakes the children. She climbs down to the studio. 'Why not wake the whole neighbourhood?' she demands, her glare so hot it leaves him only a moment to down the last of his coffee before he scuttles out the door.

Then later that morning, when Maria returns with a bleeding scrape on her knee, she scolds the girl in an almost hysterical tone before cleaning the wound with salt water. When Gerda brings up the clean linen for the baby, she accepts it with barely a nod before shutting the door. And because Willem refuses to be consoled by her teat, she deposits him in his crib before retreating to her bed and pulling the pillow over her ears.

But Vincent is his usual indefatigable self. At the end of each day, weary and spent, he does indeed begin to resemble a soldier returning from war. He brings back his spoils – studies of trees, their roots and trunks like enemies slain, their skins crusty – and, having found inspiration in the intensity and depth of the paints' colours and their velvet-soft texture, he now wonders why he waited so long.

One evening, he removes from his pocket a clod of mud wrapped in his handkerchief. Earlier, while walking through the woods after a downpour, he found himself admiring the dark, rain-soaked earth, its umber shades so rich and deep he could not resist scooping up a handful so he might have it on hand when touching up the painting in the studio. Yet some of his colour choices she cannot help but find strange. Purple soil when it should be brown. Faces blank, featureless, but the ribbon of a girl's dress stark and bright.

As it was with the drawing, this painting business does not so much preoccupy him as possess him. Unstoppable, he himself is like a force of nature. It's not long before all the walls are covered with painted studies, and the apartment's air is clogged with the scent of paint. There are already nearly twenty studies, and it hasn't yet been a month. The pace he keeps up is exhausting, as if he has a quota he must fill. When he gets an idea into his head his appetite for it seems to know no bounds, no measure. It's all he thinks about, it's all he talks about, and it matters little to him whether she can understand or not.

That he has soon run out of oils confirms her suspicion that he does not paint as much as throw tubes full at the paper. He is troubled by the cost. The solution seems so obvious, she loses her patience. 'Must you use so much? I mean, just look at all this paint. The work seems caked with it. Are you not meant to dab small amounts with a brush?' she demands.

He shoots her a disparaging glance. 'You don't know what you're talking about,' he replies.

'Then tell me: is this what they want, those rich people? Is this what's going to help you sell your work? Because all I can see is crusty paint.'

'When you are immersed in the work you are not able to calculate the amount of paint you are using or how much is left in the tubes. What matters is the painting itself. Does it sing? Does it stir your heart? Are you moved?'

She sighs heavily as she considers the work, thinking perhaps she has missed something, that if she stared long and hard she would gain the power of his eyes to help her see what he sees. But nothing of the sort happens. Not that it matters, since Theo's opinion is the only one he pays any attention to, the only one he cares about. And she has been with him long enough to know that Vincent must always be right. Anyway, who is she to think she can challenge him about art?

Raising his brows quizzically, he asks, 'What is bothering you? Why are you interrogating me like this? What do you know about it? This is the way I need to do my work.'

People who buy art want paintings, not drawings, he explains, and it's going to take time for him to master the new medium. Meanwhile, she needs to be patient and look after the children, their home. She can be assured of him working hard so they can be independent of Theo.

She has no sound argument against such reasoning. She can accuse him of being many things but never could she accuse him of being idle. He works almost punishingly, his energy seemingly sourced from a bottomless well, often leaving her both awed and wearied in equal measure. It is for them, he reminds her. For their future. Because nothing can be achieved without hard work.

'I feel like I'm suffocating in here with all this paint. The smell.' She stands abruptly, rubbing her hands on her apron, looking about her as if she has misplaced something dear. How to describe this . . . this thin, empty feeling she is unable to shake? It has assailed her after every birth, turning the inside of her into a pit of black. But even if she could explain it, she doubts he would understand her. Because it is more than the smell, more than the paints, that disturbs her; it is something far more intractable, something akin to despair. She dare not mention it, though, because he would only exhort her never to give into it – as if a scolding alone could make it disappear.

A few evenings later, he enters with a tired scowl, his shoulders drooping.

'That's it,' he declares, removing his boots. 'I'm finished with painting.'

She drops her sewing into her lap and stares at him, alarmed. What has happened to all his talk? Did he not say he must paint if his work is to sell?

'It's simply too expensive,' he complains.

The bills are mounting at the art supply store, he tells her, and when he walked past the bakery, the baker came running after him to demand money.

Sien had experienced something similar. Though the grocer did not confront her in the street, nevertheless he refused to let her buy coffee and oats on credit.

Heaving a deep sigh, Vincent rubs his face briskly like he must rouse himself. 'I cannot tell Theo as much, but I would prefer to return to drawing. My fingers are itching to hold something solid again,' he says, wringing his hands. 'Paint may have colour, but it is also sly and slippery, and seems bent on disobeying my command. Yet I must persist with the painting for Theo's sake.'

There is only a half-loaf on which to live until the money from Theo is due again. And it is autumn now: the time is fast approaching when they must light the stove.

'What about the children?' she asks. 'I understand you need your paints but . . .'

He cuts her off, impatient, irritated. 'They will be hungry for only a couple of days. Sacrifices have to be made. We must not lose our faith in the greater aim. I need to demonstrate to Theo I am making progress, you see, so he thinks it worth his while to continue to send the allowance. Besides, we are hardly facing starvation.' Then, reaching for his pipe, he adds, 'As for myself, I will not need to eat until then.' As if he can live off tobacco alone.

'Theo and his money, that's all we think about,' she mutters under her breath.

'Be patient, Sien,' Vincent counsels. 'It will not always be the case. Do you have any idea how it pains me to be so reliant on my brother? How much I am longing to tell Theo one day that I will no longer need his help and be free of him forever?'

Their gazes meet and hold. He appears beaten, as if he has expended the last of his energy in uttering these words. She can see how it gnaws at him, how difficult it must be for him, the older brother dependent on his younger brother for his bread. For all his unconventional traits, it is clear he suffers embarrassment from this uncomfortable arrangement as much as any man with pride.

She has known worse circumstances, but her body will quickly weaken from the effort of making milk for the baby. Yet more unbearable to her will be the cry of hungry children. She will try to make the bread go further – soak the last bits of the dry crust in her milk. She will be sparing with her energy so she will not easily be overcome. She picks up her sewing. She is again mending his undergarments. The man seems to either pop the stitching or put a new hole in them every other day.

Glancing warily at the wet studies on the wall, she wonders: how much money is hanging there? If only they could eat the paint, they might be saved.

They have not eaten for three days.

The day before, she set off with the children to a soup kitchen near the station, but approaching the entrance, she noticed Rika and her family coming the other way, and without thinking she turned swiftly on her heel, dragging Maria along, baby slung across her chest. Did her mother not say that all of Geest was talking about her? Then to be spotted at a soup kitchen because her so-called gentleman is in possession of so little means that he cannot provide for her and the children fills her with shame.

But what is shame to hunger? That she should now care more for it than her empty belly, she scoffs at herself for her vanity. Was it not just months ago that she dared to rescue Rika? That she dared to thrust her chest out at Lena?

After arriving back at the apartment, the children crying, she regretted leaving so hastily. Before Vincent she worried less about what others thought than earning enough for her family. After all, everyone in Geest was in the same boat, doing whatever it took to survive. Now, since her attachment to a gentleman, Sien is beset with a different care; has she, as her mother accused, ventured too far from her roots, her people?

This morning, as she lies in bed, she discovers that though

she should be lighter in body, strangely she feels more ponderous than ever. As if an invisible weight pins her down, the effort of moving seems beyond her strength. She would like to return to the mind-erasing state of sleep, but Maria's tugging and demands for breakfast make her wish impossible. The baby too is awake next to her but gurgles happily, some of her milk still swilling in his belly. When she does finally sit up swinging her legs over the side of the bed, she suffers a dizziness. And looking down, the floor opens before her like a ravine. Then her body sags into the mattress because she realises it's neither the bed nor the floor; the bottomless, depthless sensation is inside of her.

Her hands pushing down on the edge of the bed, she heaves herself upright. Downstairs, remembering the empty pantry, she brews the last scoop of coffee and pours a cup for Maria, whose belly growls as she drinks it. Thankfully her own appetite is not strong; in fact, it is nearly absent. As the voices of children drift up from the street, the girl still has enough energy to rush outside to play. Woozy and just barely holding the baby at her hip, Sien drops onto her chair and opens her chemise. A breast spills out and Willem swiftly closes his lips around the nipple. Just as she and the baby are about to drift off to sleep again the girl returns hungry and crying, filthy from head to toe. Sien has nothing to offer but her other teat, which the girl clamps between her teeth as if it were bread. Sien winces, pushing the girl off her. Too faint and weak to raise her hand, she mumbles, 'Gently.'

They are all curled up together on her chair, asleep, when a pair of hands shake them awake. They open their eyes to Vincent. He stands over them, his face contorted with anger.

'Get up!' he shouts. 'What is this mess? Have you been asleep all day?'

Her body still bone-tired, and her mind too foggy and thick for thought, Sien struggles to fully wake. As she adjusts to his presence, she does not even bother to try to stand up. The baby lets out a thin wail and Maria, lifting her head reluctantly from her mother's lap, begins to cry. Sien's breasts are lolling over the front of her chemise, a pair of shrivelled udders.

'You have the day all to yourself and the children, and this is what I come home to?' Vincent gestures to the cups on the table, dirty with dregs of coffee, the clothes strewn across the floor and the soiled linen piled up in the corner.

Incensed, he accuses her of laziness. That the Devil himself is likely to make work of her idle hands. But compared to Vincent even the most hardworking labourers would appear so. After all, who is able to keep pace with him?

'What kind of mother are you?' he demands, hands on his hips.

'A hungry one,' she shoots back.

'Ha, it has been a mere three days – that's nothing. The women in the Borinage could go for a week without as much as a slice of bread and still find the energy not only to haul sacks of coal but to keep house.'

'How would you know? They probably found a way to eat something,' she scoffs.

'You don't know anything about those women; you wouldn't last a day there,' he says, waving his hand in disgust.

She tells him that for all his talk about women needing

protection, he was doing a poor job of it himself. 'Can one live on air?' she cries. 'Or the smell of paints?'

As a reply he makes a din with the crockery he has decided he will clear from the table. Sien tucks her sore breasts back into her blouse before lifting the baby over her shoulder to put him in his crib. The girl follows her, refusing to let go of her mother's skirt, sucking her thumb.

'Oh, I should have drowned myself in the canal instead of taking up with you,' Sien moans, taking up her chair once more.

He spins around then. Crossing the room in just a few strides, he hauls her up by her wrists and shakes her so hard her pinned locks fly and tumble to her shoulders. Maria shrinks back in fear.

'I've told you before, I will not hear such talk, do you hear?' he shouts, thrusting his face into hers.

Of course, she should have known; that sensitive part of him has been wounded. He has turned into a raging inferno from which she is only interested in escaping. She wants to turn away, but as she attempts to do so, her efforts are as feeble as that of an insect long-trapped in cobwebs.

He grips her chin and squeezes it. 'You will not give up, do you hear?' Satisfied with her quick nod, he releases her. Turning his back to her, his hands raking his hair frantically, he paces the room, repeating over and over again under his breath, 'No, no, one must never give in to despair. *Never.*'

It is now becoming clear to her that he is talking to himself as much as to her.

His temper she knows well, but this outburst, keener and cutting, sends a shiver through her, and she feels goosebumps rise on her skin. No doubt his nerves are overstrung nearly to breaking point from living on nothing but tobacco and coffee. At this moment, he seems no different to all those men who dictate the lives of others, leaving the women and children to follow in their turbulent wake. Is this what she must endure to be with him, whether married or not? Their days and nights coloured by one argument or another, about money for now, but later about the children and God knows what else? It is not very different to the arguments she used to have with her mother. At this realisation, an admonition of Wilhelmina's returns to her: *Remember, he does all his work with promises, words.* Indeed, it seems he is doing nothing to promote her scant hopes but everything to prove right her early doubts; better not to have hopes, because one must then be prepared to weather the pain of having them crushed.

Yes, she has been saved from walking the streets, but is she any more secure here under his protection than if she were eking a living from night to night, from one man to the next? Is she not just as hungry as before? But in Geest she did not expect anything else, the hunger only routine, while the hunger she feels while living with a gentleman feels more bitter, sharper.

Yet she finds that she cannot turn her gaze from him. She realises they are no longer just two people sharing a roof but two souls united by their mutual understanding of the same condition. She suspects the reason he has been able to see beyond her body, her despair, is because he himself is so intimate with it, and the reason they remain bound together, and are able to recognise each other's struggles, is because they are their own.

Her resentment muted by this awareness, as well as her lack of strength, she discovers she has no appetite for an argument. Besides, is he not just as hungry as she is?

His own energy spent, Vincent now moves stealthily around the apartment. Eventually he fetches the jenever, which he has been using to wash his brushes because it is cheaper than paint thinners. Sitting heavily, he pours a cup and says softly, 'Tomorrow. The money should come tomorrow.'

She pours some of the liquor onto a spoon and, to help the children forget their rumbling bellies and go to sleep, gives them little sips. Maria's eyes are now ringed dark while her face seems thinner and her belly shrunken.

After the children are settled, she and Vincent finish the bottle. Her stomach, though empty, soon burns with a prickly warmth, while her head and body slosh, syrupy and fuzzy, like she is all liquid. Sluggishly yet gently, they help each other to bed and, arms entwined, they fall asleep in their clothes.

But the next day, there is still no postal delivery. Like overworked beasts too tired to move, Sien and the children hover lifelessly in the corners of the apartment while Vincent takes up a book, for his hands must hold something. He sits reading, smoking. Even these acts he performs at a frenetic pace, turning the pages as quickly as an intake of breath, each puff of his pipe as desperate as if it will be his last. She soothes the children, offering them her teats. Though crusty and dried-up, they are all she has. And so they suckle because they have nothing else to put in their mouths.

When the mail arrives the following day, Vincent hurries to the post office and returns with smoked meat, oats, bread, coffee and potatoes. He can barely look at them as he spreads the fare on the table with much show, like those travelling peddlers. Maria snatches the loaf of bread from the table and bites into it. Sien wrenches the block from the girl's grip and takes a knife to it. Vincent rolls up his sleeves and bustles around the kitchen, boiling water. She wets tiny balls of bread and drops them between the baby's lips. She offers a slice to Vincent. Their eyes meet, and she thinks she catches shame in his expression, but it was so lightning-brief she is left wondering if she made a mistake, because after a blink she is looking at his back, and he is whistling a nonsense ditty.

Twenty-two

She can hear a footfall on the stairs that is different. It has a particular weight and an irregular beat, suggesting the climber has paused for breath at the odd step. When he enters, she has no trouble recognising the tall, elderly visitor: it is Vincent's father, Dorus. She has always known it was just a matter of time.

She stands promptly, swaying and hushing the crying baby in her arms. Maria runs to her side, wrapping her small arms around her mother's leg. This imposing man, dressed in black and still wearing his hat, stares at them without blinking. So, it is true, he seems to realise. His son is living with a woman who is not even fit to mingle with his servants. He takes them in with tight creases between his brows. Then, appearing to remember something, he removes his hat and gives Sien a smile so warm and wide that it startles more than reassures her.

Vincent introduces her in a tone both bright and matter-of-fact, suggesting this visit were the result of a long-standing invitation. He fusses, selecting the best chair for Dorus. Next to this burly figure, he is suddenly more boy than man. A fresh shoot from a broad trunk. A son bent on pleasing his father. 'Coffee?' Vincent says, turning towards her.

The older man is sombre, regarding his son carefully. Clearly wishing to avoid upsetting or provoking him, he speaks deliberately, slowly. He has wanted to visit for some time but the move to Nuenen has prevented him from doing so. But there are matters that need his attention in Leiden and The Hague, so here he is.

While he speaks, the father continues to glance at his son, as if he is yet to be convinced that Vincent is indeed his own flesh and blood. But she suffers no such doubt. Are their profiles not the same but for the difference in their age? Vincent's – being younger – is sharper-edged. The men's mannerisms, too, are alike. The way they lean into each other, the way they each raise their chin and look down their nose before they open their mouth, seeming to take measure of their audience before speaking.

Even before Dorus has had a chance to unbutton his jacket, Vincent is already spreading drawings on the table. While his father inspects the work, Vincent hovers behind him and rubs his palms repeatedly against his hips.

'You know that I can say only little about your work,' Dorus says, chuckling nervously. 'Your uncles' and Theo's opinions you can trust. Even your mother's. But mine . . . well, my eyes are not very well informed about these things.' But then he adds, 'Though they seem to me . . . well, strong, promising.' He hesitates then adds, 'Yes, that's it. They are certainly striking . . . and sympathetic, I think.'

Vincent, delighted by this response, squeezes his father's shoulder. 'As you can see, I've been busy, working from morning to night.'

The older man, appearing relieved not to have slighted his son, sits straighter. Then, hearing squeals, his gaze alights on the baby in the crib. It strikes Sien that he may be wondering if the baby could be his son's, though he must know she and Vincent only met towards the end of winter.

Vincent launches into an explanation of his efforts with paint. 'It is turning out to be easier than I imagined, and believe me, though I may be the one holding the pencil or the brush, Theo's hand may as well be attached to mine, for we are in this together.'

There is no mention of the expense, nor his prevarications of earlier. Vincent is suddenly the capable son, confidently reassuring the older man about his career and the partnership with the younger brother, keen to restore his solidarity with the rest of his family.

The older man's eyes roam over the painted studies, but with a vague air. It appears the man is less interested in his son's work than the family and home he has set up without his approval. Turning to Sien, he asks her questions about the baby. 'A good sleeper? Yes, that's important. Vincent here was a cat-napper, keeping the whole household awake for many months.' The look he gives his son is guarded but not without affection.

Sien is pleased to note that, contrary to her initial impression of him, Vincent's father is nothing like the contemptuous

Tersteeg and warmer than the icy brother. In person he is not at all fearsome, as she imagined, but seems almost deferential. She has little trouble picturing him tending kindly to his poor flock in the countryside. It is now probable that his stiff and forbidding demeanour when she first sighted him at the hospital owed more to his tense meeting with Vincent than his natural disposition. She is also pleased to see Vincent's defensiveness beginning to dissolve in his father's presence. What heartache he must have caused this man at Christmas. She has no doubt that Vincent is capable of pushing even the most patient of people too far.

Vincent, now seated and more relaxed, asks about his mother, sisters and his youngest brother, named Cor like his uncle.

'Yes, yes, they are all well,' the older man replies distractedly.

'And you have all settled into Nuenen?'

The father nods and tells them about this small village with a wonderful church in the woods, the villagers all humble, peasant folk, devoted to their religion. There is a graveyard nearby which is full of plain, white wooden crosses.

'I would very much like to see that, Pa,' Vincent murmurs softly. His face has lit up, entranced, no doubt, by the picture he has already started to paint in his mind.

But when his father brings up Theo and his successful career in Paris, the light in Vincent's eyes vanishes like candlelight snuffed. The older man seems to forget himself as he recounts the story of Theo manning the Goupil booth at the Exposition Universelle in Paris a few years earlier, how he had met all sorts of important people: the president and various dignitaries not just from Europe but all over the world. Then, because he proved so impressive, he was transferred immediately to the Paris branch by Uncle Cent. 'He truly does us proud,' the father says, shaking his head to indicate he will never stop being astonished by his younger son's achievements.

'Oh, yes, what's more, is it not true that he not only met the King himself but was invited to tea at the palace to discuss a royal position?' Vincent asks. The sudden change in Vincent's voice – deep and grand – tells Sien this part of the story is not true.

The father, not deaf to Vincent's mocking tone, reddens and tucks his arms into his sides before drawing back. She guesses that the retelling of this story among the Van Goghs must be as habitual and inescapable as the ritual of taking tea.

It is then the old man puts down his cup with a clatter and clutches his calf. There is a small giggle under the table. Reaching down, Sien drags Maria out by the wrist, her palm raised. But catching the father's eyes, she quickly drops it.

'It's alright, let her be. She did not pierce the skin,' he says, patting his leg.

'She is getting better but she is still learning,' Vincent mutters by way of an apology.

'She's little, she has time,' the father says with a small smile.

The autumn day has turned out to be only cloudy, so the two men decide to take some air in the meadows. Vincent collects their hats. As the son passes his father's hat to him, his other hand lifts automatically to hover protectively over the older man's back, and this gesture warms her – that somehow, in witnessing it, she felt herself briefly included in their intimate exchange – as she is sure it must do the father. Vincent's father does not forget about her. He turns to give her a slow nod as a goodbye, his gaze wistful but not unsympathetic.

Vincent returns later that afternoon in high spirits, pleased by the older man's visit but also amused by their banter on the meadows. It seems that during their walk the father tried to talk some sense into him before losing his patience and spluttering, 'You cannot live with such a woman, it is not fit for someone of your rank. And besides, you are living in sin.' But when Vincent declared his willingness to marry Sien, the old man shut his mouth abruptly. 'You should have seen his face,' Vincent says, erupting with laughter. 'Of course, he couldn't very well say anything then. Because he does not wish me to marry, well, then suddenly my living in sin is convenient.'

His father, Vincent is quick to explain, may preach the Gospels, but when it came to his own affairs he, like many men of the church, did not hesitate to act contrary to his own advice.

The hope that had been awakened in her by his father's gentleness is extinguished. She bites her lips until they are numb, for she must shift the pain in her heart to another place. Another foolish mistake on her part, basking in the father's good manners. It was not out of any sympathy for her; rather, like Theo, he wanted to avoid any misstep with his headstrong son. At least that man Tersteeg had had the nerve to say what he thought of them to their faces. Cruel, yes, but honest.

'I assured him that for the time being, because we are

dependent on Theo, we have decided to postpone our marriage plans for now, but as soon as –'

'Yes, yes, when we are free of Theo, when you sell, when you can earn your own bread,' she mutters tersely, turning away to head up to bed.

A few days later, a package from Nuenen arrives at the Schenkweg studio. Winter clothing for Vincent, including undergarments, for they must know of his tendency to wear them out faster than a city horse of its shoes. But when Vincent pulls out a woman's coat, unmistakably meant for her, she is unprepared for the warmth that floods her – even before she has tried it on.

Vincent is thrilled. 'See, you are now in their thoughts,' he says, beaming in that way of someone who has won a hard-fought argument. He holds the garment up against her. 'I think my father has sized you up well.'

She slips it on carefully, as if afraid it might shatter. Apart from the sleeves, which are a tad too long, it fits so well it might have been sewn from her measurements.

Her first winter coat.

Twenty-three

Though it is still dark, and dawn some time away, she can hear him whistling downstairs. As she predicted, he may be painting less but there is no sign of him giving it up, returning as he does most days with damp studies. Mindful of winter approaching, he insists on venturing outdoors as often as it is still possible for him to do so.

While Vincent is lost to his work and nearly always absent, her struggle to get up from her bed proves a protracted battle. That hollowness inside her seems to be expanding rather than shrinking. The children's unflagging demands, especially the baby and his feeding, seem to gouge her very core. Some days she cannot see the edges of herself; she and the baby are melded to one, Sien existing solely to assuage his hunger.

When daylight finally sweeps into the room, she is disappointed at finding herself awake. Then, unable to move, she stares at the ceiling, contemplating the day ahead not as hours but as a dark mountain that must be climbed, with a peak she cannot see but that looms over her, resembling the one she faced the day before, and the one that is guaranteed to greet her the next morning, and the morning after.

But soon, because the children do not care about her moods, they command her to rise from her bed. They moan, they wail, they scream.

She reaches for the baby, desperate to quell the crying. Even before she offers him her swollen breast, his little lips are smacking at an imaginary nipple. She is suddenly overcome with the urge to shut those lips forever, to smother him with a pillow so that he can no longer cry, no longer suck her dry, no longer sap every ounce of energy from her.

But as he suckles, he begins to smile, looking up at her with raisin-dark eyes that tug at her heart. That such a robust creature should have emerged from her is still a mystery. Though it does not seem possible now, there were many times she did not think Maria would survive past her first birthday. But with this boy, whose cheeks are like ripened fruit, his little pupils clear and bold, and his crown lush with thick hair, she has no such doubts. She found it so much easier when they died. Bastard children. What possible future could they have without a father?

The question of whether Vincent's work will truly free them always lurks in her mind, vexingly, stubbornly. The waiting has started to feel interminable. How long is it likely to take? She can't help but wonder. As far as she can see, most of the money seems to end up plastered on the walls. But she has little choice but to hush her doubts about him. She must trust him. For his efforts do not flag, do not let up. There is no lack of trying.

What's more, she has come too far; they have both come too far. Two children to feed now, and that cruel season just around the corner. She must bear it.

That afternoon, after visiting Wilhelmina, they take the long way home, through Haagse Bos. The park has staged an autumn festival, awash as it is in blazing yellows, golds and the deepest reds, its trees laden with nuts. Beneath one such tree, there is a commotion. A crowd of boisterous boys – no longer urchins, now ruffians – jeer and laugh. Aware that Willem will soon wake, she does not stop, only slowing enough to take a peek at the object of their amusement.

It's Vincent, sitting alone, a painted study propped on his knees, trying his best to ignore the small crowd, his brows stitched together. A boy of twelve or so, having managed to get hold of Vincent's hat, tosses it to another. Airborne now, it flits between different pairs of hands. Vincent, jumping from his seat, makes a leap for it, while another pair of boys take turns spitting on the study before eventually one lunges at the paper and holds it up for everyone's view.

Sien drops Maria's hand and marches up to the boy with the wet sheet. Clutching the sling-held baby in one hand, she snatches it from him with the other. 'Shame on you,' she hisses. But taking stock of the boy's blotchy face, skin flecked with cuts and crusty sores, she immediately regrets her words. Because what can shame mean to him? To this boy who has spent his entire life growing up on the streets, stealing and fighting in order to survive.

When he purses his lips to spit at her, she shoves him away. Then, turning to the others, she yells, 'Shoo, all of you!' And they scatter like pigeons. Before running away, the boy in possession of Vincent's hat flings it behind him; it comes to rest neatly on the bench. To a rowdy chorus of hoots and claps, he takes a deep bow.

She rocks Willem, who has begun to stir. Maria squats by Vincent's side, helping him to pick up the brushes and tubes of paint strewn on the ground. Vincent, glum-faced, dusts off his hat before pressing it firmly down on his head. His workman's clothes, dust-covered and crumpled, suggest a recent scuffle. He looks worse off than the bridge pullers or the barge handlers. No doubt the bored gang of boys thought him a tramp posing as an artist.

She inspects the study he has painted. A group of women in aprons and bonnets are chatting under a tree, their baskets slung over their arms. The painting appears like a crude joke at the women's expense. Their faces are without eyes, noses; they have no human features. She is filled with dismay. How could it be so? Even their wooden shoes are drawn so large they resemble boats, their shins and ankles more matchsticks than human limbs. But their aprons and bonnets are as fresh and white as starched collars.

He snatches the painting from her and walks ahead, his feet stomping as if it is the ground that has wronged him, his every step registering as a blow to her heart. Now it seems they are cast out by those who are themselves cast out. Is this their future, whether they marry or not? Vincent always caught in such strife. Always attracting unwanted attention. But watching the hunched, brooding figure getting smaller, her eyes become tender for she is able to see past the strangeness of him. She sees a man who is as singular as he is single-minded. And a man for whom she has come to feel as protective as she does towards her children.

A week later, it is her mother's turn to visit. In the late afternoon's grey-pallid light, she appears older and more agitated than she had when Sien last saw her. The rent on her house is due again. Vincent had paid two months in advance, but the landlord has been around, she informs Sien as she pushes past her into the apartment, casting a brief glance at the baby in Sien's arm.

'Oma,' Maria shouts, holding out her arms to be picked up.

But Wilhelmina only gives the girl a quick hug before turning to Sien. 'Well, you're meant to be posing, so Vincent should be paying you, should he not?'

It is not an accusation, nor is it a demand, for her voice is sour with dejection, almost desperate. She speaks in the way of someone who knows the answer to her question but must nevertheless voice it aloud.

Sien is unable to reply or even sympathise. Not because she can't sympathise with her mother's plight – she understands it all too well – but how could she possibly explain Vincent's spending habits to her mother? That his coins always serve his art first? How they are lucky when he is tired and, forced to work less, there is the possibility of some being spared for them. Without a word, she returns to her wicker chair. Her mother's desolate countenance quickly turns scornful as her eyes scan the mess of dirty linen, unwashed dishes, her nose pinched against the smell.

Then, noticing a stone bottle hidden in a basket of soiled laundry, she holds it up triumphantly and exclaims, 'Ah, so this is what you've been doing while he's gone. He gives you money for this, does he?'

Though she has been taking stealthy sips all day, Sien shakes her head. 'It's for cleaning his brushes.'

Wilhelmina does not believe her. She slams the bottle on the table, head tipped to the side, one brow raised. The baby lets out a wail.

'Now, look what you've done,' Sien mutters, standing up to rock him back to sleep. Once he is lulled, she finally tells her mother about the cost of paints, how they suck up all the money, leaving barely enough guilders to settle their credit with the grocer and the baker.

But the woman is too distraught to listen. Wringing her hands, she looks about her furtively, as if she might spy a guilder. Then, sitting, she refuses to leave until she has seen Vincent. 'I will not return there so the landlord can come around and harangue me again,' she says, propping her elbows on the table. Closing her eyes, she begins to massage her temples with brittle fingers.

Her mother's usual sharp, quick manner seems to have been blunted by Sien's abandonment of her. Uncorking the stone bottle, Sien pours the jenever into two glasses.

'What are you doing here, Sien?' Wilhelmina asks, her voice quavering, hand shaking as she accepts the jenever. 'I expected you to have come home by now. I thought you'd only be gone a few weeks at most, but it's been months now. Now what will happen to me? Where will I go?'

'Perhaps Pieter or Karel will take you in,' Sien replies with a shrug, turning away. Surely her mother cannot expect her to go back to Geest, back to the streets. She would rather die, she thinks.

'And you believe him, I suppose, when he says that those ugly things hanging over there will sell?' Wilhelmina gestures to Vincent's recent studies with disgust.

Keeping her eyes lowered, Sien mutters, 'He only started to paint a few weeks ago. It takes time to improve.'

'How much time? How long will it be before his brother abandons him? Anyway, he took you away from me, it is only right that he should make amends somehow.'

It is dark when Vincent enters. Damp from head to toe having walked home in a fine drizzle, he could be mistaken for a streetsweeper who has spent the day traipsing the city. He shows them a group study he did earlier, outside Moojiman's lottery office on the Spui. Passing there, he was pleased to see a throng gathered as they waited for a lottery to be drawn, and he couldn't resist capturing the motley crowd of men, women and children. It touched him, all these poor people who handed over their hard-earned money for a pot-luck scheme that would have better been spent on bread.

'You should've seen them, huddled and anxious, clutching their tickets. They may as well have thrown their coins into the canal and made a wish,' he says, chuckling.

Sien and Wilhelmina exchange glances, for the people he is describing hail from Geest – just like them. Rendered by Vincent's hand, they are a congregation of misery, their bodies stooped and hunched, gnome-ugly faces turned away as if they are ashamed to be there, their desperation obvious to all. And even worse, the paint seems to have been smeared on, so the smudges of colours resemble small puddles. Why would he paint them like this? Is there something wrong with his eyes? In her mother's expression, Sien glimpses bewilderment, shock. She can almost hear her thoughts. How can this be art?

Yet as Sien considers the picture, her early horror begins to lift, replaced by a shiver of sadness. Vincent, in his usual way, has been too truthful, too rudely honest. But what good would it do? Is it for this they have been forced to nearly starve? His approach seems not only foolhardy but perilous. If this is what he thinks will save them, then he should give up now. Who would possibly be prepared to pay for such a confronting picture? Certainly not the poor themselves, for they would never have any use for it, intimate as they already are with deprivation. And the rich? Well, why would they choose to display such an unpleasant and pathetic scene in their homes?

A thick silence has settled on the room, interrupted only by Maria's little whisperings as she talks to her paper dolls under the table. Sien takes a sip of her jenever. Wilhelmina too.

'Now, ladies, you must remember, I am still practising with colours.'

Catching her mother's eyes, Sien gives her a tight shake of her head. Her mother merely dips her chin and keeps silent.

'It's uncomfortable to look at, even to us,' Sien ventures carefully. 'Yes, those people are being foolish, I can see that, but . . .' She pauses to take another sip from her glass. Instead of lottery tickets, she would rather spend her money on jenever – at least there was certainty in that. 'But your picture, well, it makes them appear not just foolish but also . . . unattractive.'

'It is only a study. I wanted to practise doing a group. I didn't . . . It is certainly not intended for sale,' he says, standing and quickly putting it away in his folio.

He returns to the table and eyes the stone bottle warily.

Sien fetches another glass and pours him a drink. After taking a gulp, he smiles, his lips shining. 'Well, I suppose your rent is due again?' he asks, turning to Wilhelmina.

Her mother's expression flickers as if she is about to utter a reply, but changing her mind she lowers her eyes and takes a sip of her drink.

Vincent pulls out a gold coin from his pocket. 'Here.'

As if afraid that Vincent might withdraw the coin, Wilhelmina swipes the ten guilders so fast she could have been performing a magic trick. Then, without looking up, she tucks it swiftly into her purse and stands.

After Wilhelmina has gone, Vincent pours himself another jenever and gulps it down.

'Why don't I start to pose for you again?' Sien says, touching his arm.

He thumps his fist on the table. The glasses and the bottle jolt. 'Remember? I have to paint if I am to sell,' he says, glaring at her.

Frightened by the outburst, Maria crawls out from her place under the table and runs to her mother. Sien soothes the girl. 'It's alright. Vincent was being clumsy.'

'But have you thought of doing them . . .' She hesitates.

'Go on, tell me,' he says snidely.

'Differently,' she says. 'Make them look nice, pleasant – even the poor and the suffering – so they don't offend.'

'Surely not you too,' he groans, more amused than bitter. 'So, you have become an expert now, have you? You should go and work with Tersteeg at Goupil.'

Since he is in that mood again, she bites her lips and holds her tongue. The man is not so much thin-skinned as to be without a skin altogether. She stands up and leads the girl to bed. As she turns away, there is the noise of glass breaking on the floor. Vincent picks the shards up straight away but it's too late – the baby is now awake and Maria has burst into tears. He crosses to the crib and takes Willem in his arms, clutching him so tightly she fears he will suffocate the child. Then, releasing him, he peers longingly at the baby as if he alone has the power to console him.

Twenty-four

It being darker and colder now, Vincent must spend more of his days indoors, leaving Sien little choice but to rise promptly from her bed. Her inward struggle is far from over but in Vincent's presence its hold on her loosens. One wet morning, as he lingers over his coffee, he tells her, 'I must put aside the paints for the time being.'

He has said as much before, but this time it seems more serious. 'You are to give up painting?' she asks, her voice thin with panic. If he gives up painting, is he not defying Theo's orders? Would Theo then continue to support him?

'No, not at all, but it's difficult now, with the weather.'

'But . . . but when will you . . .' Her hands, which had been combing out the knots in Maria's hair, grow still.

'It takes years to master the paints, not just months,' he says, picking up his pipe.

Her hands jolt, and she yanks the girl's hair so hard Maria's head lurches backwards. She lets out a yelp. Quickly abandoning the task, Sien sets the girl's breakfast of porridge in front of her, her movements tight, brisk.

'Years?' she repeats, voice almost a whisper.

He glances at her but avoids her eyes. 'This is the lot of an artist. Look at Mauve; it took a long time for him to become as successful as he is now. It will happen one day, but I warned you that it would not be easy.'

'You did not mention years. And you say it will happen "one day". How long is this one day going to take?'

He shrugs, puffing impatiently on his pipe. He then explains it is clear to him that, contrary to Theo's advice, he is not quite ready to tackle paints after all. He must return to the line. That's where the answer lies. If he directs all his energy towards drawing once more during these cold months, he is sure that by next spring or summer, when he can work outdoors again, he will be in a better position to do battle with the paints. And there's no doubt in his mind that next year he will emerge the victor.

'What about Theo?'

'Don't worry I will explain the matter to him. He will understand. He knows more than anyone how long these things take. And we can work here together through the winter. You can help me again, Sien.' He peers into her face searchingly. Meeting his eyes, she does not doubt his determination; he will be nothing short of a machine, a tireless drawing device. Yet she is unable to reply, her disappointment still too sharp.

'I'm not saying I am giving up. Far from it. I believe in my work more than ever – because I believe in us.' He takes her hand. As he gently squeezes it the contraction in her chest eases. 'Let's have a productive winter, full of studio work. Besides, paints are expensive and we are going to need more money through winter, burning the stove and whatnot.'

It is true. The merciless months of winter are bound to make more demands on the purse. Little can compare to the agony of being cold as well as hungry, forced to listen to the groan and rumble of small bellies. She lets out a deep sigh as her eyes wander around the warm, comfortable room. She glances at the glowing stove, the sleeping baby, the girl slurping the last of her gruel. She sips her coffee, its taste on her tongue still invigorating. Vincent is already reaching for his drawing board.

She begins to sit for him again, but it is not as before, with every attempt interrupted by the hungry baby or Maria disturbing her sleeping brother. Unable to concentrate, Vincent abandons his station in exasperation. Just as well that she has an excuse to move, because if posing was hard before, it is even more so now following Willem's birth, her body more battered than ever. The baby may not have torn her but below things are not quite as they were. The nerves, mangled and stretched, pinch her so that she may as well be sitting on a bed of nails.

Sometimes Vincent will persist while she has Willem at her breast, or whenever he happens to find her sitting – sewing, peeling potatoes – though it is never long enough to satisfy him.

'I need other models,' he says, shaking his head and storming out of the apartment.

Soon, he is again indulging freely in his habit of hiring anybody who happens to catch his eye. Those imperfect but living, breathing works of art, as he calls them, whose fetid scent, far from bothering him, enlivens his senses. Passing them in the street, he can't help but double back. Those who accept his offer – not all of them do – are soon parading through the Schenkweg studio. Delivery boys, sweepers, porters, diggers. They usually come just once, because they find it too tedious to pose when they have their own work to do and their own homes to return to.

But when he brings Jacob to the studio, Vincent is so elated he seems to be walking on air. The old man, who lives in an almshouse for the elderly, wears a long, tattered military coat as if he has forgotten that whichever war he fought in is long over. He wears it with pride, and she finds herself forgiving him its shabby, forlorn condition. Because Jacob is hard of hearing, Vincent has the perfect excuse to use his hands as animatedly as he likes. And while Jacob is around there is no opportunity for them to be idle, as he chaperones him like a child, motioning him to stand there, hold the coffee cup to his mouth, directing him endlessly in a voice that nearly shouts.

Now, happy to have discovered so amenable a model, he no longer chafes at being confined indoors – and Sien is only too glad to have Vincent's new friend pose in her place. The man sits for hours at a stretch without complaint, more patient than a statue, giving the impression this business of posing is what he was born to do. His expression, like his bearing, is stolid, and his eyes and brows, like those of a hawk, seem not so much to follow but seize everything in his sight, making up for his flawed ears. The man is drawn from every position possible, from the side, the front, standing, sitting, drinking, eating, kneeling in prayer.

They make quite a pair, Sien muses, touched by the men's deep-felt regard for each other. Vincent treats Jacob with more care than he has shown his own father, his gaze tender one moment, eager-charged the next. They are opposites in every way: the slender man, with never-ending speech and too much energy, and the quiet older man who behaves like a rock in the middle of a stream, leaving it to others to swerve around him.

It's not difficult to see why Vincent is so fond of him, this poor man who, alone in the world, never argues with him or upsets him. How happy Vincent is when he is rescuing outcasts. He seems to forget himself. Just like when he is drawing.

Even Maria has taken to this heroic model. The only time Sien has seen Jacob's expression change – a hesitant smile creeping across his face – is when he gazes at the children. He and Maria regard each other silently, seemingly reading each other's thoughts, communicating in their own secret language.

'Just look at his face, Sien,' Vincent exclaims one evening after an all-day sitting. 'Just like the old veteran in Herkomer's *Last Muster*.' Another artist he is intent on copying, she supposes. But this time there is no frustration, only a deep satisfaction. In this picture, Jacob's sideburns are like the pelts of lambs, covering not only his cheeks but his ears, and his nose appears as curved as a bird's beak, while his crooked top hat sits on his head as if it landed there by accident. One would have been tempted to laugh if one were to pass Jacob on the street. But here, in Vincent's drawing of him, he is a man you'd think twice about mocking. Trapped in his silence, he is simply there, so comfortable in his skin that he seems to hardly be aware of himself. She is reassured to see there's no sign of those irksome, ill-looking faces outside the lottery office. This is what she knows of Vincent's work. Thick, coarse lines but confident and precise, the person life-like. Perhaps he is right. Surely the line will lead to him making a saleable painting sooner rather than later.

Filled with hope, she nods encouragingly and asks, 'Can you make a painting of him?'

'Yes, eventually, but I will have to think of a scene to put him in, I suppose, make him part of a story,' he replies, sighing. 'Perhaps, if those who run the home will allow it, I can draw him with some of his fellow residents.'

Jacob's fellows at the almshouse, he tells her, those forgotten, shrivelled creatures, shut up in their small rooms while the rest of the city bustled and hummed just beyond their walls, had raised his spirits in a way he has not felt in a long time. 'In some ways, they were even more heartening than the coalminers of the Borinage,' he says.

But next time she asks about them, he tells her no one else was willing to sit for him – and what's more, those in charge of the home have now barred him from the grounds.

'Why?' she asks, dismayed but also not surprised.

Lips tight, he does not answer but shakes his head and turns away. In all likelihood, he probably pestered the residents with his usual irrepressible manner, hovering not shyly but too eagerly, too hungrily. Still, at least Jacob is at their door most days, unflappable, darting keen glances into the apartment, like a man who only wakes each morning in order to return there. A place that, for the first time, must offer him a family life. He reminds Sien of herself in those early weeks, when she too arrived at Vincent's studio each morning brimming with anticipation, drawn to the irresistible attention of the artist. With Jacob's presence in the Schenkweg studio, not only has Vincent's enthusiasm for his work intensified, she finds her own hopes also undeniably returning, persuaded even to forget her dark mood.

Twenty-five

'How would you like to go and live in England?' Vincent asks one afternoon. Earlier, prompted by Theo's latest letter, he had rushed out to make some type of inquiry at the printers, and he has returned now with his eyes shining.

Sien gapes at him. He might as well have asked her to go with him to the moon. But, her curiosity nevertheless roused, she stops sorting the laundry and sits.

He explains that Theo, in his recent letter, had mentioned an exciting development in lithography: a cheap method that will allow him to reproduce his drawings in multiples, making them affordable to many. He will also be able to send them to his beloved English magazines with the hope of securing work over there.

'Why not? I know the place well. The English are warm people. And there we can make a fresh start. Perhaps find a little house with a garden. Would you like that?' He is almost breathless at the prospect. 'I'm sure if those publications can see my work, they, unlike our friend Tersteeg, would appreciate their fine spirit.'

She wonders if this is what they have been waiting for: a way for Vincent to finally secure an income of his own. She can see that his longing for this to be the case matches hers and that, buoyed by the possibility, all his focus is now consumed by this new thing. As for her, excited more by the prospect of lithography providing them an earning than his mention of England, she does not bother to dwell on the absurd idea of moving there.

He rushes off to the printers again. After some discussion there, he returns not just pleased but triumphant, suggesting the method has already proven itself a success. 'I have booked a stone with the printer,' he says. 'I want to try one of my drawings.'

Over the next few days, he is busy experimenting with this new technique. His hands and clothes, even his hair, become smudged with printer's ink. Even after they have been laundered, his clothes, as if they were washed in the canals, are darker than before. After striking his first print, he reports happily that even one of the workers at the printers was so taken with it that he seemed to want it for himself. 'That's what I'd like: for my work to be cheap and plentiful enough that ordinary people can hang it in their homes.'

She can't help but wonder if the worker meant it in jest.

His enthusiasm soon begins to wane, however. The results have been disappointing, he informs her not long after. He begins to complain that the ink runs, that it refuses to comply with his designs. 'Because it is not in my hand, I cannot control it.'

What's more, the cost of securing the stones has proved more expensive than he anticipated. And he worries about Theo's reaction, because he fears Theo's disappointment even more than his own. Then his gloom turns to resentment, implying it was Theo's fault for making such a poor suggestion to him in the first place.

'I mean, he should have known how tricky it is. He should have known that it is not suited to my style. It will be the last time I let him meddle.'

He goes less and less to the printers. She does not bother to ask him any more about it. And as for that other country across the sea, he does not mention it again.

Taking up his pencils, charcoal and chalks once more, those reliable implements he holds in such affection, he is happier. The days now shorter and colder, he has good reason to stay indoors and gorge on as many drawings as his energy will allow him, his appetite for them again seeming bottomless. Jacob and other souls from every nook and cranny of the city appear at the studio.

And the coins leave his pocket with them.

When she remarks that he may as well walk around with his pockets turned out, he reminds her that it is for this very reason his brother sends him the money.

They manage to scrape by – just.

If his pace of work is exhausting for her to behold, how must it be for him? People are not machines, she reminds him; they need rest. But her advice falls on deaf ears and the unceasing work finally takes its toll on him. He falls ill – despairing at the loss of time.

The only consolation is Willem. Besotted by the growing boy, Vincent is forever bouncing him in his arms or crouching by the crib to coo with him. And the boy responds on cue, gurgling, his face lighting up whenever Vincent approaches. Nearly six months old, he now sleeps through the night in his crib, and is as plump as a bird being fattened, often rocking himself on his back, talking endlessly to his new companions – his toes. And Vincent, though not yet recovered, can't help but draw this happy model.

'Is he not remarkable?' Vincent murmurs, mesmerised. 'I see in his eyes something infinite and pure.'

'What could he have to complain about?' Sien replies, opening her chemise yet again to the smack of the baby's lips.

'Just think, we were all like that once, free of every care,' he says, sketching him at her breast. From his tone and yearning gaze, it seems he would not hesitate to swap places with Willem.

And so later that night, she is again woken by Vincent's mouth suckling her marble-hard nipple. This time, her body yields, stirred by his desire. But more than that, it is during these moments when he surrenders to her, to his need of her, that she is reminded of his vulnerability. Further, this intimacy between them, according to Vincent, is the very yardstick for how to live. And at that moment, in the blackest part of night, when they are breathing in each other's air, when they are almost one, she finds that she believes him.

Early December brings the Feast of St Nicholas, and as soon as Vincent enters the apartment with his satchel bulging, the mood begins to crackle with excitement. Even the stove flares, a minor inferno. Though it is a festive time of joy and presents, Sien is not able to recall a year when they were able to celebrate the occasion let alone indulge anyone with gifts; the Hoorniks were content if there was enough coke to burn and some butter to smear on the potatoes. But this year, as Vincent unpacks the goods from his satchel and spreads them on the table with great fanfare, his cheer irrepressible, she is reminded how wanting her previous feast days were.

There is bread filled with sweet almond paste, a bag of licorice and wooden blocks for Willem. Sien's eyes fill with tears at the sight of such plenty. Maria, clapping, jumps up and down for the candy, but Vincent teases her, hand bobbing up and down like a fishing line. When the girl finally snatches the small paper bag from his grasp, Vincent smiles and says, 'Well, a bird of prey could not have done better.' The girl peers into the bag greedily before taking it to her hiding spot behind the wicker chair.

Sien is taken aback when Vincent wordlessly hands her another parcel, his eyes glinting with anticipation, like a schoolboy waiting to be praised. There is a corduroy dress, with a proper flounce, for Maria, and a piece of green ribbon. They are far from new, but they may as well be, for the girl's thrill hardly suffers for it as she strips off her clothes without taking her eyes off the dress. Sien helps her into it and ties her hair with the ribbon. Besotted with her gifts, Maria twirls like a spinning top before falling to the floor, giggling. Sien knows the girl will not remove the dress even for sleep, and no doubt there will be a tantrum when the time comes for the thing to be washed.

But it's the green-striped worsted jacket he has bought for Sien herself that sends her emotions reeling. Holding it up for her, he insists she try it on. It is a little big, but it is near enough her size. She fondles the smooth wooden buttons, then extends her arms in front of her to admire the neat tailoring. But a darkening realisation jostles for her attention. 'How much did all this cost?' she asks, looking up at him, unable to help her scowl.

'Why do you always harp on about the costs? I should be allowed to buy you a jacket for the feast day if I want to. Can we forget the money for one day? Why should we not enjoy this day like everyone else?' But his expression also carries a trepidation, as if he is disappointed that the excitement he felt at the shops earlier has proved to be so short-lived. Then, eyeing Maria with her bag of candy, dressed to the nines, his face transforms instantly to that of a proud father, wide and entranced.

Sien is about to tell him that today is just one day. Just another day that will pass like every other day, and what is the use of these temporary fancies when the bills are always mounting, when there are still many days ahead of them that must be accounted for?

But of course, Vincent is not listening, smiling and cavorting with the children, who, caught up in his inescapable energy, are only more than willing to be his happy allies. She supposes if there is one occasion when one can be forgiven for being a spendthrift, then surely it is this day. Sien's heart feels both light and heavy. It is the first time anyone has bought her such an extravagant gift, and she struggles to remain annoyed at him. She can picture him swept up in the giddy atmosphere of feast day and succumbing to the mood of goodwill, determined to walk in bearing gifts like every other head of house, recalling fondly as he peers in the shop windows that he too has a family awaiting him at home. Surely the man lives on the whims of his heart, from moment to moment, from feeling to feeling, not sparing a thought for tomorrow, never mind the future – for both may be attended to when the time comes.

And for now the stove is blazing. They eat the sweet bread with jenever, their cheeks glowing like the red-hot coals.

'A time for stories,' Vincent says, standing and plucking a book from his pile in the cupboard. 'By one of the best, Hans Christian Andersen,' he murmurs, leafing through it. 'For Maria, "The Ugly Duckling", then perhaps for you, Sien, "The Story of a Mother".'

The book is one of Vincent's favourites. Its pages are stained and curled, its cover tattered, spine wobbly. How many times has she seen him read it late at night, so engrossed it seemed only his body was at the Schenkweg studio, his mind somewhere else entirely? Watching him, she wished she too could read well enough to escape into a book, to become lost in another world.

He reads to Maria, who has now settled on his lap but is more interested in playing with her dress than the book in front of her. Soon yawning, by the time the ugly duckling learns that it is actually a swan, she is fast asleep.

'If only real life were like that,' Sien murmurs, thinking, how lucky for the duckling. Who wouldn't like to wake up one day and find themselves meant for a different life, a better one?

'But why shouldn't it be so?' Vincent replies quickly. 'Think about us, how our paths happened to cross that night, nearly a year ago.'

It is just like him to believe in fairytales. The jenever swimming in her, she is overcome, because last winter, when she found out she was carrying another child, more than anything she wanted to leave this world. In fact, she was convinced she would not survive the season. That year's St Nicholas Day had passed with only a trip to the soup kitchen.

She wipes the corners of her eyes with her sleeve. Though she is less willing than Vincent to believe their meeting was fated, nevertheless she can't deny its strangeness. Some days, she wrestles with the question of why: why her? Why should Sien Hoornik be singled out when there are so many of her ilk in this city?

Vincent nods. 'This time last year, I too was alone. I was at the parsonage with my family, and yet I had never felt so miserable, nor so alone.'

The story for her is about a mother who loses her sick child to Death. Grief-stricken, inconsolable, she decides to follow Death to demand that he return her child. On her journey to find him, she faces many tests: in one she encounters a thorny bush that she must embrace, causing her to bleed, and in another she is left without her eyes. When eventually she confronts Death, he recounts the two fates awaiting her child – a happy one and a miserable one. She begs to know which her child is destined for, but he tells her that this decision is up to God and that no one can know. The child will only be returned to her if she is prepared to accept God's will, whatever it may be. But she rejects his offer. That her child may be burdened with a life of suffering is unbearable to her. So, she resigns herself to never seeing her child again.

'I don't think my mother would have undertaken such an arduous journey for me,' he says, closing the book.

'How can you be sure of that?'

He does not answer, instead looking past her, lost in some thought. Then, looking at her once more, he says, 'Perhaps for Theo, the favoured child on whom God's light shines brightly.'

He praises the story's fearless mother, who was prepared to walk to the ends of the earth, braving all sorts of harm, to search for her child. 'The mark of a true mother,' he observes. 'That's how all mothers should be. Though I don't agree she should have refused God's will like that. She should have trusted Him. If God deemed suffering more desirable for her child, then she should have accepted His decision.'

'But you are a man who worships suffering for its own sake,' Sien counters. 'As for me, I have no doubt she did the right thing. If it were my mother, I would have wished for her to save me from misery. And what's more, if I could have returned my children to God to save them from my fate, I would not have hesitated to do so.'

She thinks he is about to start an argument, but he merely blenches, lips parting but not uttering a word. Still, a moment later, she catches him glancing at her with a deep, reproachful frown.

Twenty-six

In the shadow of the doorway, the woman standing at the threshold holding a large hessian bag does not at first resemble Sien's mother. But when she steps into the light Sien, seeing that it is unmistakably Wilhelmina, shuts her eyes in disappointment. When she opens them again, it is to see her mother's dry, chalky face, her expression a picture of anguish. Then, from behind Wilhelmina's skirt, Wil appears.

But Sien cannot be surprised. Has she not always known in the back of her mind that her mother would turn up any day like this? And an actress could not have bettered Wilhelmina's performance just now, all her features conspiring to express a helplessness. If Vincent were here, he would be less interested in the reason for her arrival than her willingness to sit for him. Her sister, too, has changed in the few weeks since Sien last saw her. Her dark eyes have become dull and the only hint of life evident in her shrivelled frame is the tremble of her fingers as they clutch her shawl.

Wilhelmina tries to embrace Sien. 'Oh, you've no idea,' she mumbles, dropping her head on Sien's shoulder. Then, quickly pulling away, Wilhelmina puts on a face so sweet and pitiful – and so rarely seen – Sien can't help but cock her head to the side. She is hardly in need of an explanation.

Wilhelmina and Wil remove their shawls and warm themselves next to the stove. Maria, pleased to see them, is busy with her singsong chatter, tugging Wilhelmina's skirt and clamouring for her attention. Wilhelmina beams brightly and bends down to hug the girl, fussing about the dress and ribbon. Oh, presents from Vincent? Then, turning to Willem on the floor, she picks him up. The boy, smiling, shows off his toothless, milk-varnished gums.

'Ah, he will be teething soon,' exclaims Sien's mother looking pleased, suggesting the sole purpose for her visit is to confirm this fact.

'So, Karel has thrown you out.'

Instantly, Wilhelmina's smile vanishes and she fixes her daughter with a withering stare. Sien, out of habit, reddens. That her mother's scorn can still make her blush, even at her age, will always remain a mystery to her.

Then, remembering why her mother has come, she crosses her arms and asks, 'Well, where are your sons now?' Those sons she adored do not want her, no longer need her, looked after as they are by other women. Women younger and better than old Wilhelmina.

By way of an answer Wilhelmina turns her back to Sien to move closer to the stove.

Vincent returns from his walk. He is more sympathetic than Sien on discovering why her family has come. 'They can sleep in the room with the art materials next to Maria. I will rearrange things and make more space.' When she groans, he says, 'What else can we do? We can't turn them out onto the street.'

'But what will Theo say?'

At the mention of his brother, Vincent's face darkens. 'Look, there is no need to tell him, is there?' he mutters, avoiding her eyes. 'After all, Paris is far away.'

Since he cannot pay the rent for Wilhelmina, she supposes there is no other option. But the apartment is cramped as it is, with the studio, the children, and Vincent spending more time indoors. How will they survive the winter together, all of them trapped inside, without coming to blows? Especially Vincent, a man whose nervous energy needs the outdoors as much for walking as painting. But, excited to have two extra models at his beck and call, the next day a pallet arrives for Wilhelmina and Wil to share.

The first couple of weeks are busy and lively. The older woman, besides posing for Vincent, makes herself useful, helping with the children and the housekeeping, allowing Sien to do some posing without the previous interruptions.

Vincent tells her the two extra mouths are worth every guilder because they will help him to improve his work through winter. But with a roomful of models – including Jacob, who continues to turn up unannounced – it is not long before the paper stock runs low, and so too Vincent's money and patience. Hours of posing the Hoornik women may offer, but nothing towards the already stretched credit at the grocery store and the bakery.

Nevertheless, despite the ebbs and flows of money, they are all busy taking turns posing for him, alone and together, including Willem, who shows all the signs that he intends to crawl any day now. When he is not asleep he is a single-animal, never-ending circus, crowing and peering eagerly at all the commotion. He makes them forget the cold, their nagging hunger.

'Why should he not find everything agreeable?' Vincent cries in delight.

It's true. Willem behaves as if he has been brought into this world to provide nothing other than cheer, and as he tries to make his body move, Vincent, admiring his determination, sketches madly so as not to miss even the smallest part of his progress.

But just as Sien predicted, it is not long before the crowded apartment and ceaseless noise shatters Vincent's winter-fragile sanity. And because Willem has started teething, his pained wailing disturbs the household at all hours of the night. One morning, not only air- and light-deprived but sleep-deprived as well, he explodes at Wilhelmina.

'What are you good for, woman? This tepid coffee?' he shouts, as he storms out of the apartment, cursing them all under his breath.

Overwrought, his nerves frayed, Vincent again falls ill, more seriously than before. This time too weak to work, he huddles in their attic bedroom, reading thick volumes in English, French, turning the pages as if he means to count them rather than read them. She tries to persuade him to rest, to stop with his reading, but he is deaf to her entreaties, not even bothering to look up. Then, as a new year begins, he does not get better but worse. His cheekbones hewn, his body wilted, he begins to resemble an old man, in fact death itself, the dry wrinkled flesh on his face appearing merely a shroud for his skull. His teeth aching, his breath reeks foul like the canals in summer and his lower lip, etched with a deep crack, bleeds steadily like stigmata, and because his eyes weep a sticky white pus, he struggles to open them. Sien wipes his eyes, helps him to drink, to eat. Yet despite his wretched state, he is not able to put those books down.

Then, despairing that he has not, in a year, made a single saleable work, his condition worsens. 'How disappointed Theo must be, Sien,' he mutters darkly.

'No more than us surely? I don't see why he hasn't sold your work. How is it possible?' she blurts out.

He recoils, almost wincing from her touch as she cleans his eyes with a warm cloth.

What about me? What about your promise to me? she wants to ask him, but she stops short, his changed appearance being almost unbearable to witness. Still, after what seems like hundreds, if not thousands of drawings, that Theo has not managed to sell a single one, in spite of the down-at-heel models, staggers her. She begins to wonder if Vincent's work will ever sell.

'I must let Theo know how sorry I am,' he murmurs.

'Yes, you should do that. You should apologise to him. Apologise to him from all of us for letting him down,' she says under her breath as she takes leave of him.

That evening when he finally emerges for his supper, he is so pleased with a book he has just finished reading that he begins to talk enthusiastically about the impression it made on him even before he has sat down, not noticing that no one is listening, not noticing that he is talking to himself, forgetting that none of them can read. Sien shakes her head. It's one of those times when his thoughts are not with his body but somewhere else – England, it seems, since the novel he speaks of, *Middlemarch*, is an English one. 'The writer is just as good as Balzac and Zola, you see,' he says, taking his place at the table.

Then his eyes adjust to his surroundings and, meeting the blank stares of those around him, he pauses, blinking rapidly as if the faces are unfamiliar to him. Wilhelmina, holding a restless Willem on her lap, regards him with such stern-faced suspicion that Vincent, on catching sight of it, withdraws from the room abruptly, almost fearfully. To Sien, he appears like a man heading out from shore, receding into the horizon as the expanse of water between them becomes ever wider. Strangely, from such a vantage she is able to see him more clearly, more coldly: a man who has departed from her not only physically but in every other way, a man so far away from her that he is unable to see her tears.

Twenty-seven

Wilhelmina has just returned from Geest. Pale, her lips dry from the wind and her expression grim, it is obvious she has something on her mind.

'Vincent is not right in the head, Sien.'

Presuming this is just another of her mother's complaints, Sien doesn't reply but carries on with her task of folding the baby's linen.

'I saw him on the train tracks,' her mother continues. 'He was stumbling, as if he was drunk. Then' – Wilhelmina swallows – 'he . . . he lay down on the ground and pressed his cheek against the cold iron. Can you believe that?'

Goosebumps spring up on Sien's arms, though the room is warm, and she can feel the colour draining from her face. She fights the urge to go up to the bedroom and crawl under the blankets. But the children are waiting for their supper, and there is no place to hide from her mother's eyes, which at that moment are wider than normal.

'I mean, there's a way to die, Sien. There are all sorts of ways. But . . . but what I saw . . . well, only mad people would do it like that.' She frowns, making it clear Vincent's actions have offended her deeply, then describes the scene that followed. The railway workers running towards Vincent, waving their arms and shouting at the top of their voices to alert him to a train that was due any moment. Vincent finally standing up but appearing dazed, looking about him like a man who had just been shaken awake from a deep sleep.

'If you could have seen the sorry sight of him running away, trying to dodge the stones the workers were throwing at him,' Wilhelmina finishes.

'You made a mistake,' Sien says sharply. 'He was probably studying something on the tracks. Something that interested him. Something he wanted to draw.'

She turns her back to her mother and hurries to the kitchen. Despite her automatic impulse to defend Vincent, she feels stiff and clumsy, as if she is dressed in armour. How could he contemplate such an act? What about her and the children? What about his fierce talk about never giving in to despair?

She gulps back tears, her heart stricken – not just for Vincent but also at the dawning realisation that, despite his ardour, despite his best intentions and efforts to be a man of whom Michelet would approve, it would seem he is incapable of fulfilling his wish.

But, then, how can he? And, more importantly, how can

she expect him to, when it is clear his first concern is to save himself, never mind her and the children. Has she not observed his overwrought condition often enough? Those moments when his nerves appeared to be on the verge of snapping? When his accusations of her weakness were no more than an expression of his fears for himself. And if he is prepared to so readily give himself over to death, how can she continue to believe him, or rely on him, no matter how persuasive his speech, no matter how passionate his pledges? Though he may mean every syllable he utters, his words now seem as impermanent and immaterial as hot air. It seems as her mother said: he likes to throw his authority around with promises, promises. But it is easy for him. After all, what did he risk, other than her disappointment?

That evening, he returns late, still enveloped in the cold night's air. She is already in bed, the candle flickering in its stub. Unusually, he is in a shy, thoughtful mood. He has spent the day walking the city, he tells her, beginning to remove his clothes. He went to Geest.

'What business did you have there?' she asks suspiciously. 'Did you visit a brothel, did you?'

He smiles and shakes his head. 'I was thinking about us. How it has been a year since we met.'

She looks up and, meeting his eyes, which shine softly in the waning glow of the melting candle, she is arrested by their magnetic pull; too naked and too tender, his gaze still succeeds in overpowering her.

'And what a year,' he goes on. 'Look at all that we have done together. A newborn, a new home. And all the drawings. It has been far from dull.' He sits on the edge of the bed to remove his boots. Then, sighing heavily, he falls back on the mattress.

For the rest of her life, it will be a year she will never forget, she thinks, as if they have already parted.

'And you got the family life you always wanted,' she offers.

He stares in silence at the ceiling for some moments, unblinking. Then he says, 'Yes, now I understand what it is to have a family. I thought it would cure me of loneliness but I have to admit it has made me crave solitude.'

'You should not have to kill yourself for it, though,' she mutters, unable to help herself.

He turns to her, eyes panicked.

'My mother told me.'

'Oh, that. It was nothing . . . I was feeling feverish and just wanted to feel the cold of iron on my face.'

She is about to challenge him but decides against it, wishing to preserve that very last ray of hope granted to every person: the possibility of the end and the desire for it. How many times has she found it so tantalising that she contemplated throwing herself in the canal?

He turns his gaze to the ceiling once more, but his brows are furrowed. He is a man who sees the world only through the colour of his feelings, and though they may be as turbulent and unpredictable as the sea, they are his religion, the only truth by which he lives – she understands that now. But what their purpose might be, other than feeding his art, is a mystery to her. Yet, she concedes, the intensity of them is probably why he has been able to force his way into her heart. Why he has been able to make it beat louder than anyone before him.

He climbs under the blankets and takes her in his arms, squeezing her so tightly she is reminded of their early months together when he couldn't get enough of her, when every embrace left her gasping for air.

'I feel no less for you now than I did last year,' he whispers into her ear.

She shudders, unable to banish from her mind the image of him lying prone on the tracks.

Yet here he is, holding her close, as if he were another man, and not the one who, hours earlier, wanted to end his life beneath a train. She meets his body and, to her surprise, she yearns for him more than ever, clutching his familiar body even tighter than his grip on hers.

Then a remedy better than any a doctor could have prescribed arrives – a letter from Theo. Its contents cure him almost overnight. At first, Sien thinks one of his works has finally sold, but no, rather it is some startling personal news from the younger brother.

'At last, he's finally got himself a woman,' Vincent reports, grinning. A woman Theo rescued in the street, apparently. 'Does it sound familiar, Sien?' he asks, his poor health seemingly forgotten. The circumstances are so similar to their own meeting, Vincent is convinced that, far from being a mere coincidence, it is a sign of the brothers' close connection. 'It is clear neither of us can ignore a woman in trouble,' he says with pride but also glee. Theo had discovered the woman feverish and unwell on a bench. Unlike Sien, however, this was a woman from a respectable family in the provinces.

'It seems rather serious. He seems to have truly fallen for her. But it is just what he needs rather than only slaving away at Goupil.' His eyes are shining for the first time in many weeks.

'Has she recovered?' Sien asks, as astonished as Vincent by the similarity of their meeting.

'Well, he is caring for her, so I'm sure she will.'

In the coming days, he writes Theo more often than usual, filling sheet after sheet of paper. 'I need to offer him advice, share with him my experiences,' he explains.

In the following weeks many letters are sent back and forth, aiding Vincent's recovery. Soon, his energy restored, he is again drawing all day, all night, and she fears he will exhaust himself and fall ill again. Models begin to appear at the studio once more, Vincent now dressing them in all sorts of costumes as different character types. Jacob is back, tasked with posing as a fisherman with a sou'wester, of all things. 'Look, it still has fish scales stuck to it,' Vincent points out, beaming from ear to ear. The apartment is noisy but warm. There are endless cups of coffee to prepare, and their credit at the bakery and the grocer begin to run down again. Vincent, however, shows no sign of slowing, no sign of tiring. And this time, Sien knows better than to protest.

*

With too many mouths to feed, and money from Paris still a couple of days away, they have no choice but to visit a soup kitchen. Even if the entire Geest were to turn up there, she no longer cares, cannot afford to care. The hopes she held the previous year have begun to fade, their outline as faint as a drawing rubbed out. This gentleman is one who does not pay attention to money in the same way others do; he does nothing to accrue it and, when he has it, does not know how to manage it, let alone hold on to it.

Though the pea soup they are served is so thin they can see the bottom of the bowls, Vincent takes little notice, more interested in the long, bleak room and its patrons.

He finds the scene so moving he endeavours to recreate it at the studio. But the apartment's windows flood the room with too much light. After all, the soup kitchen was not a brightly lit place. He attempts to cover the windows with cardboard, but the result fails to please him.

After many visits to the landlord's house in Voorburg to make his case for timber shutters, he finally succeeds in persuading him. After their installation, she can see that Vincent was right. They allow him to let in as much or as little of the light as he likes, either from above or below. As if they are new toys, he can't help but play with them, marvelling at their clever mechanism. 'They provide chiaroscuro. You see, one must have mood, grey as well as black.'

He then goes to exhausting lengths to replicate exactly what he saw at the soup kitchen, even drawing a service hatch on canvas for a backdrop. The Hoornik family play various roles. Wilhelmina, holding Willem, stands to one side of the hatch,

Sien on the other, and Wil in front of it, while Maria stands facing him, holding a bowl of soup. Sien knows well his fussy ways but this zealous labour seems not only needless but irritating. How many times has she visited these gloomy sad places, with everyone huddled over the steaming bowls, eyes downcast, too miserable to be grateful? Too many times to count, and too many times for her to believe there is something beautiful about them, as Vincent insists there is. It is only him who would think so, she argues. Only someone whose family has always employed a cook, only someone who has never had the need of charity.

Wilhelmina can only shake her head in disbelief.

Twenty-eight

It is near winter's end, and yet Sien feels not even a glimmer of the hope she'd felt this time last year. Instead, her wariness is accompanied by a darkening realisation: they are colder and hungrier than a year ago.

Wilhelmina returns empty-handed from the grocery store. Shaking her head in annoyance, she tells her daughter, 'They will not let me have anything. Vincent has not settled the bill.' Removing her cap, she says icily, 'I know there are models, but still, what does that man do with all his money?'

The children run up to her, complaining they are hungry.

'Maybe I can do better,' Sien replies, tying the laces of her bonnet and picking up her shawl. She knows what her mother is like. In Geest she would have had no qualms about haggling with the grocer for half a bag of flour, just to help tide them over, but in this new neighbourhood she is likely to be as meek as a young girl.

At the store, she pleads with the brothers who own it. 'You know Vincent will come by and pay you soon. Money always arrives from his family.'

But still they refuse. One of them, the baby-faced youngest, suggests there are other ways to settle the account. She glares at them, her temperature soaring, but they only stare back, indifferent, their arms folded across their aprons.

That evening, she confronts Vincent in their bedroom. He is sheepish, avoiding her gaze, fumbling with one of his beloved magazines, flicking the pages impatiently, nervously.

'Can we eat that?' she asks, pointing at the tall stack of *The Graphic*, that English publication he never stops talking about. The day before he had brought home an armful from some bookseller in the city: twenty-one of them. But at what cost, she'd like to know. Could he not have bought just one? Maybe two? Or even three?

'I need them for my work,' he insists. 'Besides, he gave them to me at such a good price. If you must know, they were, in fact, a bargain.'

When she continues to glower at him, he tells her, 'You just don't understand. These are more important than food for me.'

'But what about the children? Can they live off pictures? Bread is what they need. It's what *all* of us need – other than you, of course.' She clenches her hands into fists, trying to repress the urge to snatch the magazine from his grasp and tear it in half.

How can he deny them bread for this blasted magazine? She rubs her breasts, hoping there is still some milk left for Willem, at least.

Finally, dropping his reading onto his lap, he screws his eyes shut and clamps his hands over his ears, as if to block out the sound of her accusations, the crying of the children. She leaves him, returning to the mayhem below. Then a moment later, he descends the ladder, walking past her with head and shoulders bowed and a deep scowl etched on his face. He heads for the door and, without glancing once at the children, unhooks his hat and coat and disappears.

Yes, how lucky for the men, Sien thinks; they can always leave.

Paints, paper were one thing; these he needed to improve his work, improve his chances of selling. But how can he expect them to go hungry for magazines, of all things?

Listening to him scuttling down the stairs, she is about to curse him and his magazines when a piercing realisation swiftly quietens her fury. Slowly she lowers herself in her chair. 'You fool, Sien,' she mutters to herself. 'You silly, silly fool.' What difference would the selling of his work mean in the end, when he would always spend his money as he saw fit: not just on art supplies, but magazines? And if they could not manage on the money they receive now from Theo – an extravagant sum, far more than any working family with a large brood earned and lived on – could the income from the sale of his work provide them any better? The cold truth of this strikes her so deeply that it seems to penetrate her very marrow.

As a shudder travels down the length of her, she closes her eyes and sinks further into her chair.

*

Wilhelmina has had enough. 'I'm leaving,' she announces after returning from a visit to Geest. Her mother has just seen the comfortable rooms Karel has set up there, and she and Wil have been invited to stay with him. They are in a house that faces the street, with a lovely courtyard garden, she says.

'He has a few girls using the rooms already,' she announces proudly as she begins to pack her and Wil's belongings.

Yes, Karel, always was her mother's favourite. But he was also the one who invariably managed to produce a stolen loaf of bread or much-needed coins when the family was about to give up. And now, it seemed, he had established his own makeshift brothel.

Sien merely shrugs at the prospect of her mother's departure. Though the woman has been useful with the children, Sien is pleased to be rid of her and her constant criticisms of Vincent. It will also mean they have fewer mouths to feed.

'I'm sure you will like it better there,' Sien says. 'There won't be a shortage of beds, I expect.'

Wilhelmina pauses in her packing and eyes her daughter not with her usual contempt but with pity. 'Vincent is no good, Sien.'

Sien bristles. 'He has fed all of us through winter, has he not? Since Pa's death, what other man has there been who would do as much?'

'That may be,' Wilhelmina concedes, 'but I guarantee you, he will be gone before the year is done.'

Sien turns away, her face burning. Yes, the woman is probably right, but Sien will never give her the satisfaction of admitting as much; to do so would be to admit her worst fears.

'You could help Karel,' her mother suggests.

'Karel doesn't need me.'

'Well, you will be needing him soon enough,' her mother predicts.

'No. If it comes to that, I'll walk the streets somewhere else. Or work in a laundry.'

Wilhelmina tut-tuts and shakes her head. Then, as though pressed for time, she flings her shawl around her shoulders, gives Maria a quick hug and smiles in the direction of the sleeping baby. For Sien she has only a curt nod as, trailed by Wil, she almost scurries for the door.

Twenty-nine

Spring arrives again and, as always, when the weather is warmer the world seems kinder; one can almost smell the promise of better times in the blossom-scented air. With the apartment less crowded, Sien and Vincent are arguing less, and Vincent, having resumed painting with his usual zeal, insists he is bound to make a sale soon. Soon. He does not notice that, having heard such promises before, she does not greet his assurances with much enthusiasm. Even if he did manage to earn a living, the money would soon go on art supplies, magazines and whatever else took his fancy – not food for her and the children.

Day by day she is becoming ever more convinced Vincent will not change, will never change. He simply is not capable of it. And, she realises sadly, nothing will persuade him to do so. Not her love, not the children, not their future.

A new voice inside her seems to be growing louder. *You must prepare yourself to walk the streets again*, it says. She does not doubt its rightness, but she doubts her will to heed it. How can she undo this past year with Vincent? After what he has done for her and the children? Yes, she is afraid and reluctant to return to the streets, but it is because she is unsure whether she can return to her former self. The woman who had no choice but to venture out night after night so she may provide. The one who could afford neither fatigue nor fear. As she struggles to recall this woman, she is alarmed to find that it is pity she feels for her and her lot. How will she overcome this dangerous sentiment in order to walk the streets again?

Vincent, meanwhile, cannot leave their bed quick enough in the morning. Tiptoeing downstairs before dawn, he gathers his materials in the deep grey light and heads out, heeding the call of the outdoors like nature's faithful servant. Most days, he does not return home until well after dark, turning up merely to sleep. In the morning, there is new work hanging on the walls: works that are as grim as the previous year's, and no doubt they will prove equally unsaleable. Among the usual sowers, peat diggers, potato gleaners and coal yard workers, she is astounded to see that he has depicted rag pickers sorting through the rubbish at a junk yard. Workers may be one thing, but what can he possibly see in such desperation, such wretchedness? She knows better than to ask. What has she learnt in the past year if not that, while others spurn such misery, Vincent is captivated by it?

As far as she can see, the only real progress unfolding in their studio is Willem. She is pleased the boy is growing more independent, no longer a weight to be carried everywhere.

He crawls around the apartment, revelling in the discovery of his agile limbs. A few times, he has pulled himself upright, his hands planted on the seat of chairs or on Vincent's knees while he works.

'A most energetic fellow,' Vincent marvels as he picks Willem up and shakes him in the air so the baby laughs and kicks his fat legs like a frog.

'All I know is that he refuses to eat porridge,' Sien says, wiping his mess from her blouse. While her other babies probably died for lack of food, this one has the gall to spit it out because he doesn't take to it. What can she expect? Spoilt even before he entered the world; spoilt by Vincent while he was in her belly.

'Is that so?' he asks, more impressed than dismayed.

Willem, in return, has eyes only for Vincent. Their adoration for each other stirs her, and she worries that the baby, though he does not have Vincent's name, thinks him his father. He even gazes at the art on the walls with a seeming admiration, as if he knows something about it.

One evening, Vincent pulls a painted study of a field of bulbs from his satchel. It pleased him so much that he found himself excited about tackling oils once more and he went off to Van Kleef's to purchase the jenever because he will need it to clean his brushes. 'In any case, after enduring the trials of winter, do we not also deserve a drink?' he says, already uncorking the bottle.

'There's money from Paris again then?' she asks eagerly.

He nods, telling her all the accounts are settled. 'You can stock the pantry again.'

Showing off his crusty painting, he is adamant that a rosy future awaits them. As long as he does not give up, as long as he continues to make progress, the work will sell, he repeats over and over again, pacing the studio. 'It's just a matter of time. Just a matter of time. It might be any day now, Sien. Any day, do you hear? Wait and see.' He is so enthusiastic, as if it were a new story he was weaving, that he fails to notice that she has turned away.

It is not his endless chatter but the warm pull of jenever that comforts and cheers her. They find themselves finishing both bottles as the children sleep. They sway, stumbling to their bedroom, and in the soft glow of a flickering candle, they fall together on the bed, giggling.

Because they are not themselves, they are not afraid to talk of death. Vincent describes a three-day journey on foot from the Borinage to France that nearly killed him.

'I started on a train, but after my money ran out, I walked all the way to Courrières.'

'Why?'

'To seek out the studio of Jules Breton, an artist I admire greatly. But when I reached there I was so disappointed that it was newly built, and so lacking in warmth or charm, that I turned around again.'

'Did you meet the artist – Breton?'

'No, I didn't dare knock on the door. I arrived there looking worse than a tramp. I probably would have frightened him.'

'Why did you go? What did you want with him?'

'Oh, I don't know. I . . . I just had this wild feverish urge to . . . I suppose just to *see* him. I didn't really have a plan. But it was quite a journey there and back. I slept outside for three nights, suffering rain, frost. I passed the first night in a carriage, and the next two in a woodpile and a haystack. Then one evening, overcome with fever, delirious, I was convinced I'd slip away overnight. And when I put my head down on a log to wait for death, I found I was calm, ready. But then the next morning I woke to the bright pink inside of my eyelids, and I was sure I felt the hand of God in the sun's rays. It seemed He was urging me to open them, telling me that it was not my time, that I still had much to do. And finding myself very much alive, I discovered I was filled with more purpose, more drive than before.'

Sien confides, 'I have always imagined a watery grave. It would be a struggle but only for a short while, then swift and certain.' She feels weightless at the thought. There is always death, she thinks dreamily.

'You're smiling,' he says.

How can she not? 'This is how I would like to die,' she murmurs, closing her eyes and crossing her hands across her chest. It's true. It would be a pleasant way to go, especially with her blood swimming with jenever.

Vincent chuckles. She can smell his pipe, feel his eyes on her. He sits up quickly, making the mattress rustle, and leaves their bed. She can hear the ladder creaking as he descends. He returns with his drawing materials. 'I will give you a peaceful death,' he announces, bringing the candle near.

'If I were rich, I'd drink jenever all day in a beautiful garden,'

Sien murmurs. 'Yes, I would like to be lazy, that's my nature. But you, no. You would still work and do nothing else. And instead of twenty models you would hire hundreds of them.'

'Because I'm afraid I will run out of time, I don't want to spare myself.'

'Is that why you work so hard?' she asks, opening her eyes.

He nods. 'You see, if I have to choose between my work or my health, I will always choose work. It's better to sacrifice one's constitution for something that will endure than worrying about our bodies which, in the end, will be no more anyway.'

'How would you like your end to be, then?'

'It must be outdoors, in nature.'

'Yes, I can see it now. Exhausted from all the drawing and painting, you will simply drop dead in a polder.'

'Perhaps.'

He sits at the end of the bed and begins to draw. He does not have to tell her to keep still; she has no desire to move, nor is she capable of it, because when she opens her eyes the room sways and spins.

Just as she is about to succumb to sleep, she can smell his jenever breath near hers, then his body is on top of her. Like a young man, he is hungry for her again, body thrashing with nervous energy, gripping her too hard, fumbling, impatient. The bed rocks as if it were battling the violence of the high seas. Tasting salt on her lips, she opens her eyes and sees that he is weeping.

Afterwards, like a drowning man clinging to a piece of shipwreck, he refuses to let go of her.

*

The next morning, still groggy, a fresh drawing greets her downstairs. So that's how she looked last night. Unlike his other drawings, this one shows her happy. At the prospect of death, she lies contentedly, her eyes closed, her smile wide. But she winces at the size of her feet, which are so large they appear as if they might belong to a giant.

As spring draws to a close, the warm weather, so convivial for travel, brings Vincent's father to the Schenkweg once more. Unlike the previous year, this time there is no fear, no concern about his arrival. Vincent is now the charming son, for Sien is no longer a dreaded secret.

When the father acknowledges her, she does not go red but meets his eyes and returns a greeting. Glancing at the children, who are making a small racket, he smiles. But he seems troubled, his expression tense with some worry. Vincent fusses around him as if he were unwell. She prepares the coffee and quietens the children. And when the two men sit and drink together, she realises that this time the father's downcast face has nothing to do with her and Vincent; he is upset about Theo. The elder Van Gogh, distressed by the younger son's latest romantic entanglement, has come to seek Vincent's opinion.

At this unexpected turn of events, Vincent grows so cheerful, his mood so giddy, he makes her dizzy.

What does Vincent know about Theo's Marie, and what does he make of Theo's plans to marry her? the old man asks. Is it not too rash?

'I do think Theo should wait,' Vincent replies. 'There really is no harm in taking one's time in these matters.'

Sien looks up, so startled she almost drops her cup. Vincent had done nothing but encourage Theo from the very beginning of his affair with Marie, urging him to defy their parents and marry her. Did Vincent not accuse them of trying to ruin Theo's life? Did he not advise Theo that, given his good, solid career and income, he should be allowed to marry the woman he loved? What objection could their parents possibly have, she remembers him asking, especially since she is from a respectable, religious family in the provinces? But she also recalls Vincent delighting in the prospect that, rather than him, it is Theo who is making their parents suffer.

'I know Theo thinks he is in love, but he is young, and we all know that sometimes, on looking back, we realise we acted not only hastily but unwisely,' he says now.

Sien can only guess he is referring to that business with Kee, though he speaks like a man who has much experience in matters to do with women and affairs of the heart.

It is obvious Vincent's counsel sits well with his father, that it is what he had hoped to hear.

'After all,' Vincent continues, 'Theo has an established career, a serious professional reputation, so yes, he has much at stake, and your objections are reasonable.' He nods gravely. 'In my own case, Sien and I have decided to be sensible, putting off the question of marriage until I have my own income.'

Catching her astonished stare, Vincent's eyes become so frigid they almost command her to lower her gaze.

She is shocked to discover how skilful he is at playing these games. That he can pretend so convincingly. His bitter criticism of his parents now forgotten, he acts as if he has always been the favoured son, obliged to dole out advice to his father about his younger brother, suggesting Theo was prone to stray, needed Vincent's steady, guiding hand. How quickly things can change. Poor Theo, who must still be under the impression he continues to have Vincent's support.

And she would also like to know: what has happened to Vincent's feelings of guilt about his dependence on Theo, his fear of letting him down? Is this how he intends to repay his brother – by betraying him? The matter is hardly her concern, and yet it seems that for the first time she is seeing Vincent with her eyes fully open. The more she listens, the more she is shaken by this other Vincent: a man who enjoys gossip as any fisherwoman who sells her catch door to door, and just as fickle. Saying and doing what will make him look best.

If Vincent can spin such stories about Theo to suit him, and if he can so readily change his mind regarding the delicate matter of his brother's heart, would he be any different when the time came to deal with her? The wound to her heart is deep and painful, but this time her eyes are completely dry.

Vincent steers his father's attention to his recent drawings, and the paintings that are still drying. He explains excitedly that it would not surprise him if all the hard work of the past year will soon lead to a sale. But the older man's attention is elsewhere; he seems preoccupied. Vincent sighs and suggests they take a walk in the meadows to clear their heads.

As she farewells Vincent's father, she is certain they will not meet again. She will stay here for as long as she can, but she will no longer be fooled by Vincent. She can see that he will always put his own needs first – and, as her mother was fond of reminding her, Sien's children did not belong to him. Despite his affection for them, he did not consider them his responsibility. Indeed, would Vincent take her and the children with him to his parents' parsonage if his brother stopped sending money? Would his good family take them all in?

Wilhelmina's dire prediction of her future would prove true: she was sure of it now.

She is being shaken. Reluctantly, she opens her eyes to find Vincent looming over her.

She takes a deep breath, and swallows to be rid of the sour after-taste of jenever. Then, her vision bleary, she glances at the children, who are laughing and squealing. Her nose detects a stench before her eyes have had a chance to focus. Lifting her head, she can see Willem, having managed to wriggle free of his linen, smearing himself and the crib with his faeces. Maria, his delighted audience, is jumping up and down and clapping her hands, urging him on.

Sien can't repress a laugh.

Vincent lifts her by her arms and shakes her. 'What is the meaning of this? What has become of you?'

She pushes him aside and goes to the boy. Fetching water and plucking towels from the pile of dirty laundry, she wipes him clean, ignoring Vincent's hot glare. She can feel his rage even without looking at him. It is enough that she can hear his thick, noisy breathing, as if he is walking in a strong wind.

Later, after she returns from the laundry, Vincent mounts one of his attacks. What kind of mother falls asleep drunk? What kind of mother would let her child play with his faeces as if it were a toy? Only one who is lazy, only one who is willing to give in to bad old habits. 'Don't you understand? We must never give up trying. Never! Don't you see? That is the Devil in us.'

Though he is more savage than usual, his words have little effect on her, ringing hollow in her ears. And because she makes no attempt to be contrite, instead sniggering, he becomes angrier, his flustered face growing redder and hotter, resembling one of those preachers on street corners, impatient and desperate to be heard, to be heeded. They glare at each other. His mask has been ripped off, but so has hers, and she realises they have reached a new depth, a new understanding in their relationship: there is to be no more hope for a shared future, and no more pretence of wishing for one.

Thirty

It is no longer just warm but hot. With the return of summer, he is seldom at home, working outdoors, making the most of the longer days. Unusually, he has also been spending time in the company of other artists, those few who did not entirely shun him. Though he still complained about them the year before, this summer, they seem to have stopped bothering him. But this about-turn neither surprises nor disturbs her.

'De Bock has kindly offered to let me store my gear in his studio,' he says, arriving home without his usual equipment, only his drawings of diggers in the sand dunes. 'You have no idea how this will help me. It will mean when I'm working in the dunes I won't have to lug my stuff around.'

Then he talks fondly of De Bock, implying he has become reacquainted with an old, dear friend. But is De Bock not the same artist he accused last year of being dull because he only painted landscapes without any sign of human life and therefore no soul? As if remembering this, he says, 'And for my part, I am trying to encourage him to draw the figure. Though he will resist.'

He also disappears on painting trips with Van der Weele, and with some students who are taking lessons from him. He mentions other artists he would like to see and of his plans to visit them at their studios. 'I wonder what Breitner has been up to through winter?'

Though he enthuses about these painters, he talks less about his own prospects. It seems he is at last beginning to suspect the truth: that the possibility of him selling his work is as remote as finding a gold coin in one of Geest's alleyways. She can tell by the way he regards her and the children, one moment soft-eyed, the next tearing his gaze away, unable to meet their eyes, the quantities of drawings and studies piling up around them so that indeed – as he once dreamt – they seem tall enough to reach the rafters.

But then the very next morning, as if waking from some stupor, he charges around the apartment, gesticulating with his pipe, smoke trailing from him like the heated breath of some beast on the run. Soon, he will truly master the colours. And this year, he is sure, they will obey him, especially after the improvement in his drawings of the past year. Yes, he can feel it in his bones. This will be the year that he makes a sale. Not just one or two either – a few. He intends to hire different models, more interesting types from Scheveningen. He will buy more costumes. 'I need one of those fisherman's jackets with the high collar, and more hats for women, and a Scheveningen women's cape too.'

But he has stopped talking about the two of them and their future altogether.

Because it is Willem's first birthday, Wilhelmina and Karel turn up, bringing a felt cap as a present. Karel strides in, his manner like that of a landlord as he eyes the apartment and its contents. He has grown fat over winter, Sien notices – probably from all the beer he consumes while carousing with the young girls, despite his marriage.

'So, this is the famous studio, then,' he says, glancing amusedly at Vincent's work on the walls. Shaking his head, he barks a laugh loud enough that the children stop their play and look up at him.

'Has he sold anything, this artist of yours?' he asks, grinning now. Then, without waiting for an invitation, he plonks himself on a chair, one arm hooked over the back, knees spread wide.

His tone implies he does not expect a reply. No doubt Wilhelmina will have told him all about the soup kitchen visits, the mounting debts, the scant food, the endless stream of models through the studio. And, of course, the art. Stacks of drawing, all of dubious quality.

'So, now that you have seen them for yourself, would you like to pose for him too?' Sien asks, head tipped to the side.

Wilhelmina has made coffee and she offers a cup to Karel. He ignores her, his eyes instead narrowed on Sien's. She drops her gaze, resenting him. He has always had this power, this effect on her, even when they were young.

But when she looks up again, he is all smiles. 'Well, I think you're wasting your time here, that's all. There's no future for you with this so-called artist.'

She shrugs.

Wilhelmina taps Karel's arm, no doubt reminding him of something.

Karel puts his cup down and tells her how well their rooms are doing. Sien could work there too, and not necessarily to screw every night – though she will have to work this way some nights to cover her and the children's board.

'Sien, you don't have to walk the streets anymore. You will be comfortable, warm. We all know Vincent is not going to marry you, don't we? I mean there's no difference between screwing him for this apartment or screwing anyone else for a bed at my place, is there?'

She launches herself from her seat with her arm raised, ready to strike him. But Karel's arm is already there to meet hers.

Wilhelmina intervenes, pushing her son down onto his seat. 'No, no, let her be,' she murmurs. 'She will come around.'

Karel snorts. Then he smiles and nods in the way of someone who is confident of being proven right in time.

Sien turns her back on them and crosses to the window. It may be true, but to have Karel tell her so, well, she may as well just go off and take up streetwalking again, live from hand to mouth, live from night to night, from one drunken soldier to another. But at least she can earn a living without anyone telling her what to do, and if she were to fall in a heap again, as she did the night she met Vincent, well, next time she wouldn't be stupid enough to go home with a gentleman who promised her the world.

Vincent arrives just as Karel and Wilhelmina are taking their leave. As if intuiting the reason for their visit, he eyes them with open hostility.

When they have gone, he accuses her of plotting to abandon him, going behind his back so she can return to her crooked old ways. That it seems as if all his good deeds, all his well-meaning efforts of the previous year to set her straight, have been in vain.

'Didn't you tell me when we met how much you liked prostitutes?' she retorts. 'How they were the only women who understood you, who comforted you over the years? Karel is only trying to make a living.'

She may not like her brother and will always fear him, but she will also defend him. Have they not survived Geest together, fending for themselves in those narrow streets? How can she hold out against him, her own blood? And how would a man who has always had parcels and postal orders arrive on his doorstep possibly understand?

'Well, instead of making money from selling women, why doesn't he get a job at the gas factory then, just as you said I should?' he sneers.

She stays silent as she clears the table. Let him be right. She won't deny him, because his need to be right is more important to him than to her; he acts as if his very life depends on it. For her, it makes little difference. More clear-eyed than ever, she understands they are simply biding time.

Yet as she glances at the children, she knows her cavalier dismissal of the future rings false, for she can see how far they have come. Thriving now, they seem to demand her assurance. Perhaps she also has come too far to turn back. To have been persuaded they matter is no small thing. He may have helped her to see her life differently, see herself differently, but what use will they have for such insight once he is no longer with them? How much will they count then?

On a rare day when Vincent is working at home, she opens the door to a burly man. Pushing her aside, he barges into the apartment and marches up to Vincent. Knocking his easel to the floor, he seizes him by the collar and demands, 'Where is the money for the pottery you took from me?'

She recognises him now as the shopkeeper who sells household items in the neighbourhood and to whom Vincent took a lamp for repair some weeks ago, returning with recently fired earthenware that was attractive but which they hardly needed. But Vincent had found it too charming to resist, and begged to be allowed to take it on credit, since he did not have the funds to pay for it straight away. And now it seems the shopkeeper, having learnt that the cobbler has been paid while he has not, has understandably become enraged.

'Well?' the man demands.

'Look here,' Vincent stammers, 'you . . . you almost . . . did . . . did you not demand that I take it?'

'Demand? I showed it to you and you took it. I didn't know that you could not pay.'

'But . . . but that's where you are wrong, my friend. I can pay – I just . . . I just need another . . . another week or so.'

'You think I can sit around and wait for money to come from somewhere? I have to earn it, *my friend*,' the shopkeeper thunders, red-faced.

'You . . . you made . . . you made me take it.'

'Made you?' The shopkeeper pushes Vincent against the wall, making the windows rattle.

Sien is used to this type of spectacle – fists drawn like weapons, ready to pummel flesh, break bones; it is a regular, almost legitimate entertainment in the streets of Geest. Still, she is filled with horror when Vincent struggles in the man's grip and gasps for air.

She lunges at the shopkeeper but he is too large, too strong. With one arm, he casts her aside, sending her stumbling back.

Vincent, having lost his stammer, shouts angrily, 'You worthless bully.'

But Vincent is no match for the shopkeeper, who throws him to the floor then plants his knee on Vincent's chest. As Vincent writhes and squirms, Sien hammers the man's back with her fists.

He turns and snatches her by the wrist. 'And you, pretending you are a wife and mother. I know what you are.'

It is the baby's high-pitched scream that brings a close to the scene. He is standing in his crib, his linen hanging heavy as the room begins to fill with a smell.

'I'll pay you first, before the grocer, the baker,' Vincent promises, speaking rapidly.

The man leaves but not before thrusting his chin in Vincent's direction menacingly. 'If I am forced to come back here, you will not be able to stand up when I am finished with you.'

Sien, her nerves shattered, seeks out her chair when the man has left.

She expects Vincent to regret his rash purchase, but instead he lays the blame entirely on the other man, moaning about the meanness of shopkeepers and their narrow-minded pettiness, preoccupied as they were with money. The man had begged him to take the earthenware, and he felt he had no choice but to oblige, since he appeared so desperate. Did he have to be such a brute about it, though? When Vincent's own intentions were perfectly good? He would have got his money eventually.

In his usual way, Vincent had followed his heart when he should have used his head.

Now it is no longer for herself or their future she is frightened, but for him. How can this man survive, here in The Hague or anywhere else, trusting only the whims of his heart?

Thirty-one

Vincent is in a frenzy. Pacing the length of the room, he is scowling as he reads and re-reads the latest letter from his brother. His face is as white as the paper he holds and Sien assumes there has been a death in the family, but no, it is to do with a financial crisis in Paris. It has forced Theo to tighten his belt; he is no longer in a position to promise Vincent his allowance.

'Theo says he can give me no hope,' he says, falling into his chair so heavily that it rocks.

'Has he lost his job?' Sien asks, drying her hands on her apron.

He shakes his head. 'No, he makes no mention of that.' Then, his voice anxious, he continues, 'Or does he mean he can give me no hope about my work? Has he given up hope on that?' Agitated, he scans the letter again, brows twisted. 'He mentions that he found some of the recent work *meagre*. Can you believe that?

Meagre! How dare he?' Exasperated now, he fumes, 'Well, given the constraints I have, with a family to feed, of course my work will be meagre. What does he expect? Because at times my energy is meagre – my body too, for it is not made of iron, though I wish it were.'

Lighting his pipe, he stands and resumes his pacing.

Then he spins on his heel and reaches for his pen and paper. 'I must make my case. He must understand I am prepared to double – no, *treble* – my efforts, just as he must do the same with his work. I mean, selling art is easy for him. One only has to use one's mouth, never mind getting one's hands dirty. Surely he can talk those dim-witted, rich Parisians into buying more of those Gérômes.'

He sits hunched at the table and writes, his hand not lifting from the paper. As the pages fill with endless waves of words, she understands the moment she has been waiting for has finally come, and she finds herself feeling more relieved than sorry. The previous eighteen months have allowed her a life beyond anything she could ever have wished for, yet despite the unquestionable ardour of Vincent's love, his company has proved altogether too exacting, almost beyond bearing.

She stands and returns to the kitchen to deal with the tub of dirty dishes.

'I've been thinking we should move to the country – perhaps somewhere north, like Drenthe, where things are bound to be cheaper,' he announces a few days later.

Sien is sitting at the table with Willem perched on her lap; he is feeding himself bits of bread.

'I suppose there will be less shops and so less shopkeepers pushing their goods on you.'

They have not spoken of the incident since, and she has not asked him whether the man has been paid or not.

Ignoring her remark, his voice climbs with excitement. 'Just imagine. A small, honest village somewhere far from the city. Where the rent will be lower, the price of food too. Everything will be simpler, inexpensive. I'm sure of it. Even the models.'

She has expected something of the sort; she has been rehearsing in her mind this very scenario for many weeks, but still she is not prepared, her heart plunging like an iron anchor to the sea floor.

Leave this city that has been her home for her whole life? His mention of England the previous year did not trouble her because she deemed it one of Vincent's idle fancies that was more an expression of his love for those English artists than anything practical. But his proposal of Drenthe seems considered and plausible enough she finds it difficult to dismiss in the same manner, and though the place is closer than England, it is nevertheless sufficiently far from The Hague for her to be alarmed by the possibility of her and the children left stranded there. She might as well set sail for the other side of the world. And who was to say she will be free of her past in Drenthe if the folk there catch wind of the children not belonging to Vincent or that she and Vincent were living in sin? They could move to the country, but she cannot change who she is, who her children are.

But more than abandonment she fears Vincent's inability to change. She is convinced they will never escape the debts which will always continue to soar, because for him art will always come first, above everything else, and he will be just as reckless with money in Drenthe as he was in the city. On top of this, the threat of Theo cutting them off will no doubt follow them all the way to that far northern part of the country.

'Just think, there will be less temptations too.' He gives her a meaningful look, and she knows he means there will be no distillers where she can buy her jenever. But then he adds, 'I don't just mean jenever, but expensive paint shops where I can run up the bill. I will then have to learn to use the paints more sparingly.'

'It's no use, Vincent,' she sighs. 'I can't see what good moving somewhere else will do.'

'You must admit, getting away from the bad influence of your family will help you.'

'Because you saved my life, now you would like to save me from my family. Is that it?'

He loses his patience. He accuses her of shamelessly, knowingly choosing her sinful family over him. Here he is, offering her a chance to escape their evil clutches – for they will only lead her astray and send her out whoring again; how can she contemplate refusing him? All he wants to do is move away from the city, live cheaply until his work improves and sells.

She should be angry but she cannot see any point to it, given they never really had a future. Despite their hopes, despite their efforts, despite their love. Besides, she has difficulty rousing ire. For she has come to know him with all his different layers and shades. Because of all that has happened between them, anger seems too easy, too lacking, too dishonest for their story, and for better or worse, she has been changed. Yes, by all the things he did for her but, more than that, his belief in her has allowed her to see herself as not just a whore but as someone worthy of love, of a better life.

Yet she can see now that she was also expedient to him. He needed her love, as well as her body, and she willingly gave herself to him – because she also needed to.

But she is less worried about her broken heart than the loss of its strength. Again, she has no choice but to ask herself: how will she go on, in this new, sorry husk of herself? How will she survive?

Vincent is still outlining arguments in favour of his latest scheme. 'Sien, any fool could see we can't go on like this, especially since Theo is having difficulties and must send less. In the country, where costs are not so high, we can make do. I'm sure of it.'

Her heart begins to stir again. 'It is no use, Vincent. What you say is true, but it makes little difference. I once believed that selling your work would change everything, but it won't. I have lived with you long enough to have learnt that the likelihood of you changing is as impossible as undoing my past. Whether life elsewhere is cheaper, you will always spend your money on art before us.'

She does not look up, concentrating all her attention on tearing more bread for Willem. She can hear Vincent's heavy breath, feel the hot air expelling from him.

'My mother warned me that this would happen,' she adds.

'What did your mother, that *good woman*, say then?'

She lifts her head and tells him that her mother saw through him many months ago. Saw that he was a man no different to all the useless do-gooders. Wilhelmina had seen people like him before, from families with money, who could afford to say what they wanted, could afford to indulge themselves in saving others, using others' souls to save themselves.

'Ha, so you believe that woman, do you? The one who sent you out prostituting? The one who led her own daughter down the crooked path?'

But she knows from his tone that he is hurt.

'At least I would be prepared to return you and the children to The Hague if we had to part ways.'

Oh, how kind of him.

And in this promise she detects the truth: he has made his offer out of duty and not because of any genuine desire for her company. The air between them now quiet and still, she holds his gaze coolly, steadily, and asks him, 'Why do you insist that we come with you when you know in your heart that you do not wish us to?'

He reaches for his beloved pipe, but fumbling, it clatters to the table. Snatching it again, he packs it with tobacco, pushing his thumb down harder than she has ever seen him do. 'How . . . how can you . . . It's not true . . . Why . . . why would I not want you by my side?' His tic is trembling.

Catching the panic and terror flickering in his eyes, she knows she was right. She need not say any more. So, though she had intended to point out he was only interested in assuaging his guilt, only interested in making his leaving easier, she changes her mind, because the possibility he may have behaved without honour would be unbearable to him. After all, honour is the cornerstone of his very being – as his belief that he alone is a true Christian: one who, instead of just spouting catechism, actually dared to stick his neck out for her. And yet despite his best efforts to emulate the type of man Michelet extolled – a man who should have no trouble keeping a woman by his side, protected, near the family hearth – had he not failed? In any case, whatever Michelet said, love was not enough in their situation. It was never ever going to be enough.

'You must do what you need to do, Vincent. As you said, art is your calling. And you should understand I have to protect myself and the children against any further false hopes. Our love was never possible and we were naive to think it could hold. But since you have been the only man who has been generous, kind and loving to me, I bear no grudge. Yes, my family is no good, as you say, but I have nowhere else to turn. They are my fate.'

His jaw drops. For once, he has no words; his bluster has deserted him. His shoulders slump, and he appears half his size. She should be pleased to see him like this, but the time for blame and regrets long past, she is filled instead with an emptiness, all her energy used up by the mad efforts of the previous year; setting up house, rearing the children, sitting for countless drawings, fighting the hunger, fighting the cold, fighting what seems like the whole world.

When his eyes finally meet hers, they are damp. 'You've spoken with your heart,' he tells her, voice hoarse and dry. 'And it is pure and true. That it should be so, despite the life you had before you met me, tells me that I was not wrong about you. That you did indeed deserve all my help, my sympathy, my love.'

It is so like him to think that his guilt has been absolved because of her. He certainly has a knack for turning the tables to suit himself – a skill that no doubt would continue to serve him well, leaving him with little room for self-doubt, propelling him ever forward. Yes, despite his abandonment of her, since she was worthy of his efforts, nothing has been in vain, and he has been vindicated. How fortunate for him.

But she lets him be, for he is in more need of this than she.

'But I must urge you to go into service,' he says. 'Don't work for your brother and mother. I'll help you to find a position. There are plenty advertised.'

She scoffs. What does he know about being a maid? A few girls from her neighbourhood, wishing to try out respectability, went into service. But when their bellies began to swell, they came home and said there was not even time to point their fingers at the men of the well-to-do family they worked for before they were thrown out.

'No,' she said. 'Perhaps Gerda can use a helper at the laundry.'

He has made the arrangements. A wagon will take his belongings to Drenthe next month. But he remains overwrought, the lines on his face as heavy and deep as those of his drawings. When he looks at her, he struggles to hold his gaze. He continues to advise her to apply for a service position, but in a vague sort of way, without conviction, without any seriousness, as they share a silent understanding: they have been hiding like children in this apartment, away from the adults, away from the real world. Pretending as if they were characters in a Hans Christian Andersen story.

Now the destiny she long predicted and awaited is within a hair's whisker of her, her life in the apartment appears a long, exhausting dream, one from which she is only too glad to wake. After all the arguments, the endless work, the drama, the effort, what remains? This room cannot speak for what took place here, cannot know the stories she and Vincent made here, and she feels nothing for it. She is sure in time she will remember little, if anything, about the place. Unlike the ache in her heart.

As the time for his departure draws near, they are kind and gentle to each other. They speak in near whispers, their heads lowered. His eyes, always moist, seem ever ready to shed tears. Especially when Willem tries to climb onto his lap or sits at his feet and coos at him.

Their lovemaking is charged and restless. He seems determined to tunnel into her body, as if the answers to all his problems might be found between her legs. Then he struggles to fall asleep, tossing and turning, his body satiated but his conscience not, clinging tightly to her one minute and then, seemingly spooked by her touch, withdrawing and turning his back to her.

As for Sien, inside, she is trying to run from him, trying to widen the distance between them. And once more that clever part of her has found its wings and now floats just below the ceiling, looking down at the lean, pale man as he wrestles with the tangled sheets and blankets. The woman stares, her dark eyes not blank but wide, rippling with a fear that will not allow her to close them.

She stands on tiptoe, craning her neck above the crowd to search for Vincent. They had said goodbye at the apartment, but after he left, she wandered from room to room. Finally she had taken Willem on her hip, grasped Maria by the hand, and set off for the station.

Bobbing in the sea of heads, she glimpses a familiar, crumpled hat.

'Vincent,' she calls out.

Though the platform is noisy, he spins around straight away, like a man who has received a tap on his shoulder. Scanning the crowd, he spots her, and his face lights up.

She approaches him awkwardly, as if they are strangers meeting for the first time. But Willem is not fooled. Pulling away from her, he stretches not just his arms but his entire body towards him. Vincent doesn't hesitate. He drops his case by his side and relieves her of the baby, holding him up exuberantly above the crowd, grinning. Then, cradling him with one arm, he picks up his case with his free hand and marches towards his train, leaving Sien and Maria to follow.

In the third-class carriage, he finds a corner seat and, holding the baby on his lap, bounces him. Then, at the sharp blow of a whistle, he hands the boy back to her. As he does so, his gaze, glistening wet, hovers over her face. He then leans forward and kisses her deep for the last time, not caring who is watching.

She whispers, 'Remember, don't listen to the shopkeepers.'

He wipes his eyes, lips quivering as they attempt a smile.

'And you must remember to go and see the carpenter next door for my address in Drenthe,' he replies. 'I'll write to him when I get settled. Ask him to help you send me news. I've spoken to him.'

She nods, though she is sure that, whatever he has promised Vincent, he will do no such thing for *her.*

She takes the children and turns away without a word, without a backward glance.

Rotterdam, November 1904

The name outside the gallery stops her short. *Vincent van Gogh*. Her heart in her throat, Sien stares at the large letters in disbelief.

Before she knows what she is doing, she is already at the gallery's entrance, taking a peek inside. There, through the gaps between the visitors, she is stunned to see, on the walls, paintings. The colours seem to dance and leap from their frames. Bright blues, yellows, greens, pinks. She forgets to blink, unable to believe they came from his hand. What happened to the drawings? *What happened to that cursed black line they all suffered for?*

She notices a young man frowning at her. For a moment she thinks it's Theo before quickly realising that Theo would no longer be young. He eyes her up and down and seems ready to approach her. But before he can do so, she turns and retraces her steps.

So, he has managed to sell his work. And since he is painting now, he must have conquered the line, after all.

As a successful artist, she assumes he has a large house somewhere in the country, with servants, horses and the woods nearby. Has he ever given a thought to her? Has he ever spoken of her? Does he recall how she sat for him and how she helped him, in order for this success to happen?

Pausing at the corner near the gallery, she lingers. To think that he is somewhere nearby . . . She is too overcome to be still. As she paces back and forth, the long-buried memories come rushing out of the darkness. They are sharp, like shards of broken glass. The smell of paints, the walls covered with art, the hunger, Vincent constantly working, writing, reading, living on nothing but air and tobacco. And his moods. Just remembering those months wearies her.

The last time she saw him, the Christmas of the year they'd parted, he returned to The Hague with a slight stoop, as if the sky in Drenthe was low enough to bow his back, his face all angles, clothes appearing as if he had not changed them, let alone laundered them in the three months he was there. And taking him in, she kept her arms fastened by her side; it was all she could do not to embrace him. But he left again, teary-eyed, sorry, promising never to forget her.

Well, she'd like to see if that was true.

So, with some trepidation, she waits; he could arrive at any moment. What would she say to him? Would he even recognise her? Or would he walk straight past her?

Over the years, catching a glimpse of a face that reminded her of him, she'd imagine meeting him again. Then the questions would come. *Did you find it, Vincent? Did you find your truth in those black lines, in the paints?*

The waiting proving unbearable; her need to know whether he is here, whether she will see him, prompts her to return to the gallery. Perhaps he has been inside all along. She stands by the door, eyes darting keenly over the throng. A man turns around, and her heart skips. But no, it is not him. The young gallery attendant cuts into her line of sight. Stepping outside, he asks, 'Are you looking for someone? Is something wrong?'

He is more puzzled than annoyed.

'Is he here?' she asks, looking over his shoulder into the gallery.

'Who?'

'Vincent.'

He gives a small shake of his head, appearing confused.

Exasperated, she points at his name and blurts out, 'The artist. Vincent van Gogh. Is he here? I . . . I would like to see him.'

The shake of his head is no longer hesitant but emphatic. 'He died more than ten years ago.'

'Died? He is dead?'

He nods slowly, studying her face with a deeper curiosity.

Her legs about to give way, she lowers herself onto the step. Immediately she feels his hand grip her arm.

'Please, you cannot stay here.'

'No, no, it can't be true.'

He tries to help her up, but her body suddenly feels so heavy she cannot make it rise.

'But how?' she asks. 'How could he be dead?'

'I'm afraid he shot himself, in France.'

She cannot remember how she managed to stand, to walk, but she finds herself at the corner once more, dazed, clutching her skirt. She hears his voice as clearly as if he is standing next to her. *You are to never give in to despair. Do you hear?* How many times had she recalled his words when she felt the presence of that shadow companion drawing too near?

And yet he himself had given in.

For all his talk. For all his defiance. But there is no greater truth than death. And because of him, did she not also carry on the fight? Now she asks herself: why? Was it for him? So that she might feel his gaze pierce her heart all over again? To know those months hadn't been a dream? That they hadn't been in vain?

She looks up at the banner above the gallery once more. Vincent was right. Though he may be gone, it is just as he said: his work has endured.

As for her, she realises what has remained for her is not the art, nor the suffering, but the imprint he left on her heart. This is what has sustained her. What she has been carrying around with her all this time.

She glances at the well-to-do people hurrying past her. Though she is no longer the streetwalker of Geest – is married now, to a kind, younger man who gave her children his name – she is as invisible to the gentlefolk now as she was then. They do not see her, not as Vincent saw her. But it no longer matters. Clear-headed, clear-eyed, she takes their measure. It is the same for them all in the end. Nothing changes, really. Only time: which does not forgive, which does not show mercy. And it will march on, leaving them behind.

She can feel a darkness growing within her, feel her shadow companion's warm breath on her neck.

She can still hear his voice from that first night. *Are you alright?* Looking up to see a lean face, crooked hat and eyes too naked. She can see his wiry body bent over his easel, his mood tense, nerves taut. And then she feels the sigh of his last breath on her cheek, untroubled and soft – yielding, finally.

And with that thought comes an inward elation, a lightness, as if her flesh too has already passed on to somewhere else.

Sien Hoornik's body was found in a canal in Rotterdam, early on the morning of 23 November 1904 by a public gardener. Two policemen confirmed her death.

An exhibition of Vincent van Gogh's work was held at Rotterdam's Oldenzeel Gallery, a kilometre from Sien's home, between 10 November and 15 December 1904.

Author's Note

Recently I picked up a book about Vincent van Gogh in a bookshop. It declared him the most famous artist in the world. When an artist attains such a reputation, one assumes his story has been anatomised to the degree that very little remains to be known about him. So, on my first visit to Amsterdam a few years ago, overfamiliar with both his work and his personal life, I relegated the Van Gogh Museum to the bottom of my to-do list.

When I did reach there, the first work I encountered was *The Potato Eaters*. I knew the painting but was unprepared for the way it moved me. Crudely rendered, with a sombre palette portraying a peasant family eating a humble meal, the painting expresses a powerful dignity and humanity that belies its modest size and indelicate execution. It was nothing like the refined work of Van Gogh's Dutch contemporaries, lauded and celebrated during his time, some of which I had just admired at the Rijksmuseum.

I became curious about the artist's unique style and the originality and boldness of his vision. This led me to Van Gogh's years in The Hague and his relationship with Sien Hoornik. I was surprised to learn he had had an intimate partner, but the crucial role she played in his development as an artist, and as a man, was immediately apparent to me, and I became fascinated by their story. After reading Vincent's account of their relationship – the only one we have – there were too many questions raised in his telling for me to trust his version entirely, and I felt compelled to write Sien's story.

Acknowledgements

In the course of my research for this novel, the scholarship of a few key authors proved invaluable: Carol Zemel's *Van Gogh's Progress: Utopia, Modernity and Late Nineteenth-Century Art* helped me to understand Vincent and Sien's relationship through a particular cultural lens, *Van Gogh: The Life* by Steven Naifeh and Gregory White Smith was breathtakingly comprehensive, and Martin Bailey's *Living with Vincent van Gogh* provided ground-breaking information about Sien's death.

Ken Wilkie, author of *Van Gogh Files*, generously read an early draft and provided much-appreciated feedback.

I owe a huge debt to several Dutch historians who shared their knowledge and expertise, in particular, The Hague-based historian Pieter Stokvis whose research about The Blue Press unlocked the key to the coalface realities of prostitutes' working lives. And to Cor Smit, the Leiden-based historian who provided numerous articles that explored sex work for many poor women during this period. I could not have read the Dutch-written articles without the kind assistance of Eric Ruijssenaars of Dutch Archives. I am particularly grateful to Mieke van Baarsel, the author of *Geleerde Zorgen*, a history of Leiden University Medical Centre, the hospital where Sien Hoornik went to have her baby, for her close reading of the manuscript and kind suggestions.

The Vincent van Gogh Museum allowed me to spend an unforgettable day in their storage room up close with those drawings Vincent completed in The Hague – thank you to Hans Martijn, who hosted me that day. The letters of Vincent van Gogh were the 'master' resource for this novel. They are available online at www.vangoghletters.org.

The staff at the archive offices of The Hague and Leiden, in particular, Jan van Wandelen, who guided this non-Dutch speaker through their files with infinite patience.

To Pamela Peelen, who thought my proposal perfectly reasonable and did not hesitate to reach out to her cousin, Tom Kluen, who in turn led me to those historians mentioned above.

My agent, the inestimable Grace Heifetz. Her enthusiasm and belief in the work were unequivocal from day one. I knew my work found the right home when my publisher Ingrid Ohlsson helped me to find new layers in the story. Ali Lavau for her rigorous yet sensitive editing. Rebecca Lay for her guidance and reassurance through the editorial process.

A special thank you to Nadine Davidoff, who was there from the beginning as not only a vital sounding board but a critical one, challenging me at every turn. To my readers: Arathi

Menon, Rick Bland, John Antony, Rachel Harris, Rod Woolley and Leonie Khoury, whose championing of the work enabled me to continue to the end. To Tim Collins for providing me refuge from domestic chaos at his Cloud studio.

And to the Malcolm Bradbury Trust, whose bursary enabled this writer to be UK-based at UEA while undertaking the kind of research that can only be done 'on the ground'.

This book could not have been conceived or written without the support of my family – Zach and Michael Amarant.